LOST
IN
LAKEVIEW

LOST
IN
LAKEVIEW

COLLEEN BITE

Cover Design by Damonza.com

ISBN: 979-8-9941644-0-2

First edition 2025

This book is dedicated to my husband, Tadas.
Your daily sacrifice has not gone unnoticed or unappreciated.
Your support and motivation have made
this book what it is today.
Complete.
Now, time to celebrate!

AUTHOR'S NOTE

My Dear Reader,

Your mental health is extremely important to me; therefore, if you find any of the following topics to be triggering for you, you may want to reconsider reading any further.

*Trigger Warning *

This book contains mature content including scenes depicting cancer, stillbirth, physical and emotional domestic abuse, child abuse, self-harm, suicidal ideation, suicide, and general violence.

CHAPTER 1

MARK

THE NOTE SAID: *I can't do this without you anymore.* He signed it, *only Mark*, as in, "It's only me, Mark," which was how he began all his voicemails to her. It had become their inside joke. He signed all her birthday, anniversary, and "just because" cards with it. There were often "just because" cards.

This would be the last time he used the sign-off. Someone would find it. Or would they? After all, it was just him—only Mark.

He looked around their apartment, the place that used to hold so many happy memories. Now, all he could see were the last days of her life after the cancer had withered her away to almost nothing.

What was once their cozy living room, lit with ambient light and furnished with their big soft couch, adorned with the novelty throw pillows they'd collected throughout the years (ones with *Do Not Disturb* and *This Is My Happy Place* on them), was now a makeshift hospice. Where her pumpkin spice candles had once permeated every piece of furniture, there was now a smell that only victims of cancer could describe. Sweet, almost fruity, but also chemical.

He looked around but said nothing as he closed the front door for the last time.

ᢙ

Mark Peters drove his light blue Toyota Yaris down what had once been his favorite highway: Highway F in northern Wisconsin. He was headed to the Lakeview Resort, where they'd spent their honeymoon and many subsequent vacations. It had been their favorite place, but that seemed so long ago now.

As he drove, Mark reminisced about their first trip to the resort. They'd made an impromptu stop on their journey to Minneapolis. It was their first year together, and the resort looked like it had come straight out of a movie—a horror movie, Isabel had said at first, like the cabins at Camp Crystal Lake. Fortunately, instead of being murdered by a hockey mask-wearing psychopath, they had fallen in love.

He could see her in the car with him now, though he saw her everywhere, really. He only wished he didn't see her this way, thin and frail, her chemo cap covering the scalp once rich with long, silky golden hair.

"You're going there?" she asked from the passenger seat.

"Where else?"

"I don't know. I guess there is nowhere else."

"Not for me."

The town of Loomis Falls was your typical small town, comprising a wood mill, a small grocery store, a bank, a post office, a laundromat, a lumber store, a bakery, a few gift shops, and more than enough bars, most of which were scattered up and down Main Street. There were also two gas stations, one overpriced, selling nothing but gas and cigarettes, and the other, Fred's, which was still overpriced but offered many more conveniences, and which most locals used for groceries.

Mark pulled into the latter one, knowing the drive would soon become miles of nothing but woods and cabins. He was at a quarter of a tank—enough to get him there, which was all he needed. He parked in front of Fred's and reached for the door handle, then remembered her.

"Do you need anything?" he asked, but she was no longer there, just as she hadn't been for the last nine miserable months.

Fred's kept the hard liquor behind the counter, perhaps to embarrass whoever wanted to buy it on a regular basis.

"A bottle of Jack, please," Mark said to the young girl behind the counter as he pulled cash from his wallet.

"Um, hold on, please." The curly-haired blonde strained her neck searching for someone else in the store.

"Dad?" she shouted. "I need you for liquor. Sorry."

"Sorry" came out "Sharry" because of her braces. This girl was nowhere near old enough to sell him his bottle. Her name tag said *Becky*, and she looked only thirteen or fourteen. Almost too young to be working, unless her dad owned the store, and Mark guessed he did.

A man in his mid-forties rushed up from the center aisle; his hair was gray at his temples, and he looked a lot like Tom Selleck. The man's name tag confirmed his guess. The tag said *Fred Niemeyer*.

"You must be Fred?" Mark said. *If Izzy were here, she would've giggled.*

"That I am," Fred said. "Sorry about that. My daughter is not old enough to sell the hard stuff. What can I do ya for?"

"A bottle of Jack, please."

"The old Mr. Daniel's, coming right up."

The man may have looked like Tom Selleck in *Magnum, P.I.*, but he acted more like Gomer Pyle. Mark couldn't hold in the chuckle.

"What's funny?" Fred asked, genuinely curious.

3

"Mr. Daniel's is right. Never heard it called that before."

Fred smiled and grabbed the large bottle of whiskey. "That'll be forty-two."

Mark pulled three twenties out of his wallet, handed them over, grabbed the bottle, and walked away.

"Wait, your change!" Fred called out.

"Keep it," Mark said. "Actually, give it to Becky, if you don't mind."

"Wow, thanks, Mister!" Becky squeaked.

"Have a good one!" Fred yelled as Mark walked out.

He climbed back into his Toyota; Izzy had picked out the color for it. She said it reminded her of the sky when they lay in the grass together, making shapes out of the clouds.

"What's that smile for?" Izzy said in her "almost there" voice, the one he remembered from her last days.

"That girl reminded me of you," he said, then drove on.

For someone who didn't know where it was, the resort would be difficult to find. Mark and Izzy often wondered how it drew any business, being so hidden away. Had they not gotten lost and used the driveway to turn around, they likely never would've found it. Their phone signal was spotty on the back roads, and they'd lost their directions over two miles before.

The resort's driveway was eerie, with its gravel road and overgrown landscaping. Tree branches brushed the top of the car as he drove down the path. After a quarter of a mile, the driveway opened up to a clearing, and the resort came into view. It had a main office and six cabins. Beyond the cabins was Mill Run Lake, spanning a mile across and about seven miles long, something they'd learned on their first visit.

Today, as before, sunrays glittered on the surface of the lake. "It looks just as beautiful as it did on our honeymoon," Mark said, but she was no longer there.

CHAPTER 2

ELLIE

SHE STOOD FROZEN in place, bare feet on her bedroom carpet as her mother flitted around her, grabbing clothes from her dresser drawers and stuffing them into her backpack. Her mother didn't ask her to help, nor did she bark orders at her like she normally did before school—or when Ellie had been less than motivated to clean her room. She just grabbed what she needed. Ellie ran the last few moments over in her head. *What happened?* She looked at the fronts and backs of both of her hands; they were trembling, but they looked just the same as before.

"Pajamas," her mother mumbled, reciting the impromptu list of what was needed. She opened the top dresser drawer, pulling out the items and stuffing them into Ellie's backpack.

The dresser drawer stood open, her mother having been too preoccupied to worry about closing it.

Dad would've been mad about that... but not anymore, she thought.

Then something occurred to her. Ellie focused her attention on the drawer. She thought about the consequences of leaving it open. Anger rose like lava in her belly, and while she would've normally doused it, she let it rise instead.

Close.

Close.

Close!

Nothing.

Although she'd tried many times before, it was never something she was able to do. Not even a shake or rattle of an object, like you would see in the movies, when a child attempted to move things with their minds.

It was too late, as her Aunt Laura would sometimes say, her *choo choo had fallen off the track*; the anger was extinguishing itself, replaced by introspection.

It wasn't anger she felt when it happened; instead, she felt fear, desperation, and that other feeling. The one she had when things got scary, when *he* got scary. Like a bubble of safety or a shield.

It was her, she thought. *The woman, my protector.*

Her mother didn't ask her to follow her down the stairs. She just shouldered the backpack and scooped up Ellie in her arms. At eight years old, it wasn't a common occurrence for her mother to carry her down the stairs, but it wasn't unheard of either, especially when she was sick, or had fallen asleep on the couch. Right now, though, all she wanted was to feel her mother's arms wrapped around her.

"Close your eyes, baby," her mother said.

Ellie did as she was told. As her eyelids closed, the tears she'd been holding back found their way out and slid down her cheeks, soaking her mother's warm shoulder.

"What about Dad?" Ellie said as her mother placed her in the back seat of their car and made her way to the driver's seat.

"I'm going to text Aunt Laura. She can come over, okay?"

Ellie watched her mother's panicked face in the rearview mirror and nodded.

"Okay," her mother said. "Okay. Good."

But Ellie wasn't sure it was good, because her mother looked like she could rip the steering wheel off the car's dashboard. She knew her mother wanted to ask her something by the way she kept glancing back at her. Sensing the question, Ellie gave her an answer.

"I can't feel him."

Her mother nodded. "Good."

CHAPTER 3

LAURA

LAURA MAYFIELD WAS driving to work when the text came through. She almost checked it, but as an ER nurse, she'd encountered too many victims of texting and driving. Also drinking and driving, reading and driving, eating and driving, not to mention the many other inconceivable things people thought they could pull off behind the wheel.

She made a vow to herself and her husband that she would only drive while driving. Because of this, she didn't see the jumbled autocorrected mess of a text message from her sister Julia until her forty-five-minute drive was over.

Julia: *Can you plead checking on ted? He is not answering his phonics.*

Laura texted back: *Where are you? I just got to work.*

She wasn't sure if she should go inside and start her shift or wait for her response. This was not like her sister; in the eight years she'd been married to that rat bastard, Julia had never asked her to check in on him. She had never even wanted her near him. So, why was she asking this now?

Laura watched her phone, the animated ellipsis of her sister's forthcoming text.

Julia: *He bought me flowers.*

Laura's hand raised to her mouth. It'd started as a joke: "If I ever text you, 'He bought me flowers,' you'll know that something is wrong." They'd laughed about it at first, but as the years went by and the incidents with her and Ellie increased, the joke became a warning. Laura now clearly understood that she would not be going into work today.

Laura: *Call me. I'm going to drive. I'm headed to you now. Where are you?*

Julia: *Can't call; got Ellie with me. Going to that resort you mentioned; it sounds like fun!*

Laura couldn't wrap her mind around what was happening. If Julia were really in danger, why was she acting so cheery? An ellipsis popped up again, and Laura bit at the skin surrounding her fingernails. She'd quit biting her nails a while back, but the trade-off was that she had perpetually bloody, torn skin around the tips of her fingers.

Julia: *listening to the podcast you machined the other day; you were right. It's right up my alley.*

Podcast? Machined? So, is she fine? Just then, Laura remembered the podcast. The one she almost jokingly told Julia to listen to: *The Only Way Out,* a true-crime podcast following the gruesome murder of a man by his abused wife. Laura's heart raced. She tried to text, but her fingers were shaking. Another text popped up.

Julia: *Will you please check on him and make sure he is okay? I will be worried until I find out.*

It clicked. What kind of true-crime junkie was she? Why hadn't she figured it out sooner? Her genius sister was covering her tracks. *But, oh no. What the fuck am I walking into?* she wondered.

By the time Laura pulled into the driveway of Julia and Ted's two-story McMansion, it had been at least an hour and a half since Julia's first text. *If he's dead, he is very dead,* Laura thought, *and if he is not, he is probably furious.*

Her thumb hovered over Evan's name on her recent call list. But before she pressed the call button to ask her husband for advice, she had an idea, one she wished she had thought of before coming here.

She scrolled through her contact list, found Ted's number, and pressed it. The phone rang and rang until his voicemail started up: *You've reached me. Leave a message.* He even sounded like a prick on his voicemail.

"Hey, Ted; it's Laura. Julia was concerned that she couldn't get ahold of you, so she asked if I would stop by and check in. Call me if you get this, please. You know Julia; she is worried."

She ended the call, stepped out of the car, and walked to the front door. The longer she waited, she knew, the odder it might look to anyone in the neighborhood. So she did it in a rush before she could stop herself.

Laura rang the doorbell first, then rapped on the door. She called his name between knocks, but there was no response.

She could try the back door; she *should* try the back door, but she had the spare key, so why would she? If this were any other day and her sister asked her to come by, would she check around back? Mind racing, Laura wasn't sure what would look right.

She grabbed her key and opened the door.

Peeking her head inside, she wondered if Julia had wanted her to catch Ted cheating. Maybe she and Ellie were going on a little trip, and Julia knew Ted would be alone, so she needed her sister to catch him in the act. Then she would indeed have grounds for a divorce, because she would be a witness to it. *Smart,* she thought, *but what if he gets mad and tries to hurt me?*

"You owe me big time, Julia," Laura muttered.

"Ted! It's me, Laura! I'm coming inside. Jules wanted me to check on you!"

The door pushed open—but something resisted. She caught it just before it hit her in the face. Then, with a harder shove, she opened it further.

As guessed, the obstruction was Ted. He was lying at the bottom of the stairs, his arm bent behind his back. There was congealed blood on his face and head, and some pooling beneath him, the origin of which she couldn't determine. She felt every beat of her heart as she pulled out her phone and shakily dialed 911.

"Nine one one," said the dispatcher, "how can I help you?"

"There's been an accident." Her voice quavered.

"Do you need police, fire, or an ambulance?"

"Ambulance, I guess."

"Okay, ma'am; can I have your name?"

"Laura Mayfield."

"Thank you. We are tracking your location. Can you tell me what happened?"

"My brother-in-law is lying at the bottom of the staircase. I think he fell."

"Okay, ma'am; can you tell if he is breathing?"

"It doesn't look like it."

"Okay, would you be able to check his pulse? All you need to do is take your index and middle finger and—"

"It's fine. I'm a nurse. I'll check his pulse." Laura pressed her two fingers to Ted's carotid artery and waited. She almost let the next word slip out: *Fuck.* But she caught herself and said, "It's slight, but he's got a pulse."

CHAPTER 4

JULIA

JULIA STEPPED INTO the office, Ellie at her heels. She could smell the cedar before even seeing the wood paneling lining the walls. There were a few reasons she'd chosen the Lakeview Resort—one, it was off-grid, and two, Ellie always felt safe near the water. Julia always wondered if her daughter's love of the water stemmed from her father's fear of it. Maybe she felt safe in the water because it was a place he would never go. Whatever the reason, she was happy that her daughter had a refuge, and if she could, she would help provide it. Also, these types of family-owned resorts tended to be less strict with providing an ID and credit card.

Her sister had stayed here once after a patient at the hospital recommended it to her. Laura mentioned its "seclusion," and Julia knew she had chosen that word specifically and intentionally. It had always turned her stomach, the thought of her and her daughter needing a secluded place, but here they were.

The woman behind the counter looked to be in her mid-sixties. She wore her grayish-brown hair in short curls, and her skin looked as though she had spent years in the sun.

She looked friendly enough, but right now, Julia was wary of everyone—no longer trusting her judgment of character.

"Good afternoon," the woman said cheerily. "These look like some new faces."

Julia smiled, relieved that the woman seemed to be kind and welcoming. "Yes, it's our first time here. My sister recommended your place to us."

"Well, thanks to your sister, then. I'm Mary Beth Langsted. My husband, Dave, and I own the place."

"It's nice to meet you," Julia said, praying that it didn't seem strange that she hadn't introduced herself and her daughter.

"Taking a girls' trip?" Mary Beth said, more to Ellie than to her. Ellie looked at her mother, not really knowing what to say.

"Yep, we just needed, er, well, wanted, to get away for a couple of days, and this seemed very relaxing. My daughter loves the water."

"Well, the lake is beautiful right now, clear as a bell." Mary Beth's focus remained on Ellie. "You can see right down to the bottom and all the little fish swimming around."

"That sounds great," Julia said.

"As a matter of fact, I have the perfect cabin for you. It's called the Lakeview Cabin. Can you guess why?"

"Because you can see the lake?" Ellie responded with a big, proud smile, and her mother's heart felt lighter seeing it.

"Smart girl, you have won yourself a candy," Mary Beth said, pulling a basket of Dum Dums from behind the counter. "Do you mind, Mom?"

Julia nudged her daughter with her elbow. "It's fine with me."

"Thank you," Ellie said, taking more than a few seconds to pick her flavor.

"Now, let's get you set up. I'll need a bit of information, as well as an ID and credit card to book your room."

Julia's smile fell. She didn't want to let on that she had no intention of giving this woman her ID or credit card, so she opened her purse and dug around. She dug past her wallet and looked at the envelope of cash she had gotten from the bank after they'd left their house that morning. How was she going to justify having enough cash to pay for a cabin, but no credit card or ID?

"Oh no," she said, looking up at Mary Beth. "I can't seem to find my wallet."

Julia waited for Mary Beth's response, but Ellie spoke up. "Maybe it fell out in the car? I can go check."

Please don't be helpful right now, baby, Julia thought. *But then again, this may work to our advantage.*

"Sure," Julia said, fishing out her car keys and handing them to Ellie.

"I'll be right back," Ellie said, skipping out of the office and out to their car parked in front of it. Julia watched Ellie through the large picture window at the front of the office, which was an add-on to the main home. Mary Beth's residence, she guessed.

"While she's doing that, would you mind filling out this paper for me?" Mary Beth said, handing over a clipboard with a half sheet of paper attached. It was a standard form—name, address, email, reason for a visit. Julia took it with a smile, glancing over to see that Ellie was still searching the car.

She wrote the first name that came to mind, Jane Douglas. For the address, she listed one of the houses she grew up in. Email, jdouglas@gmail.com, easy enough. There had to be someone with that email somewhere who would assume emails from the Lakeview Resort in Loomis Falls, Wisconsin, were nothing but junk mail.

A small bell chimed as Ellie came through the door looking disappointed. "No luck?" Julia asked, noticing her daughter's defeat with a twinge of guilt for sending her on a wild goose chase.

"You know what?" Julia said, handing the clipboard back to Mary Beth. "I'll bet I left it at the bank. We stopped to get some cash for our trip, and that was the last time I had my ID. I have the cash," she said, reaching into her purse to show the envelope. "Is there any way we could pay cash for now? I can call the bank and ask if they found it? Maybe they would fax over a copy of my ID?"

"We don't have a fax machine," said Mary Beth. "Never cared for them."

"Email? I can leave a large deposit."

Mary Beth looked at Julia and Ellie with what looked like both sympathy and hesitation.

"I don't want to ruin a girls' trip," the woman said at last. "I guess it will be all right for one night."

Just then, Julia exhaled, realizing she'd been holding her breath. "Thank you so much. I will call the bank right away."

"You'd better hurry. I don't know about your bank, but mine closes around this time." Mary Beth pointed at the clock, which read 5:45 p.m.

"Yes, you're right, thank you," Julia said, then noticed Mary Beth's gaze darting quickly away from her. Julia's hand brushed her throat as she remembered what it had endured earlier that morning. Had it left more of a mark than she remembered seeing? Her appearance hadn't been her top priority at any point that day.

"That's one-fifty for the night," Mary Beth said, waiting as Julia fished out the money from the envelope.

"I can leave a night's deposit as well."

Mary Beth raised her hands in a shooing gesture. Addressing Ellie, she said, "I can't very well take all that fun money from you now, can I?"

15

Ellie smiled a confused but genuine smile.

"I insist," Julia said, handing over another hundred and fifty dollars in cash.

"You two look honest to me," Mary Beth said, winking at Ellie. "I trust you."

Mary Beth folded the money over into Julia's hands. "Plus, you're going to need the cash if you go into town. Most of these places still only accept cash."

She's right, Julia thought. Not wanting to be in this office arguing any longer than she had to, she simply said, "Thank you."

"You're very welcome. We are glad to have you; you'll be safe here," Mary Beth said, handing over the keys to the cabin and holding on to Julia's hand for just a moment longer than expected. A tear slid from Julia's eye, and she quickly wiped it away with her free hand. Mary Beth gave a knowing nod as she released her hand, and Julia gratefully returned it. The tightness in her chest released just enough for her to compose herself and head for the door.

Just as the two were about to leave, a man entered the office from the house. "Howdy folks," he said, tipping an imaginary cowboy hat in their direction. Ellie giggled.

Mary Beth gestured to him. "This is my husband, Dave, and this is Mrs. Douglas and her daughter. You know, I'm not sure I got your name, sweetheart."

Ellie opened her mouth to speak, and Julia cringed, waiting for her response. There was an instant shift in the room's energy. Julia shivered.

Ellie paused for a moment and said, "Kinsley; it's nice to meet you, sir." And with that, she gave him a curtsy, holding on to her imaginary gown. Now it was Dave's turn to laugh.

"Wonderful to meet you, little lady. I see you're all set." Dave pointed to the large key chain in Julia's hand.

"Yep, all set. Thank you again." Julia placed a hand on her daughter's shoulder and guided her out. Ellie turned and gave the two a little wave; delighted, they smiled back at her.

Julia was relieved that Ellie had given them a fake name but couldn't for the life of her figure out why. Was it possible for an eight-year-old to be so perceptive as to realize that, if her mother had given a false name, she should too? Or was there something or someone guiding her to do so?

Julia couldn't help but think of the time when three-year-old Ellie had gotten away from her at the park and climbed one of the tall landings. Julia ran up the stairs and still couldn't find her, and when she reached the landing where her daughter had stood moments before, she'd looked down to find her daughter sitting peacefully in the mulch, like she'd been there all along.

Hadn't there been times throughout Ellie's childhood when she felt like she had been given an extra hand? Sure, but Julia always considered that to be the universe's way of balancing scales. She wasn't sure, but Ellie was much more intuitive than Julia had been at her age. Much, much more.

Julia and Ellie were about to get into the car to drive over to the cabin, which was visible from the parking lot, when suddenly, Mary Beth rushed out from the office, catching them before they hopped inside. "There's a problem," Mary Beth said, and Julia's heart sank. *How could they have found out so soon?*

"I can explain," Julia began.

"I completely forgot," said Mary Beth, "the Lakeview Cabin has already been reserved for the night. We have a regular, and I seem to have forgotten that it was his night. But I am going to give you the Evergreen Cabin instead. Now, you won't have the same lake view, but it's bigger, with a separate bedroom, which is nice. Consider it a free upgrade for my mistake."

With that, Mary Beth handed over keys that looked identical, save for the name on the attached strip of wood. Julia handed her back the Lakeview Cabin keys and took the new set.

"It's no problem," Julia said, still not sure she was hearing her right. "Thank you for the upgrade."

Mary Beth grinned. "It's my pleasure, and I promise if you take a walk to the back of the cabin, you'll get the same lake view."

"Sounds great," Julia said, her pulse slowing after the startle. She wasn't sure how much more stress her poor heart could handle, but she would soon find out.

CHAPTER 5

MARK

MARK FOUND HIS cabin as he remembered it. The smell was the same too—mothballs. Who would ever believe that a person could grow to love the smell of mothballs?

He wondered if anyone would think it was strange for a man staying at a resort to have nothing more than an attaché case and a bottle of Jack Daniel's, but he didn't think there was anyone here to care. He, a woman, and her daughter were the resort's sole occupants. It was the offseason. Families returned home; kids resumed school. Except for that little girl, apparently.

"What little girl?" Izzy asked, as if responding to his thoughts. She now stood in the doorway to the bathroom, clutching the frame for balance.

"There's a little girl staying here with her mother, at least I think it's her mother." Mark noticed the similarity in looks between the woman and the girl, both with long brown hair; *it's longer than it should be*, he thought, but wasn't sure why.

Mark went to the window and pulled back the curtain. "They almost stole our cabin," he said, watching the woman grab a single backpack from the trunk of their hatchback.

Surveying their surroundings, the woman took the girl's hand and hurried inside.

"That was strange," he said. "I guess I'm not the only one packing light."

When he turned around, though, he was alone again.

"Why do you keep leaving me?" he said through gritted teeth.

The cabin looked more like a large room than an actual house. Walking in, one found a large log bed frame with a queen-sized mattress and a handmade quilt adorned with woodland creatures. There was a small couch against the wall, and a wood-burning fireplace stood in the corner with a stack of wood beside it. The Langsteds had added a television in the past few years, and as much as Mark loved the nostalgia of a cabin cut off from the modern world, he also loved cuddling up with Izzy before the fire, watching movies from the collection of DVDs that the resort had collected over the years. Their favorites had been the *Sister Act* movies.

He thought of it now as he walked around the cabin. He saw the small kitchenette on the right-side wall, where they'd prepare Jiffy Pop over the hot plate on movie nights; it was always burnt, but they ate it anyway. There was a table big enough for the two of them and two more guests—which they never had—and a small bathroom with enough space for a toilet, a sink, and a shower, one they'd christened on that first night, not caring how tight the fit was. Izzy's ghost was everywhere in this place, and Mark was now even more eager to join her.

He grabbed his attaché case off the small dresser by the door and brought it to the kitchen table. He opened it up and turned it over. Out fell half a dozen prescription pill bottles, all labeled with the name Isabel Peters. He was supposed to give them to the hospice to dispose of, but neither of them had remembered to do so. Although it may have been less of an accident on his part.

He picked up the fallen bottles and placed each of them upright. Doctors had prescribed Isabel numerous pain pills over the last few months of her life, but almost none relieved her pain.

Once the bottles were in place, he went back to the dresser for his bottle of Mr. Daniel's and placed it next to them. He sat in the kitchen chair and contemplated his last meal. After a few minutes, he ripped the plastic off the bottle, opened the cap, and took a drink. He gulped it as if it had been Coke, and when he didn't taste the sweet burn of carbonation—rather the burn of what he thought lighter fluid might taste like—Mark remembered why he'd never been able to take shots of alcohol without gagging. Why, then, had he thought he could wash down these pills with something he couldn't wash down on its own?

He liked Jack Daniel's; it had been his favorite drink, but he'd always added Coke. Sure, that might make him "less of a man," but who was there to care, especially now? The only problem he could see was that he didn't have any Coke. But there was the office vending machine.

The last thing he wanted was to end up in an awkward conversation with either Mary Beth or Dave, but, unwilling to drive back into town, he was willing to take his chances.

Just before he reached the vending machine, the woman in the adjacent cabin walked up to it with her daughter. He waited behind them as they made their decisions. A few long seconds went by before she realized Mark was behind them.

"Oh, shoot," she said, moving aside. "I'm so sorry; you go ahead, please."

"No, it's fine. Take your time. I'm in no hurry." That was a lie, but he thought he'd already inconvenienced them enough with the cabin situation.

"There isn't a huge selection," the woman said.

"Beats driving all the way into town," he added.

"That's for sure, and yet Ellie still takes forever to decide."

Mark blinked. "What did you say?"

"What?" she asked, taken aback.

"I mean, what did you call her? Your daughter, what did you say her name was?"

"Kinsley," she said, wringing her hands together, but her daughter placed a hand on hers, calming her.

"I thought you said something else. Sorry," he said, wondering if the shock of mistaking the familiar name showed on his face.

"It's okay," the woman said, beginning to dig through her purse for coins. She grabbed some quarters and handed them to the girl. Instead of landing in her hand, though, the coins dropped to the ground and rolled. The girl chased them and grabbed all but two, which ended up under the vending machine. She dropped to her knees and tried to reach under, but her arms were too short.

Mark looked around and found a tree branch. He grabbed it and joined her on the ground. He struggled for a few moments to get low enough, then wound up lying on his belly. After some work, he scooped the coins out of their hiding spot.

He raised up onto his hands and knees and met her face-to-face, taking in her deep brown eyes. He handed her the coins, and the touch of their hands produced a little shock of static electricity. Mark pulled away quickly, scraping the girl's hand with one of his too-long fingernails.

"Sorry, I really have to trim those," he said, knowing full well that he hadn't focused on self-care for months, nor did he intend to.

"Who are you sad about?" the girl asked.

They rose to a standing position, and she continued her inquest. "I'm sad, too, about my dad."

At this, the woman grabbed her shoulders and pulled her back and away from Mark. "I'm sorry. Kinsley has never met a stranger," she said, embarrassed.

"You should teach her to be careful. There are a lot of not-nice people in this world."

"I know," Kinsley said, her eyes still penetrating his. It was off-putting, but in a way that made you want to stay and figure out why.

"She has a sixth sense about people," the woman said, and then told her daughter to make her choice. She chose a Coke.

"Good choice," Mark said as they were about to walk away. He placed his dollar in the cash slot.

"Thanks," Kinsley said, "and I'm sorry about your wife."

Mark stiffened, his heart in his throat momentarily. He turned slowly to look at her and ask her how she knew? But they were already walking away. Mark's dollar sat in the slot, getting sucked in before getting shot back out again, over and over, until he remembered what he was there for. He pulled the dollar out, straightened the corners, placed it back in, and then made his choice.

Mark made it back to the cabin, two bottles of Coke in hand. He walked to the kitchen table and sat down.

"You're really still going to do this?" Izzy said from the bed. She was lying on her side facing him, under the covers but still shivering, her chemo cap askew on her head.

"Why wouldn't I?"

"After that?"

"After what?"

"That little girl. I know you heard what that woman called

her daughter. Doesn't that mean something? Doesn't that change things?"

"No, why would it?" he asked.

"I don't know. They seemed off somehow."

"How do you mean?"

"Like standoffish. Or scared."

"Probably because of the strange man frantically asking a little girl's name," he added.

"So you *did* notice," Izzy said.

"Fine, yes, I noticed, but it doesn't change anything."

"Doesn't it?"

"Okay," Mark said, turning his chair to face his wife. "Elaborate."

"Well, it seems like maybe they have gone through something. Packing light, the comment about the little girl's father…"

"And what does that have to do with me?" he asked.

"I wonder how traumatized that little girl would be to wake up to a bunch of flashing lights, only to find out that the nice, sad man who helped rescue her coins was dead inside the cabin next door."

Mark winced. "Do you really believe that?"

"No, but you do. Because I'm not here."

He thought about this, staring at his empty bed. He didn't know that woman and her daughter and didn't owe them anything. It was a supremely selfish thought, yes, but once he was gone, he wouldn't have to see her ever again, right? He wouldn't see the damage he caused, the aftermath of the trauma he left behind. Would he? That was what he didn't know. He saw Izzy all the time, but part of him understood she was built from his memories of her, that she was his only coping mechanism.

Right?

Ultimately though, it would be better to wait. He could watch a movie, live in his memories for a day or two. In the worst-case scenario, he would wait until they left. If they were on the run from something, which he felt they were, they would be gone soon, and he could do what he came here to do.

He thought about popping *Braveheart* into the VCR; it was their favorite movie, but it was also more than his heart could handle, so Mark fell asleep to the sounds of Whoopi Goldberg singing the songs of The Supremes.

⁓

A few hours later, Mark awoke to a frantic knocking on his cabin door and jumped instinctively out of bed. His brain was still wired to wake at the slightest sound—in case Izzy needed him. He searched the dark room for his clothes, but he remembered he was still wearing the only clothes he'd brought with him—gray athletic pants and his favorite, faded navy-blue Up North T-shirt, because, well, who cares?

He looked around for Izzy, struck every time by her absence, her *gone*-ness. The knocking got louder and quicker, and now there was a voice behind it.

"Hello! Could you help me, please?"

It sounded like the woman from next door.

Mark swung the door open, and before he could say a word, she began rambling. "I'm so sorry to wake you, but I didn't know what to do. I need help." Her eyes darted toward her own cabin, then back to Mark as she spoke.

"Whoa, hold on a second," he said, rubbing his eyes. "Slow down; take a breath. My brain hasn't started working yet."

She did what he said and took a deep breath. It seemed to help a little.

"Good, now tell me what happened."

"I went outside to make a phone call because I didn't want to wake Kinsley. When I tried to go back inside, the door was stuck."

"You mean you locked yourself out?"

"No, that's the thing. The door isn't locked; it just won't open."

Mark gave her a quizzical look.

"Come see for yourself," she said rather defensively.

"Let me get my shoes. I'll be right over."

As he walked toward their cabin, he could see her struggling with the knob and pushing her shoulder against the door. "Here, let me try," he said, now standing next to her. She backed away so he could try opening it. Mark turned the knob... and it didn't catch; instead, it turned as far as it would if it had been unlocked. He bent down and looked between the frame and the door itself. The sliver of light that shone from within the cabin proved her claim. The deadbolt wasn't engaged, and when he turned the knob, the entry latch cleared the space as well.

"Huh," he said, standing and looking at the door. "You're right; it's not locked."

She nodded at him. "So, what do I do?" she asked.

"I guess it's just stuck," Mark said. "I'm going to try to push it open." He turned the knob, rested his arm and shoulder against the door, and pushed. When that didn't work, he tried a series of small pushes. The woman began pacing and mumbling to herself, something about her being so stupid and how did she manage to do something like this?

"It's not working," Mark said.

"Oh, my God! Oh, my God!" she said.

"It's okay, don't panic," Mark said.

"How? If she wakes up, she is going to be terrified. She's going to think I left her."

"Or she will wake up, and if she can't find you, she will open the door. Problem solved."

She thought about this for a moment and seemed to realize he was probably right. "I don't hear her in there," Mark said, putting his ear closer to the door. "She must still be sleeping. Did you try any of the windows?"

"I locked them all when we first arrived," she said. The mention of her locking all the windows confirmed Mark's suspicion that the two were running from something.

"Well, it can't hurt to check anyway," he said, walking to the window on the side of the cabin. The woman followed. It was an old hand-crank window, so even if it hadn't been locked, which it was, they likely wouldn't be able to climb through it.

"Well, at least you have your phone," he said. "We can call the local police or fire department, and maybe they can pry it open."

"No!" she said, as if he had just asked her to kick a puppy. "No, we're not doing that."

"*Okay*, I guess we could try to wake Mary Beth and Dave. Maybe they have a trick for getting it open."

"Okay, yeah, that's a good idea," she said.

"Great," he said.

"Great," she repeated.

"It's your cabin, so you should probably go and wake them."

"What if Kinsley wakes up? I need to be here."

"I'll wait here," Mark said.

"Don't you think it would be a little scary if she woke up alone and found a strange man standing outside?"

"I'm not exactly a stranger." *And yet, if I went, I would be the one to walk over and wake up the Langsteds at... What time is it?* he thought and checked his watch. "Shit, it's eleven thirty. I'm going to give them a panic attack if I wake them up now."

The woman shrugged.

And with that, Mark was off.

Distance-wise, the main house was only half a city block away, yet it seemed to go on forever. Mark glanced back at the woman, who was now much farther away, then back to the Langsteds' house, which appeared to be even farther away than when he had started. He shook his head. *That one sip of whiskey couldn't have affected me that much.*

He walked on, then looked back again. Now he was so far that he could no longer see the woman, yet the house was even farther in the distance.

Mark jogged ahead, continuously looking behind him, growing frightened. His heart raced just as his shoulder struck a hard surface. It was the office door. Somehow, he'd run into it.

"Where the fuck did that come from?" he said. *I must be out of it.* Mark looked back at the woman and saw her waiting there.

He knew there was a doorbell outside the office that rang to the main house for emergencies. He remembered using it only once—actually, it'd been Izzy who'd used it. It had been their third or fourth visit to the resort. Mark was showing off his lumberjack skills by chopping—or trying to chop—some wood for their fire, when he missed and sent the maul straight into his foot. Thankfully, he'd not been any stronger than he was, because instead of slicing off one of his toes, the blade had only cut through his toenail. It was not a pretty sight, and his gym shoes were no more for this earth.

Izzy and the Langsteds had concluded there was not much to be done for a big toe sliced part of the way down the toenail. There would be no way to stitch it up, and Mark, by his own admission, was not in too much pain. Thus, they settled for using a centuries-old first-aid kit, which the Langsteds agreed to only after Mark convinced them he had recently gotten a tetanus shot. He did, however, promise to let them call an ambulance the moment he started showing symptoms of lockjaw.

The memory stopped Mark in his place. It was not a happy moment—it had hindered their intended vacation, after all—but the laughs they'd had in the years since more than made up for the trouble, which was why Mark couldn't help but smile as he pressed the doorbell.

He waited; sure it would take a while for someone (Dave, he assumed) to come to the door. After a shorter time than seemed possible, the door swung open on its own. Mark entered the office, and instead of finding a dark, quiet room, he walked into a bright, lively space.

Mary Beth stood at the desk, wearing what looked like an old-fashioned poker dealer's uniform, along with a puffy-sleeved button-down shirt covered by a red-and-white checkered vest with red bands surrounding each arm just above the elbow. On her head sat a green plastic visor that made her curly, chin-length grayish-brown hair stick out in all directions.

The strangest thing about her appearance, though, was the large lit cigar jutting from the side of her mouth. Mark could see her holding it in place with her teeth, lips parting with every puff as she clacked away on an old typewriter.

To his left, he heard a whirring sound and turned to see Dave Langsted frantically pedaling a stationary bike that, most assuredly, had not been there this afternoon. Dave wore a burgundy-colored bellhop uniform, complete with gold buttons and a matching pillbox cap. Sweat dripped down his face as he stared blankly ahead.

Mark knew immediately that this was not something he wished to interrupt, but instead of backing out of the room slowly, as he wished he had, he cleared his throat. Mary Beth's gaze shot up, and when she saw him, she didn't blink.

"How can I help you today, sir?"

"Um…" Mark didn't know what to say. Not because he couldn't remember what he was there for, but because he could hardly hear what she'd asked him over her continuous typing and the cigar causing her to talk out of only one side of her mouth. She never stopped, and he wasn't sure she would even hear him over the noise. But he tried anyway.

He cleared his throat again loudly and spoke up. "Ahem, I'm sorry to disturb you, but I think one of your guests needs some help. Her front door seems to be stuck, and her daughter is still inside."

Mary Beth blinked again, which Mark thought might have been an acknowledgment. Yet, instead of stopping, her typing slowed down dramatically, clicking every few seconds like a slow, methodical pulse.

She smiled wide, but the smile didn't reach her eyes. One of her eyes glistened with what looked like tears. "Did you try the doorknob?"

Click. Click. Click.

"Yes," Mark said, confused at the absurdity of her question. "Is it locked?"

"That's the thing. It isn't locked; it's just stuck."

"I would suggest trying again. Maybe even jiggle the handle next time."

"And if that doesn't work?" He looked over at Dave, still pedaling, then back at Mary, smoking, smiling, clicking.

"If that doesn't work, come back and I'll send Dave to help." She looked toward her confused-looking husband. Mark followed her gaze.

As if Mary Beth's words had broken a spell, the man who Mark would never have described as agile abruptly leaped from the bike, clapped his feet together, and offered Mark a salute.

"Okay... thank you," Mark said, backing away until he bumped into the door. He reached behind his back and turned the knob to exit, not wanting to turn his back on the two.

Mark left the office, but as he was walking away, a thought came to him. He walked back inside and looked at Dave, who was still frozen in salute. Mark raised his flat hand to his own head and saluted the man back, then brought his hand back to his side. Dave relaxed his arm, then climbed back on his bike.

CHAPTER 6

MARK

"What's wrong?" the woman said, eyes widening in concern as he walked toward where she still stood outside of her cabin.

"I think I interrupted some weird shit," Mark said.

"Were you able to wake them?"

"They were already awake, and they weren't much help."

"What did they say to do?"

"Jiggle the doorknob."

"You're kidding me."

"Nope."

"So, what do we do now?"

"I'm not sure," Mark said, giving the doorknob a shake sarcastically. He turned the knob and pushed. The cabin door swung open. They looked at each other, mouths agape.

"No fucking way," Mark said.

"Oh, thank you, Jesus," Julia said, rushing past him to go inside the cabin.

She was about to call out, but Mark grabbed her arm before she could. "Why wake her? She doesn't have to worry about any of this."

She pulled her arm away at first, then seemed to realize

he was right—after all, nothing had really happened. "You're right," she said, taking a deep breath that seemed to slow her down momentarily. "I'm going to go check on her."

Mark nodded, then realized that he had somehow made his way into her cabin. The decor was the same as his, though instead of a queen-sized bed, there was only a couch in the living room. *There must be a separate bedroom*, he thought, and wondered why he and Izzy never inquired about a larger cabin. Mark was just about to leave when the woman rushed back into the living room.

"She's not in there!"

"What?"

"She's gone. I can't find her!" She ran to the bathroom, which was the only other room in the house. "She's not *here!*" The woman moved like a hummingbird, zipping from one place to another, unable to stand still, her eyes wide and searching, her body visibly shaking.

"Call out to her? Maybe she got scared and is hiding somewhere."

"Right. Um... Kinsley?" she called out hesitantly.

"Kinsley!" Mark said, more confident.

"Kinsley, baby, you can come out now. Everything is okay," she said, walking around the cabin, opening closets and cupboards. "Where could she have gone?" She began to tear up. "The door was stuck; she couldn't have gotten out!" After a beat, she said, "Fuck this! Ellie! Ellie, baby! It's okay, please come out!"

Mark stood dumbfounded. To the left of the woman stood Izzy, bundled up in her warm robe and still shivering.

"I told you," Izzy said. Mark just shook his head. *What's the point of pushing a woman who's already on the edge?*

He called out, "Ellie!" The name caught in his throat. "I'm

going to check outside," he added, also as an excuse to hide his own tears.

After a short time, she followed him outside.

"Wait, wait!" he shouted. "Don't close the door!" Mark ran to her before she could pull it shut. "Just in case."

"Good idea," she said, looking around for something to prop the door open with. She found a small shoe.

"Oh, my God, she doesn't even have her shoes." She wedged the shoe in between the door and the frame, and when she rose to her feet, Mark could see her face crumble as she began to weep.

"It's okay," he said, moving closer to her. Instead of embracing her, he put what he hoped was a comforting hand on her shoulder. "She couldn't have gotten far. Is she the type of kid to wander alone in the woods at night?"

"No, not at all. That's why I'm scared. She wouldn't have left." Her sobs grew stronger, and Mark decided a hug was necessary, after all.

"We will find her. I'm going to help you." Julia took a moment but allowed him to hug her as she tried to catch her breath.

"I just realized that I don't even know your name. I'm Mark." He wondered if she would give him another fake name.

She thought for a moment, then said, "Julia."

"Julia and Ellie?"

She nodded.

"All right," Mark said, stepping away from who he now knew as Julia. "As much as I don't want to go back into that office, I think we need to get Mary Beth and Dave to help."

As they walked toward the office, a look of realization crossed Julia's face. "Maybe she went to look for you when she didn't see me; she seemed to have a connection with you," she said, running toward Mark's cabin.

"Shit," he grumbled, jogging after her. "Wait!" he shouted, just as she turned the knob and walked inside.

"Ellie!" she cried as she searched around the cabin, once again opening doors and cabinets, her daughter still nowhere to be found. Julia walked into the kitchen and saw that the tabletop held a slew of prescription bottles standing under the watchful gaze of a bottle of Jack Daniel's. She brought her hand to her mouth, realizing her mistake.

Mark rushed in—too late.

"This is not what you think," he said.

"It's none of my business. I'm so sorry. I wasn't thinking." She walked toward the front door.

"It's just my wife," Mark said. "This is all her medication." Why he felt he had to explain all this to her, he had no idea.

Julia waved a hand at him. "Like I said, not my business. Let's just forget I saw it, okay?"

She was already back outside by the time Mark caught up with her. Neither of them said a word, just walked at a steady speed toward the office.

Mark began, "Listen—"

"All I care about right now is finding my daughter," she cut in. "After we do that, I will worry about what I just saw in there, okay?"

"No," he said, touching her arm to stop her. "Listen."

Mark looked all around them, at the trees, the grass, the sky, then back at her.

"What am I listening to?"

"Nothing. Do you hear anything?"

Julia focused on the surrounding sounds. He was right: nothing.

"Where are the insects? The animals?" Mark asked. They looked at each other, then back at the office before picking up their pace.

When they reached the office door, Mark gestured for Julia to go inside, then held both hands up as if to say, *Not it.*

She shook her head and opened the door. Instead of finding Mary Beth and Dave in their strange role-play costumes, they walked right into Julia and Ellie's cabin. As Julia stepped over the threshold, she tripped over Ellie's shoe, which she'd propped in the doorjamb.

"Did we go to the wrong building?" she asked Mark as he moved the shoe out of the way and walked inside.

"No, we didn't," Mark said, searching the cabin.

"Ellie! Are you in here?" Julia called.

"Ellie!" Mark echoed.

"We must've gotten turned around," Julia said. She walked over to the front door and pulled it open. She took one step outside and, instead of being outdoors, wound up right back inside the cabin. Mark walked toward the open door and looked through it. Instead of seeing the darkness outside, he saw what looked like a mirror reflection, though it wasn't of himself but Julia.

"What the fuck is this?" Mark said. Julia shook her head, not wanting to believe what she was seeing. She rushed back toward him, and they took each other's hands, standing together in the cabin, regarding only each other, afraid to look anywhere else. Mark counted one, two, three, then pulled her through the doorway and over to his side.

They both looked back through the open door and saw their own reflections on the other side. Mark reached for the door and slammed it closed, then guided Julia over to the couch and sat her down.

"We need to think," Mark said, sitting down next to her. "We just need to think this through."

"Think what through?" Julia buried her head in her hands. "What the fuck *is* this?"

"There has to be an explanation for all of this."

"Great, what is it?"

"Maybe it's some kind of prank? Do you know someone who may want to trick you?"

"Yes, but even if they did, how? How could they possibly do this?"

He frowned. "Maybe it's some sort of sound stage or something?"

"How would we end up on a soundstage? What is this, *The fucking Twilight Zone*?"

"I don't know! I don't know!" Mark said, standing and pacing the floor in front of her. "Maybe we were drugged and brought here."

"That seems kind of elaborate, don't you think?"

"I don't know!" After some hesitation, Mark asked, "Just what kind of trouble are you in?"

"Me? I don't think you have the right to say anything to me about trouble."

"What is that supposed to mean?"

"Oh gosh, I don't know. Maybe it has something to do with the little pill party you have going on over at your cabin."

"And what about you, 'Julia'?" he said, making air quotes. "Or 'Kinsley'?"

"You know nothing about us! And don't you dare say anything about my daughter! Why don't you go back to your cabin and finish what you started?" As soon as the words came out of her mouth, he could see the regret on her face. "I didn't mean—"

Mark held a hand up to stop her. "Wait a minute. I bet that's it."

"What's it?" Julia asked, gritting her teeth.

"We're drugged, or not drugged exactly, but I bet this is

some kind of gas leak. I'm probably still in bed hallucinating all of this. You're not even here."

"Then how do I wake you up?"

"Pinch me."

"Gladly," she said, grabbing the skin on his forearm and squeezing it hard.

"Ouch, all right—enough."

"Any other theories, Einstein?"

"At least I'm thinking instead of panicking."

"Says a man who obviously doesn't have children." The look on his face told her she'd struck a chord. "And I put my foot in it again," she said, looking down toward her feet, avoiding his saddened face.

"I can tell you that bickering will not help the situation," he said. They were sitting together in an uncomfortable silence, trying to figure out their next move, when a little voice sounded from the bedroom.

"Mommy?"

Julia jumped to her feet and rushed toward the bedroom. Instead of finding her daughter in the doorway, however, she came face-to-face with him.

CHAPTER 7

TED AND IZZY

TED. HIS NAME fit his face, especially his 1970s mustache and feathered light brown hair. He looked like he ought to be on a motorcycle. With his looks and charm, medical sales were the smartest, most lucrative way to go without a degree, and man was he good at charming the office staff, or anyone for that matter. He was tall and muscular—he worked hard on his physique; his body looked good, and he knew it. He looked like he could wreck a person and probably had. Many times.

Ted and Julia had been married for eight years. She would recognize him anywhere, but the version of Ted walking toward her now was at least five years younger, more handsome with those sharp, enviable Hollywood features.

Julia stumbled backward. To Mark, it looked as though she were cowering. The tall man paid no mind, as if he didn't care, or maybe he didn't see her. She looked as if she expected a blow, and when she didn't receive it, she turned back to him.

As she opened her mouth to speak, another voice issued from the bedroom. Her voice. Mark and Julia both watched in dumbfounded amazement as another, younger version of Julia exited the bedroom.

"Look what you did," younger Julia growled.

"What did I do this time?" Ted asked, exasperated.

"You're going to traumatize her!"

"I just told her that big girls sleep in their big girl beds."

"How dare you!"

"How dare I what, Julia? All I'm doing is being a parent to our daughter," he said in a seemingly patient, non-condescending tone.

"What the fuck am I seeing?" Mark asked, sidling up to the version of Julia he knew to be the real one.

"It didn't happen like this," Julia said.

"What are you talking about?" Mark asked.

"I don't know what's happening. But that night... it didn't go like this."

They stood together, watching the scene as if it were a Lifetime movie playing out before them.

"I understand you want to be close to her, Julia, but if you keep letting her sleep with us, she will never learn to get over her fears," Ted said, reaching for younger Julia's hand. Before he could grab it, she yanked it away.

"You're trying to turn our daughter against me!" she shouted.

"I would never—"

That same tiny voice they'd heard earlier—now closer—startled all four of them. It was Ellie, but she couldn't have been over three or four years old.

"Daddy?" she squeaked, hugging a yellow blanket close to her face.

The other Julia, her younger self, whipped around to find her daughter and swiftly picked her up. "Don't you fucking come near us!" she spat, seemingly unconcerned about screaming in her daughter's ear. Spittle flew from her mouth—she looked almost rabid. She turned and marched away, with Ellie clinging to her side.

They found another door further down a hallway that hadn't existed moments ago. They went inside, and she slammed the door shut and engaged the lock, leaving Ted behind standing at the out-of-place kitchen counter, shaking his head.

"You know that's not how it happened, you son of a bitch!" The real Julia reached for a knife from the block on the counter and rushed toward Ted.

Mark realized what she intended to do and grabbed her by the wrist before she could thrust it into Ted's back. There was no need for his heroics, though, because Ted was no longer there, the countertop was gone, and Julia herself no longer held a knife. Once again, they were back in the small kitchenette of the cabin.

Mark and Julia could only stare at one another.

"Mark?" a weak voice squeaked from the living room. Mark didn't turn to look where the sound had originated— he knew it was Isabel. What surprised him was the gradual turning of Julia's head.

"Um… I'm not sure, but I think this one may be for you," she said, slowly backing away from the scene before her, stumbling over her own feet as she did.

"You can see her?"

"You mean the woman in the hospital bed where a couch should be?" she asked, not looking away from the obviously sick woman in front of her.

Mark nodded.

"Yes."

The scene unfolding before them now was one he'd been trying to escape for close to a year. Mark took a step toward Isabel but was cut off by a figure. He knew it well, by the clothes it was wearing: ridiculous Snoopy pajama pants and a plain white undershirt. He remembered how foolish he'd felt wearing them when the funeral home came to pick up his wife's body that same evening. He also remembered thinking that Izzy would've found it hilarious.

They both watched now as he went to her bedside and sat in the recliner, the one he'd placed next to her and used as a bed in those last few weeks. Mark watched himself check her pulse. He remembered doing it, as the hospice nurse had told him what he should be feeling for in the end, and because of this, he knew the time was near.

But something unusual caught his attention. She'd called out to him just moments ago; when in reality, Izzy hadn't spoken a word since that morning. In that moment, inside the strange hybrid cabin and condo, Mark could only think of how grateful he was that they were not reliving that moment, which was his and hers alone.

"This is wrong," Mark muttered.

"No shit," Julia said.

"No. I mean, yes, but the memory. It's wrong."

Mark stepped closer to the scene so he could hear the conversation better. Julia, although hesitant, followed beside him.

"I don't want to go," Isabel groaned. "I'm not ready. Please. Please, Mark, I don't want to die. I love you. How could you do this to me?"

As Mark watched his past, exhausted self grab a vial of medicine from the nightstand, he covered his mouth and shook his head. He didn't say a word to her as she pled with him. He grabbed her IV port and rested it on the bed next to her. Then he picked up a syringe and held the vial upside down, drawing the liquid into it. Izzy's eyes looked frantic. She searched the room for someone or something to help her. She grabbed the port and tried to hide, but the other Mark, his past self, saw her and grabbed it away from her. Izzy continued to plead with him.

"I'll get better, I promise," she said. "We can start a family like you wanted. Please don't do this."

The other Mark, his past self, grabbed the port and injected the needle into it, staring at her with cold, uncaring eyes as he pushed the plunger.

"Please," she begged. "Is it going to hurt? I'm so scared it will hurt."

Her fear was what wrenched the real Mark. He leapt at the version of him standing in front of them, intending to rip the IV from his dying wife's vein... but he landed face-first on the living room couch instead. The two extra people were gone, leaving Julia with a man who had his head buried in the couch cushions as he sobbed. She moved closer to him and paused for a moment before taking a seat beside him, where she placed a hand on his back and rubbed in a circular motion, just as she had with Ellie when calming her after many childhood slights.

"I'm guessing that's not what really happened," she said.

Mark could only shake his head. There were no words.

CHAPTER 8

ELLIE

SHE WAS DREAMING about the ocean; it was her safe place. The place she went to in her head when real life got too scary. She had never seen it in person, but somehow knew exactly what it looked like, even smelled like. Over the years—well, the more recent ones at least—she had trained herself to think hard about it before falling asleep.

Eventually, the water seeped into her dreams. The sound of someone crying woke her from her dream. It wasn't her mother. It sounded like a man, but it wasn't her father, either.

"Mom?" she called out, expecting her to come running, especially tonight. When she didn't, she got scared.

"Mommy!" She hadn't called her that in at least a year, but tonight, Ellie felt at least a year younger. She peeked around the open bedroom door into the living room area. She couldn't see anyone, but as she entered the room, she could feel a presence.

"Mom!"

Once again, no response. Panicking, Ellie ran to the bathroom and threw open the door. Nothing. She flipped the light on in the bedroom, wondering if maybe, in her haste, she'd missed her mom sleeping right next to her. No. She even checked the bedroom closet.

Ellie ended her search in the kitchen and saw her mother's purse on the floor with its items scattered all around it. She went to it, finding it strange... not only her purse being dumped out on the floor, but for her to have gone somewhere without it. She sorted through the mess, searching for her mother's phone. If she found it, she could call someone for help. If she didn't, it meant Mom had it with her, and if that were the case, she likely left to make a call.

When she didn't find the phone, she felt relieved. She had probably just gone outside to make the call. "Thanks a lot, Mom," she said to no one, but she looked toward the middle of the room when she did.

Next, Ellie looked for her shoes. She could've sworn she'd left them at the front door. She had always taken her shoes off upon entering anyone's house, especially her own. It was one of her dad's pet peeves, but where had they gone? She reached for the door handle, swung it open, and stepped outside.

"Mom!" she called out as she began her search. She was brave; she knew she was, because her mom reminded her all the time, but shivers still ran through her body. She couldn't help it; she was still a kid, after all. Every time she called to her mother and didn't get a response, she felt a familiar sting in her eyes, the rush of emotions just before a breakdown, though this time she was able to prevent it with a thought.

The water. She would go to the water. Ellie turned and headed toward the lake.

She wiped at her eyes with her shirtsleeve as she walked, feeling at least a little more hopeful. But then again, how long had she been walking? She turned around to see how far away she was from the cabin.

It had to have been at least five minutes, but she was still right next to the cabin. And the lake still looked like nothing but darkness in the distance. At this time of night, she thought she would be able to see the moon shining on its surface. The lake was just beyond the office, and that was right ahead of her.

She started to run, which wasn't easy without her shoes—except, she wasn't feeling sticks or rocks or weeds. The grass felt almost fake, like what you would imagine movie grass would feel like. It had a definite bounce to it, but no matter how fast she ran, she didn't get anywhere; she was still the same distance away from the cabin.

"Mom!" she screamed as she collapsed onto the... what was it? Foam? She allowed herself to catch her breath, refusing to panic. She wondered what time it was, then remembered her Apple Watch. She slapped her forehead.

"How stupid am I?" she hissed. She didn't have her own iPhone, but her mom did get her a secret Apple Watch for Christmas last year, which she could only wear when her dad wasn't around.

She hadn't remembered putting it on, or even bringing it with her when they left the house, but there it was. Her watch was linked to her mother's phone, and there wasn't much you could do on it without Wi-Fi; but you could call for emergency help, and what was this, if not an emergency? She checked the time.

5:36.

"What the...?"

She pressed and held the button on the side of the watch, like her mom had taught her to do in case of an emergency, but instead of the SOS slide bar popping up on the screen, a tiny silver ball released into the face of the watch, a watch that was no longer a piece of tech wizardry but one made of cheap plastic.

Her mind raced back to the time she'd asked her parents

if she could get an Apple Watch. They had been at a birthday party for one of her father's co-worker's children. The party took place at a local arcade, and the boy they were there to celebrate was a year younger than Ellie. He showed off his favorite birthday gift, a new Apple Watch, and Ellie had fallen in love with it. The boy's mother was what she had heard her daddy call a "nurse practitioner." Ellie wasn't exactly sure what that was, but she figured if this lady could afford to get one for her kid, her mom and dad should be able to as well.

It was later that night when her father told her he had a surprise for her. He'd sat her on the couch, and from behind his back, he pulled out a long white rectangular box. When he handed it to her, she could see right away what it was.

Ellie looked to her mother, who looked to her father. A look of concern crossed her mom's face. She was probably worried about the money for such an extravagant gift. Her mother always had to be careful with how they used the family money. Ellie didn't care. She squealed with delight and jumped out of her seat. She leapt into her father's arms, almost spilling the drink from his hands.

"All right, all right, go ahead and open it," he said, smiling.

"I will do extra chores for a month, Daddy, I promise," she said as she slid open the box. As a child who'd never owned an Apple product, Ellie didn't notice the Apple seal had already been broken.

The packaging was so elegant and clean; she took her time and felt the smoothness of it. She pulled the packaging out of the box and opened the first flap, then the second, revealing an orange plastic watch. It wasn't a watch at all—it was supposed to look like one, but instead of a watch face, it held a kid's game, where a tiny silver ball rattled inside, and the object of which was to get the ball to rest in one of three holes. Ellie had seen one just like it in the glass prize case at the arcade earlier in the day. She guessed this was where the rest of her tickets had gone.

Ellie looked up at her father, whose face reflected pure joy. "What do you think?" he said, croaking out a harsh laugh.

Ellie's face grew red with shame and embarrassment. She let the box fall to the ground and tried to hold back a whimper.

"You be careful with that," he said. "Those things are expensive!"

Her mother looked at him with pure hatred. "How could you?"

"What? I gave her a gift. I thought you'd be happy. You two love spending money."

Ellie could no longer hold back her sobs. Knowing that crying made her father angry, she ran to her bedroom.

"Should I start on your list of extra chores?" he called out after her.

"Why don't you have another drink?" her mother said before leaving the room to comfort her child after another one of her husband's cruel jokes.

"Don't mind if I do," he said, taking a sip.

With her mind back to the present, Ellie looked down at the cheap plastic band around her wrist, then grabbed it with her other hand and crushed it before throwing it on the ground and stomping on it.

CHAPTER 9

LAURA

LAURA NEVER DREAMT that she would wish to be on shift, but that was what she was doing as she peeked around the door frame at the two suits headed toward her down the hospital corridor.

She brought her fingers to her mouth to bite them, then thought better of it. Although she wasn't working today, it didn't take a nursing degree to know you should never put your fingers near your mouth at a hospital.

Instead of watching the suited men walk down what seemed like the longest hallway on Earth, she ducked back inside of Ted's room in the intensive care unit, grabbed the chart from the end of his bed, and scanned it as quickly as she could until the sound of footsteps grew closer.

Coma, GCS-P score of one. *It doesn't get much worse than that*, she thought. She slipped the chart back in its place and sat in the chair next to Ted. Laura pulled out her phone and typed something on it, managing only a few words before she heard the knock on the open door.

She tried hard to muster up some tears for her brother-in-law, but she came up dry. Instead, tears of joy came to her at the thought of her sister and niece being free of him at last. She crossed her fingers as the officers entered the room.

She reached for a tissue, hoping the action would invoke sadness, just as one of the men spoke. "Miss Mayfield?"

"Missus," she said, standing up to greet them.

"I'm Detective Mason, and this is my partner, Detective Phillips," said a dark-haired, mustached man of average height, gesturing to his partner, who towered above them both. *He must've played basketball in high school,* she thought. He hunched his shoulders slightly when standing next to his partner, and Laura wondered if that was his way of attempting to make his partner feel more secure. She liked him a bit for that, despite not knowing if her assessment was true or not. She shook both of their hands.

"You can have a seat, ma'am. We just have a few more questions for you if you don't mind. Is now a good time?"

She glanced over at Ted, thinking how it would've been a terrible time in any other situation. But she wanted to get this part over with, so she nodded in agreement. There had been other officers at the scene when the ambulance arrived to pick up Ted, and she had already gone over everything with multiple officers and detectives, then again down at the police station, but she guessed she would have to tell her story at least a hundred times so they could check for inconsistencies, just like they did on true crime shows.

"Actually, would you like to step out into another room?"

"No!"

She'd responded too fast, she knew. She hadn't meant to, but she was desperate to be there with Ted if he woke up. In case he had anything to say. She thought of how to explain away her insistence, then realized that, in this case, the truth would work.

"I want to be here when he wakes up." She thought the "when" instead of "if" was a nice touch.

"Of course," said the detectives. Laura thought of herself as observant, but if anyone asked her about the appearance of the officers she'd spoken to today, she would not have been able to tell you. The only distinguishing features of these two were one man's mustache and their differing heights. It didn't help that it was already past 11:00 p.m., and she had been dealing with this shit all day.

In fact, if she hadn't been an employee of the hospital, there was no way she would've still been allowed to be there. Visiting hours had ended at 9:00 p.m. It also didn't hurt that Laura tended to make friends wherever she went, so she knew nurses in all the various wards.

Mustache looked around for somewhere to sit. *It must be a long day for these two as well*, Laura thought, *if they need a chair for this chat.* He found an armchair and pulled it over to where her chair was. He gestured for his partner to sit, and the man didn't hesitate. It seemed they had this routine down pat. Basketball sat perched on the arm of the chair next to his partner.

"Mrs. Mayfield, have you been in contact with your sister or your niece?" asked the man in the chair. *He must be the lead detective*, she thought.

"I received the texts from her this morning when she asked me to check in on Ted."

"Is that a normal occurrence? Your sister asking you to check in on her husband?"

No, she thought. "It's not an everyday thing, but she has asked before when she was going to be out of town."

Julia cared more about the houseplants than Ted, but these guys didn't need to know that.

"And does your sister go out of town often?"

"On occasion." Laura wasn't sure what she meant by that, but it sounded right.

"She didn't tell you about these plans beforehand?"

"No, well, she talked about going on vacation for a while."

"But you said she goes out of town 'on occasion'?"

"Well, yes, but not for vacations."

"What does she go out of town for?"

"Well, maybe not out of town, but she goes on school trips and things with Ellie."

"Are you and your sister close?"

"Yes, very close."

"Yet you don't find it strange that she wouldn't tell you she and her daughter were going on a trip?"

Yes, very.

"No, not really. We're close as sisters, but we're not up each other's butts." With that, Basketball let out a chuckle. His partner shot him a questionable glance, and he lifted his hand and coughed into it.

"Listen, I've been answering questions all day," Laura said, regaining the control she knew she'd been losing. "I really could use a break."

"The thing is, we haven't been able to reach your sister. She was able to text you earlier in the day, but since you found her husband at the bottom of their staircase, we haven't been able to reach her. Don't you find that strange?"

Yes. "Not really."

"Have you been able to get a hold of her, Mrs. Mayfield? You know, to tell her how her husband is? Since she seemed so worried about him earlier?"

"No, I haven't."

"And you have no idea where she went."

Laura shook her head.

"Okay, then. Would you mind letting us look at your

phone, just in case your sister's earlier texts could give us some kind of clue where they went?"

"I don't think I feel comfortable with that, no."

Now it was Basketball's turn to jump in. "The thing is, Mrs. Mayfield. May I call you Laura?"

She nodded.

"The thing is, this doesn't look like a simple accident. I think someone may have pushed Mr. Barnet down those stairs, and we're concerned that your sister and your niece may also be in danger. We've had cases of kidnappings before that looked quite similar to this one."

"Kidnapping? You think my sister and my niece were kidnapped? By whom?"

"That's what we're trying to find out. And we could use your help."

Lost in her thoughts, Laura didn't respond. Could that be true? Could Julia and Ellie be in danger? And if so, was keeping the texts from the police actually hurting or helping them? Laura assumed Julia knew what had happened. But what if her sister had been coerced into sending those cryptic texts?

"We're going to go down the hall, grab some coffee, and give you a few minutes to think. Can we bring you some?"

Laura stared blankly ahead.

"Laura?"

"Huh?" she snapped back.

"Coffee?"

"Sure, thanks," she said, still lost in her thoughts.

"We'll give you some time to decide." The detectives left the room, and Laura panicked. What if she was putting them in danger? How could she have been so stupid? Was her sister capable of attempting to murder her husband? If she had been, why not sooner? Why suffer for so long?

Laura brought her fingers to her mouth, then stopped

herself, looked at her fingertips, and thought, fuck it. She tore at the skin next to her middle fingernail with her teeth, pulling a chunk off and chewing on it. She stood up and walked over to Ted. "Listen, fucker," she whispered to him. "If Jules did this, you can fucking rot. But if she's in trouble, you need to wake the fuck up and tell me what happened to my sister, or I'll kill you myself."

The two detectives walked back in, holding their cups of coffee. Basketball held out a cup for Laura. She took it, thought for a moment, and then said, "I think I may know where she is."

CHAPTER 10

ELLIE

ONCE SHE FINISHED what her father would've called a "pissy fit," Ellie realized with terrifying clarity that she was alone in a dark and strange place. She shook, not from the cold—it was her natural response to fear. It was, in fact, so natural and so commonplace that the shaking almost comforted her. *At least I feel normal*, she thought, not without sadness.

What do you do in an emergency? Ellie thought. *You call nine one one. No phone. You find an adult. Where is the nearest adult?* Ellie glanced at the cabin next to theirs, the sad man's cabin. She didn't want to bother him if she didn't have to. He seemed to have enough on his mind; his sadness oozed off him. She was afraid she would catch it like a virus, as she sometimes did.

The office. Why didn't I think of that sooner? That lady was nice. She'll help.

This time, as she moved forward, step by step, she got closer and closer to the office. She was too afraid to look back. When she reached the office door, she attempted to open it, but it was locked. She tried again, because why not? Still locked; she was about to get worked up again when she saw the orange glow of a small doorbell on the wall next to the door.

Without hesitation, she pushed it, then pushed it again. She held it down, then pressed it repeatedly in quick succession. The nice lady would probably be mad, but at least she would come. Ellie crossed her fingers and waited. No one came, but they were pretty old and probably sleeping, so maybe it would take a while for them to come to the door.

Time eddied on.

She glanced at her watch that wasn't there. She didn't know why she tried to check her watch, but she had seen lots of adults do it when they got impatient, and right now she was as impatient as she had ever been. She was just about to walk around the house to find another door to knock on when she heard a *zip* behind the office door—the sound, she realized, of the front glass door's vertical blinds being drawn up. As Ellie moved closer to the door's window, she saw only darkness.

Then, as if having materialized out of thin air, Mary Beth stood there, her face eerily close to the glass. She wasn't smiling, like before. Her mouth was slack, as were her eyes. Ellie thought of the old cartoons with the dog named Droopy her father made her watch when she was smaller. He liked the dog because it was sad. The woman didn't look sad, though. She looked tired, or not exactly tired, but like she was still sleeping.

"I'm sorry to bother you," she said, "but I need some help. I—"

A series of inaudible mumblings fell from Mary Beth's mouth.

"I can't hear you," Ellie said loudly back to her. Mary Beth kept mumbling, too quiet to hear.

"I can't find my mom!" she shouted. "I need your help!" Frustrated, Ellie reached for the door handle and tried to pull it open, but it remained locked.

"Will you please open the door? I need your help!" She moved closer, her ear now pressed against the glass. She strained to hear the words behind the mumbles.

"I'm sorry," Mary Beth was saying, over and over. "We're sleeping right now. Please try again later."

It was like she was reciting a voicemail recording, with no recognition of what Ellie was saying, or even that she was standing in front of her.

"I'm sorry, we're sleeping right now. Please try again—"

Ellie moved her head away from the glass, raised her hand, and slapped the glass in front of the woman's face as hard as she could without breaking it. Mary Beth didn't even flinch, nor did she break her repetition.

"I'm sorry, we're sleeping right now. Please try again later."

Her eyelids were still at half-mast, but instead of reacting like anyone else would to a sudden assault, Mary Beth slowly closed the blinds as she spoke.

"No, no, no!" Ellie shouted, slapping the window as if her hand might stop the blinds from blocking her view. She kicked the door with the ball of her bare foot, then turned around toward her next option: the sad man's cabin.

She walked back toward his cabin at a slower pace, ignoring her anxious urge to move faster. She had one of those feelings again. The kind telling her that something wasn't right, but that she had no choice—and right now, Ellie was tired of not having choices.

Reaching the sad man's cabin, she raised her fist to knock, then paused. Even though they had only just met this afternoon, she liked him. There was something familiar about him, like talking with a cousin that you had met once before but couldn't quite remember.

But the sadness. The sadness oozed out of him like sweat she wished she could wipe away.

Ellie pushed past her hesitation, which felt like an actual physical pressure against her hand. She knocked hard on the cabin door three times and bounced on the balls of her feet as she waited. She was just about to turn away when it opened.

There he was, dressed in a pair of Snoopy pajama bottoms and a white T-shirt. "Okay, okay, what is it?" he asked, rubbing his eyes. His hair was sticking up everywhere, as if his head had been in a wrestling match with his pillow.

"I need help," Ellie said, not bothering with formality or politeness.

"What time is it?" he asked. Ellie looked at her wrist where her Apple Watch should've been and shrugged.

"Where is your mother?" the man asked, looking over Ellie's shoulder to the outside.

"I can't find her."

He gave a frustrated sigh and opened the door wider. "Well, come in, then," he said, gesturing to his cabin. Ellie paused for a moment unsure what to do. She felt sure enough to knock on his door in the middle of the night asking for help, but then why was she so worried?

Ellie always had a sense about people, and that sense had always kept her safe. Just like the time the janitor at school had asked her to help him carry some supplies to his closet, then asked her to bring them inside and place them on the shelf. Instead, she set the items on the ground in front of the small room and ran away as if her life had depended on it.

Later in the school year, when the janitor had gone, she'd overheard her dad saying something like, "Maybe we should lock him in the boiler room, set it on fire, and pray to God he doesn't show up in their dreams." Ellie had no idea what he had meant by that, but she had a strong feeling she'd dodged a bullet.

What threw her off now was the exact opposite. She

couldn't read the man, and it was strange because earlier in the day, when she and her mother had met him at the vending machine, she could, and she would've trusted *that* man without hesitation.

The present man shifted his weight from one foot to the other, still holding the door, making it obvious he wouldn't wait much longer for her to decide. Desperate, she stepped inside.

"Have a seat," he said, gesturing to the small table in the kitchen.

She did, but she was antsy, like her bones wanted to jump out of her skin. She wrung her hands together and played with the seams on her pants all while looking over the man's cabin, waiting for him to do something.

"Do you have a phone?" she asked, looking around for one of those old ones connected to a cord and attached to the wall. This place was old. They even had one of those tape machines people used to watch movies on.

"I do, but first, take it easy for a second. Let me get you a drink. Do you like Coke?"

He opened a small refrigerator. She didn't respond. *He knows I do*, she thought. *He saw me get one from the vending machine this afternoon.*

When he opened the fridge, she could see a row of Coke cans lined up within. Cans, she registered, not bottles.

"I really just want to find my mom."

"I know, and we will," he said, snapping open a can. He grabbed a glass from the cabinet above him. His back was turned, so she didn't see him pour the Coke, but she noticed he was taking much longer than it should have to pour one glass, even with giving the foam, as grown-ups said, "time to settle." She saw the empty box that once held a twelve-pack of Coke sitting on the countertop, and it bothered her, but she just couldn't grasp why. He finally turned to her, full glass in hand. He handed her the glass, and she instantly knew why none of this felt right.

The glass in her hand was cold, condensation wetting her palm.

He didn't *have* any Coke. That was why he had been at the vending machine earlier, because he hadn't wanted to drive into town in order to get some. So, why did he have a fridge full of ice-cold cans—especially when they only had bottles of Coke in the vending machine, not cans?

"Drink up," he said, standing over her, watching. Behind him, leaning against the counter, was a woman Ellie knew well. The sight of the woman comforted her beyond measure, and she really needed some comfort at that moment. She had seen her for as long as she could remember, but they had never spoken. Ellie didn't think she could speak, but somehow, she always knew what the woman was trying to tell her. She was beautiful, with long, curly golden hair. She shook her head at Ellie. And without a word, she knew what the woman was trying to say: *That's not him.*

Ellie looked at the man, then back to her—but she was gone.

"I think I'm just going to go find my mom," Ellie said, placing the cup down on the table.

"Don't be rude!" the man shouted, so out of character from earlier that she startled back into her seat. Her eyes teared up as fear set in. She looked at the glass, checking where the foam had dissipated. There was now a fine line that looked white and chalky. She glanced past him to where he had been standing moments before. Lined up along the counter were at least five little orange pill bottles, like the ones you get when you are sick or hurt.

"I'm sorry, but I'm not thirsty," Ellie said, terrified of what the man's response might be.

He only smiled and looked at her in a kind of pitying way, as if he felt sorry for her. But why? "This is going to be better for everyone, I promise," the man said. Before Ellie could react, he had the back of her head in one of his hands and the glass in the other. He pushed the rim of the glass to her lips, splashing the liquid onto her face. He forced the glass between her lips, ramming it into her clenched teeth.

She grabbed at the man's hand, trying to push it away, but his other hand grasped her hair and yanked her head backward. She wanted to beg for him to stop, but she knew that if she opened her mouth, it would give him the opportunity to pour the liquid inside; and even though she didn't know what he'd put in the drink, she knew it had to be something that could hurt or even kill her.

"I am trying to help you," he growled. "You asked for my help."

Ellie kicked her feet and tried to get in between his legs, the area her mother had always said she should aim for, but he was too close to her, and she couldn't get any real power behind her kicks.

"Open your goddamn mouth!" he yelled, slamming the glass down on the table so he could use both hands to pry her mouth open. His nails dug into the flesh around her lips. Noting the glass out of the corner of her eye, she released her grip on one of his forearms and grabbed for it, and with as much strength as she could muster, she smashed it into the side of his face. The glass broke, cutting her hand but knocking him back just enough to give her the space she needed. With all the strength she had left, she sent her leg straight into the now-bleeding man's groin. Mark doubled over in pain and let out a primal growl as Ellie ran for the cabin door, never glancing back.

"Ellie!" he screamed as he exited the cabin, hobbling in her direction. She started running toward the office but then thought better of it—too bright. She didn't want him to see her, so she ran into the darkness. Toward the water.

This time, as she ran, she saw she was creating distance between herself and the cabins—the exterior lights dimmed, but still the man called for her. "You don't need to suffer anymore, Ellie!" he cried. "You don't deserve to live in pain!"

She saw the lake and ran toward it, only slowing enough not to splash the water as she entered the bank. The resort had set up a makeshift beach with a thin line of sand at the base where kids could play and build castles. Next to it was a fishing dock, thankfully unlit at the moment. With only slight trepidation, she waded in up to her shoulders. She wasn't sure what scared her more: this man catching her or putting her head under the cold water of this dark, still lake.

She was about to make the plunge when she realized there was space enough under the dock for her to fit without going under, so she did.

Just as she slid under the deck, she saw the man in the distance, outlined by the light from the cabins behind him. "Ellie!" he called out in a singsong voice. "It's time for your medicine!"

Ellie stood as still as possible, even holding her breath as the man approached the water. She wondered if she had made footprints in the sand, and if she had, would he be able to see them in the dark? He stood on the sand, scanning the water for what seemed like forever. She shivered from the cold and prayed that it wouldn't cause ripples in the water.

The man looked like he was about to turn away when something large brushed Ellie's calf. She let out a sharp yip, sounding to herself like a dog whose tail had just been stepped on. The man turned toward the water, having heard her. He took a step toward the water, but when his bare feet touched it, he shrank back as if burned.

She looked on as the man continued to watch the water, though he didn't seem willing to risk touching it, as if he was too afraid. It went on for so long that Ellie considered moving into his line of sight. She thought about taunting him from the water just to see if he would come any further, but as brave as she felt, she was not a dumb kid, so, as her mom would say, she stayed put.

Minutes passed, and she considered her options. She didn't like any of them. Would the man stand there forever waiting for her? Would they be there until the sun came up or would she die of hypothermia before that happened? What about the cut on her hand? This dirty lake water couldn't be good for it. Was it possible for her to swim to the other side of the lake?

In the daylight, she could see across it, but not now. Still, it seemed far, even if her mom had taken her to swim lessons. If it were up to her father, she would never have set foot in a body of water, but her mom had enrolled her in swimming at school, because, as she had explained to Ellie's dad, it was "mandatory." Ellie didn't know much else. She knew only that she had never felt freer than she did in the water.

That's it, Ellie thought. Her third-grade patience wouldn't hold out any longer, and she was just about to begin the swim across the lake when she heard a sound, almost like a baby crying out for its mother, something she herself longed to do.

Then she heard it again, only closer. This time, there was no doubt about what the sound was. It was the howl of a wolf, and it seemed to be moving closer.

Do wolves swim? Would they swim if they were starving? She hoped it was starving, and that Mr. "Snoopy Pants" would be a good choice for dinner, but the man didn't wait around long enough to see if he was on the menu.

He looked as though he wanted to yell something to her, but instead of drawing attention to himself, he turned and jogged back toward the cabin. The wolf howl stopped, and Ellie decided to make her way out of the water, but just as she was knee-deep and headed for the sandbank, a black shadow emerged and stood on all fours on the grass before her. They both froze, her eyes adjusting to the sight.

This was unlike any wolf she'd ever seen. It was the size of a large man, bent down on all fours, covered with long flowing hair. Or was it "fur" when it was on an animal?

The mammoth wolf turned its gaze to her and let out two distinct cries that Ellie would swear on her life sounded like a wolf's version of "You good?" That was all it took for her to understand that the beast was no danger to her. She blinked rapidly, making sure she wasn't seeing a man instead.

"I'm... okay," she said back to the wolf, who seemed to give her a nod before continuing down the water's edge. It sniffed the ground as if tracking something, then finally made its way into the woods.

"Thanks," she called out quietly, though it was already gone. When she reemerged from the water, she tried to run, but her legs felt like two blocks of solid ice. Instead, she hobbled back toward the light.

CHAPTER 11

JULIA AND MARK

MARK SAT ON the living room couch, his eyes red and puffy from crying. Still having a difficult time holding it back, he kept sucking in air, trying to catch his breath. He hadn't even noticed when Julia grabbed the kitchen chair and used all her anger to send it flying toward the living room window, where it bounced off and landed soundlessly on the wood floor. She picked it up again, this time by the legs, and swung at the window like a tennis racket. The chair sailed across the room in the opposite direction and landed upright in its original position at the kitchen table.

Julia let out a growl of exasperation, her hands resting like claws at her sides. To Mark, she resembled the earlier animalistic version of herself they had seen moments ago.

She went to the front door and kicked it, then stopped, tilting her head just slightly. "Did you hear that?" Julia asked.

Mark didn't respond; either he hadn't heard, or he was so racked with grief he didn't care.

"I could've sworn I heard…"

Then, out of nowhere, a thought popped into her head. "Screwdriver."

Mark frowned. "Huh?"

"Is there a screwdriver in here anywhere?"

"How would I know that?" Mark said. "It's your cabin." But when she didn't reply, he realized she wasn't even talking to him, not really. She was on a mission and conversing with no one in particular.

"A quarter, then," she said, then spotted her purse on the kitchen table. She rummaged around in it, found a penny, tossed it to the ground, and kept searching. At last, she pulled out a quarter, then let her purse drop as she rushed to the front door. The purse fell to the ground, spilling its contents.

"What are you doing?" Mark asked.

"I'm taking the door off of the hinges."

"With a quarter?"

"Do you have a better idea?"

"Maybe," Mark said, getting up from the couch and going to the kitchenette. He opened a drawer, pulled out a butter knife, and held it up. "Try this," he said, walking toward her.

"Don't bother," she said, and they both looked at the screws on the door hinges, the screws that were flush to the wall, not a notch in sight.

Mark rubbed his fingers over the smooth surface, wanting to make sure he wasn't seeing things. "It wouldn't have worked anyway," he said resignedly. "The door would've just floated in midair, blocking our way."

A chirping noise sounded, and Julia's face lit up. She reached into her back pocket and grabbed her cell phone. The time on the screen was strange, 5:36 a.m., but there was also a text notification. She clicked on it.

Laura: *Coma. It doesn't look good.*

Julia clicked on her sister's name and attempted to dial out, but the call dropped. She opened the text messages again and typed: *Help us, trapped at the Lakeview Resort.*

She hit send. Not delivered, try again.

She tried again—not delivered.

"Fuck!"

She thought for a moment, let out a breath, dialed 911, and put the phone on speaker.

"We're sorry, your call cannot be completed as dialed," said the robot voice. "Please try your number again."

Again, she dialed 911. "We're sorry, you never learned your numbers. Your call cannot be completed as dialed."

She tried again.

"We're sorry," said the voice, "that you're a dumb bitch—"

Julia raised her hand to throw the phone, but Mark caught her by the wrist.

"We may need that later," he said, taking it from her and placing it in his own pocket.

Julia nodded.

"It's him. It can't be him, but it's him somehow."

"Who?" Mark asked, guiding her back to the couch and sitting her down.

"That's what he calls me, 'dumb bitch,'" she said, giving a little laugh. "He made Ellie call me that for an entire day once, instead of Mom." She leaned over her knees, head in hands.

"Who did? Who are we talking about here?"

"The devil," she mumbled into her hands.

"Who?"

"My husband. He's the reason we are here. There was an accident at home, and Ted, my husband, Ellie's father, was injured... severely. I grabbed Ellie, and we ran, and this was the only place I could think of to go." Julia wasn't sure how much more to say about what happened. This man was helping her, or trying to, at least, but what about after all of this? How much was safe to tell?

"So, I take it this Ted guy is not the nice, thoughtful person

I saw a little while ago?" Mark said, referring to the scene they both saw play out in front of them.

"That was him, but no, he is nothing like that."

"Okay, you hurt him somehow, and you were afraid, so you both came here, and now what? He's after you?"

"Not exactly. We didn't hurt him. He fell down the stairs. He is back in Illinois, in the hospital… in a coma, apparently."

"Okay," Mark said, shaking his head. "So, he has people after you? Is he connected in some way? Did I get involved with some mob shit?"

"No, it's not like that." Julia got up from the couch, finding it impossible to stay still while explaining something so ridiculous. "I don't know how to explain all of this without sounding crazy. Plus, nothing like this has ever happened before. Not exactly like this, at least."

"Listen, I am very much done playing twenty questions with you, so I need you to tell me what the fuck is going on. Now! *Please.*"

"Have you ever seen the movie *Scanners*?"

"That old movie about telepathy, where the guy's head explodes?"

"Yeah, that's the one."

"Maybe. I don't remember. Why?"

Before Julia could continue her uncomfortable explanation of what she believed was going on, the front door to the cabin flew open, and in walked her daughter, holding her shoes, which she'd found outside the cabin door. Julia's eyes widened.

"Ellie?"

"Mom!"

They ran toward each other. Ellie dropped her shoes to the floor as her mother scooped her up and squeezed her tight. "My baby, my baby," she said, stroking her head. They both cried joyfully, as if they hadn't seen each other in months— although the night had felt nothing short of it.

"Where were you?" Ellie said through wet sniffles. "I've been looking everywhere for you."

"I was looking for you, baby. Where were *you?*"

"I woke up, and you were gone, so I tried to find your phone, and it was gone, so I went looking for you." She squeezed her eyes shut as she tried to explain what had happened.

"Okay, okay, it's okay; we're together now, and that's all that matters." Julia set her daughter down and knelt in front of her.

"Why are you wet, sweetie?" Julia backed up to look at her daughter. "Oh, my God, what happened to your face?" Julia touched the raised red scratches around Ellie's mouth, scanned the rest of her daughter, and saw the blood dripping from her hand at the same moment Ellie was seeing the man that had chased her, that had hurt her, sitting on the cabin's sofa. Ellie's mouth dropped.

"What's wrong, baby?" Julia panicked upon seeing her daughter's reaction. Ellie didn't say a word; instead, she picked up one of the shoes she had dropped and whipped it hard at the man's face, missing him by an inch and striking him in the shoulder. Mark had only a moment to react before she picked up another shoe and sent it flying toward him. He jumped up from the couch, dodging the second one.

"Hey, cut it out!" he said, trying hard not to curse at a little girl.

Ellie searched for something else to throw at the man. She found her mother's purse on the floor and picked it up. She was about to whip it at him, but her mother caught her arm. "Ellie! What are you doing?"

"We have to get away from him. He is going to kill us!"

"Kill you?" Mark said. "Why would I do that?"

"Mom, run! We have to run!" Ellie screamed, looking for more things to throw at Mark.

Julia grabbed her daughter by the waist and picked her up. "Please stop this," she begged her as she carried her to the hallway, brought her into the bedroom, and slammed the door.

She set her daughter on the bed, locked the door behind her, and pressed her back against it. Ellie didn't stop; she just kept searching for either a weapon or a way out.

"Please calm down," her mother said, attempting to grab her daughter.

"He's trying to *kill* me!"

"No, he's not. He's been with me the whole time." Her mother's words finally reached her, and confusion set in. Ellie, to her mother's relief, sat on the bed, face scrunched up, as she tried to straighten things out in her mind.

"Something strange is happening," said Julia. "Nothing is right. Do you think there's a chance that whoever you're running from is not the same man sitting out there?"

She pointed in the direction of the living room. Julia knelt before her daughter, trying to plead with and comfort her at the same time. The culmination of whatever had happened to her while she was gone must've hit her all at once, because Julia no longer saw her mature daughter, who was really eight going on fifteen. She saw the toddler who would run into her arms after falling on the playground, wanting nothing more than comfort and love. And she herself wanted nothing more than to give her exactly that.

Ellie collapsed into her mother's lap, clinging to her as if she were her parachute. They both cried, releasing the pain of not only tonight, but of years past, of all the days and hours that had led them here, which they would never get back. Because of him.

"I know, baby. I know," Julia said, stroking her hair. She

kissed her daughter's head and giggled. Ellie pulled away to look at her mother, not comprehending what could possibly be funny.

"I was just thinking," Julia said. "This is not the worst vacation we've ever been on."

Ellie looked at her, clearly confused, but then her confusion turned to laughter. "You're right." At that moment, they both looked at each other and said: "San Francisco."

This time, they both burst into laughter. Julia felt proud that she could at least give her daughter something to lighten her heart. Even if it was a bad memory. She hoped it was a sign of positive things to come. She held on to that thought, because if her instincts were anywhere near as correct as her daughter's were, she knew she would need to cling to it again soon.

"He felt different," Ellie said.

"What do you mean?" Julia asked, pulling back enough to look into her daughter's eyes.

"The man who was chasing me. He looked the same as the man out there, but I couldn't feel anything from him. No sadness like before, just nothing."

"The man out there has been trying to help me find you since the moment we got separated. And even though I can't feel things like you and your father do, I think he's a good man."

Ellie nodded, understanding.

"Do you think you can give him a chance for me? I will be right there with you."

Ellie looked into her mother's eyes; she could feel her fear but also her relief. She felt the same as always, and Ellie wondered if she would ever have a chance to feel her mother's happiness.

"Okay," Ellie said, standing. "Let's go check him out."

Julia took Ellie's hand, and they both made their way into the living room. Mark was no longer sitting but searching the room for anything that might be of help to them.

"Hi," he said.

"Hi," Julia said. Ellie let her hand slip out of her mother's and went to him.

Mark raised his hands in surrender, and Ellie stared at him. Clear wonder shone from those eyes. Whatever Julia had said to her must have worked, at least a little, because he no longer saw fear there.

"You changed," Ellie said.

"What do you mean?"

"You changed your clothes. You had Snoopy pants on."

Mark looked at Julia, and the recognition hit them at the same time. Julia's hand went to her mouth.

"That wasn't me," Mark said, squatting down to Ellie's level to talk to her face-to-face. He did it slowly so as not to scare her any further. "It looked like me, but it wasn't; do you understand?"

Ellie then glanced over Mark's shoulder for just a moment, gave a slight nod at something neither Mark nor Julia could see, then pulled him into an embrace that knocked him off his feet and onto his butt. She fell into his lap but didn't release the hug. Mark looked to Julia, who shrugged and offered a look that seemed to say, *She does this sometimes.*

Mark let the hug continue, and instead of feeling uncomfortable with this stranger's child embracing him, he felt warmth rush over his body and a sense of calm he hadn't felt in what seemed like years, at least since Izzy.

When she eventually pulled away, all she said was, "You needed that." Then she walked back over to her mother.

"You were right," Ellie added. "He's the good one."

CHAPTER 12

MARK

MARK STOOD IN front of Julia and Ellie, not sure what to say or do. They must've felt the same way, because everyone was quiet.

"What now?" Ellie said, breaking the silence.

"I'm not sure," Julia said, "but we need to get you cleaned up and get your hand bandaged."

"Are you sure that's safe?" Mark asked.

"No, but I also don't think mud and lake water is good for open wounds, so we're going to risk it." Mark noticed that Julia wasn't letting go of her daughter, always laying at least a hand on her shoulder. He couldn't blame her. If he were in her shoes, he would do the same thing after the night they'd been having.

"I'll be right here, just a shout away," Mark said.

"Thanks, Mark," Julia said with a wink, easing the tension in his chest.

He gave a reciprocal nod.

Julia and Ellie grabbed some fresh clothes and went into the bathroom. Mark heard the door close behind them and allowed himself a moment to relax. After all, things had seemed pretty normal over the past twenty minutes or so.

"Normal?" Izzy asked from the couch. She looked a thousand years old, her head resting back against the cushion as if her neck could no longer hold its weight.

"Yes, even you are normal, my dear," Mark said, taking a seat next to her.

"I'm sorry I talked you out of ending things when you had the chance," she said.

"Don't be. Maybe I can help them," Mark said.

"How?"

"I'm not sure, but this all must be happening for a reason."

"You don't believe in fate," she rasped, her breaths increasing with each sentence.

"I believe in decisions, and all of ours brought us here."

"You're smart," she said, smiling.

"You're beautiful," he said, reaching for her hand.

But before they could touch, she was gone. No matter how many times it happened—and it happened often, multiple times a day, in fact—Mark still couldn't get past the pain of not being able to touch her. It was one of the driving forces behind his decision. To touch her again, he would do whatever it took.

Since Ellie had come inside the cabin, Mark realized, neither he nor Julia had checked the front door. He rose to his feet, drew in a deep breath, and went to it, wondering if this time he might find a dragon on the other side, or maybe even the sinister version of himself. What would he do then? Kill it? After witnessing himself and Izzy in her dying moments, he wanted nothing more. He wished to find himself beyond the door. He would... he would what? Slap him? He needed a weapon first.

Mark searched the kitchen, opening cabinets and drawers, looking for anything he could use to bludgeon or stab with, thinking all the while about how unreal all this was. The most dangerous item he found was a steak knife, but he could do some damage with it. He took the knife back to the door with him and turned the knob. He pulled on it.

Nothing. It would no longer open.

He looked at the cracks that separated the door from the frame. They seemed to be sealed shut with some type of caulk, almost like it was a stage door with no purpose or intention except for decoration. He was about to kick it, or stab it, out of nothing more than frustration, when he heard the bathroom door open. Out walked Ellie, dressed in pajamas. They were fitted, dark blue with thin light blue, yellow, and red stripes. She had a towel wrapped around her wet hair. Her mother followed close behind her, juggling a first-aid kit and a hairbrush while still keeping a hand on her daughter.

The sight of Ellie barefoot and cozy in her pajamas warmed a part of Mark's heart he no longer knew existed, but that warmth quickly faded, replaced by a deep sense of mourning for the child he would never have.

"Ellie is what we were going to name our daughter," Mark said, unsure what made him say it out loud. Maybe he wanted someone else to know of her before no one ever would again. The thought of her, if only that, may live on somehow.

Julia looked uncomfortable, searching for something to say, while wrapping a bandage around her own daughter's hand.

"We had her name up there on the nursery wall," he said. "I painted it myself."

"Are you an artist?" Ellie asked.

"Sort of. I'm a writer."

"What kind of books do you write?"

"I write children's books, actually."

"What are they about?"

"Maybe Mr. Mark doesn't want to talk about that right now," Julia said to Ellie.

"It's okay," he said. "I write stories about all sorts of things, but I mostly like writing children's fantasy, dragons and fairies and all that. I enjoy writing about worlds that I'd like to live in."

"How do you mean?" Ellie asked, intrigued.

"Well, maybe if I wished I lived in a castle, I would write about one and imagine that I live there. Does that make sense?"

"Yeah. Sometimes I like to imagine that I'm floating in the ocean. It makes me feel safe."

"That's it. It's like therapy and work all rolled into one."

"I went to therapy once!"

"Okay, that's enough," Julia said, unwinding the towel from her daughter's head and starting to brush her hair.

"You both have beautiful hair," Mark said. "How were you able to grow it out so long?"

"Daddy won't let us cut it. He says short hair makes you look like a di—"

Julia pulled back on the hairbrush.

"Ouch!" Ellie cried. "Can I do it, please?"

"You don't get the knots out all the way."

"But I'll never learn if I don't practice."

"She's got you there," Mark said.

"Enough outta you," Julia said, tossing the first-aid kit at Mark, who flinched before he caught it.

"Nice catch!" Ellie said.

"Thank you very much," Mark said with a little bow at the waist.

This is how it could've been, Mark thought. *This is how being a father could've been, and it would've been magical.*

Ellie looked at Mark's face and frowned.

"I'm sorry about your daughter," Ellie said. "And your wife."

"Thank you, but how did you…?"

"Remember when I said that Ellie has a sixth sense about people?" Julia asked.

"Yeah."

"Well, it's a little more complicated than that. When she was a baby, there were certain people she just wouldn't go to. I mean, if they even attempted to hold her, she would scream as if someone were trying to kill her. Not a normal baby scream, like if she were hungry or wet or sick. It was a cry of pain. I was the only one she would let hold her most of the time."

"And Auntie Laura," Ellie interjected.

"And Auntie Laura, my sister. It wasn't until she started talking that we even began to understand what she was experiencing."

She paused and averted her gaze, as if unsure of how to continue. "She kept saying I can feel your pain," Julia went on. "We thought maybe she saw something on TV and she was reciting it, but we couldn't figure out what until one day she did what she did with you. She was about four or five, and we were at the hospital. I brought her to the ER because she had a barking cough that was just terrifying. It turned out to be croup, and all I needed to do was open the fridge and let her breathe in some cold air, but I had never experienced something like that, so I had no clue that it wasn't something serious. I mean, it sounded serious.

"Anyway, when we were about to leave, Ellie saw a man sitting alone, so she walked up to him and touched his hand and said, 'I'm sorry about your son.' I swear to you it was only minutes before the doctor came out and told that man that his son had died."

"Whoa," Mark said, mouth dropping open.

"That's not all," Julia added. "It must've taken a few minutes for it to sink in, but when it did, that man became irate. He went after the doctor right in front of us, sucker punched him right in the face. He was going off about how the doctor had killed his son. I didn't know what to do. Someone called for security, and in all the commotion, Ellie's hand slipped from mine. I started screaming for her, and before I could catch her, she had made her way to the man and grabbed his leg. I swear to God that man froze like a statue.

"I was terrified, but he just looked down at her, then got down on his knees and sat on the floor next to her. She crawled onto his lap and hugged him. It was as if the anger and the pain drained right out of him. The man was still arrested for attacking the doctor. But he went without a fight."

"Is that what you did for me?" Mark asked Ellie.

She gave a small, shy nod.

"Thank you."

She smiled, not without pride.

"Can I ask you a question?"

"Okay, I guess," Ellie said, looking at her mother for confirmation.

Julia nodded.

"What do you do with it? With the pain, I mean... when you take it away?"

Ellie shrugged, and Mark imagined something—a channel of dark energy being drawn from someone and swirling around in that petite body.

"You don't keep it inside you, do you?" he asked.

"I do," Ellie said.

The look on Julia's face was that of shock and horror. Had she never thought to ask this of her daughter?

"Baby, you said you don't," Julia said, almost panicked.

"It's kind of hard to explain," Ellie said, looking like she thought she had done something wrong. "I don't feel the pain after I take it. The sadness goes away fast, but the knowing stays with me. I'm not explaining this right." She threw her arms up and dropped them to her lap.

"Okay, hold on," Mark said, taking her hands in his. "Take a breath. You have done nothing wrong, and you are explaining things perfectly."

He glanced at Julia, and she gave him an appreciative nod.

"If you don't want to talk about this, we can talk about something else. Like your favorite food, or what you like to watch on—"

"No, I want to…" Ellie took a deep breath and expelled it slowly, an action usually reserved for someone much more experienced in anxiety than she should be.

"It's like I can feel that someone is hurting," she said, "and then I have a strong feeling, like I want to help them feel better, so I hug them; and when I do, the pain gets worse for me, but just for a minute, or as long as the hug lasts. Afterward, I can still feel what that person felt, if I want to, but it doesn't hurt like it did anymore. It's more like a story inside my head."

Mark nodded as if he understood, which seemed to calm Ellie, who let out a sigh of relief.

"Does the pain you feel hurt physically? Like if you were to get—"

"I know what 'physically' means. I'm in the third grade."

Both adults smiled, which was exactly what she was aiming for.

"It doesn't feel like a cut or a bruise," Ellie continued. "It's just, well… it's kind of like how you feel if someone just hurt your puppy in front of you, like really, really badly."

"That's worse sometimes, isn't it?" Mark asked.

"Much worse," Ellie muttered.

Mark met her eyes. "Thank you for sharing that with me."

"Why do you sound like a therapist?" Ellie asked, and both grown-ups laughed.

"I guess I missed my calling," Mark said.

෴

After they passed the time with some mundane but comforting conversation, Ellie had, unbelievably, fallen asleep, her head resting on her mother's lap as she stroked her hair.

In case what he was about to say was something Julia wanted to shield from her daughter, Mark brushed her arm and mouthed the words, "Is she out?"

Julia nodded silently, noting that it was okay to speak.

Mark continued in a hushed voice. "I noticed that you two don't seem as weirded out by all of this as I am. And I guess she sort of explained why, but I still don't understand how your husband is involved in any of this."

With some hesitation, Julia replied, "Whatever Ellie has—this power, or sense, or whatever you want to call it—she got from him. I just didn't realize it until I learned about what she could do."

"He can do the same thing?"

"No, his is different. The only way I can think of to explain it is that, however good and kind my daughter is, he is the exact opposite, only stronger."

Ellie stirred, and Mark put a finger to his mouth. The last thing this little girl needed was to wake up again on this terrible night if she didn't have to. Anything he needed to know, he would ask about later. Fingers crossed, he wouldn't need to.

Mark stood up and stretched, then mouthed to Julia, "I'm going to try the door."

He walked over to it, grabbed the handle, and took a deep breath. Before he turned the knob, he looked back at Julia and jiggled the doorknob. She gave a silent chuckle. Then he turned back to the door, twisted the knob, and pushed it open.

CHAPTER 13

LAURA

"I want to go with you," Laura said after she finished telling the detectives about the resort she'd stayed at once before, the same place her sister had mentioned in a text message earlier in the day.

Basketball snorted. "You weren't even going to tell us about this place, and now you want to go with us? Sure, why not? In fact, why don't you walk into the place first? You can have a little talk with your sister, and if she's in danger, you can just tell whoever has her to quit it."

"Wow, that was really elaborate sarcasm," Laura said, surprised.

"Thanks," he said, shifting his weight to his toes and back again.

"I thought you wanted to be here when he wakes up?" asked Mustache.

For a moment, she was at a loss for words as she recalled her concerned sister-in-law act.

"My husband is going to come and stay with Ted." There wasn't a chance in hell that her husband was going to come to this hospital in the middle of the night for Ted Barnet. Evan hated Ted just as much as the rest of them did, for his own reasons, but these men didn't need to know that.

"We'll let you know if we find her," said Mustache, not even considering her plea. The men turned to walk out of the room, but before Basketball stepped out behind his partner, Laura grabbed him by the elbow. She tried to wait until Mustache was on his way down the hall before saying what she felt she had to, but she didn't really care if he overheard at this point.

"I haven't met anyone who deserves to be in that position more than Ted Barnet," Laura whispered, head nodding toward Ted's unconscious form. Basketball looked over at the man lying in his hospital bed. "Please remember that when you find my sister," she said, letting go of his arm.

The detective gave a serious nod and, with one more look at the pitiful scene, was on his way.

Laura watched him go, turned, and approached Ted's body. "What's going on in there?" she asked him. She thought about making a fist and knocking it on his forehead, but knowing her luck, someone would walk in the room as she did.

Instead, she tested him another way. She took his hand and turned it toward the ceiling. She found the sensitive part of his forearm, grabbed the skin with her thumb and index finger, and pinched as hard as she could without breaking blood vessels.

No reaction. But she continued pinching just a little while longer. When her fingers grew tired, she let go and sat back in her chair.

Laura was not yet satisfied. She scanned his body, thinking about what other tests she could perform, and it suddenly came to her.

After checking the doorway, she reached her hand out toward his breathing tube. Before she could even grasp it, Ted's eyes shot open, and she let out a startled scream and jumped back, heart racing, trying to think of how to explain what she had been doing, not understanding that there was no need.

Once she realized that Ted's eyes were staring at nothing, she moved closer, waving her hand in front of them. She thought she remembered from nursing school someone saying that coma patients' eyes could potentially open, though they weren't seeing anything in particular. She sure as hell was going to get some EyeGard tape to keep them closed from now on.

Laura drew closer to Ted to look into his eyes, certain that, if he was in there, she would be able to tell. She examined his blank stare for what must've been a minute until a nurse walked into the room.

"Hey, girl, how are you doing?" It was Kaitlyn, a short RN who had her mousy brown hair pulled back in a ponytail; she did rounds in the ER occasionally when they were short-staffed. Laura had known her for well over a year, but today she didn't even acknowledge her.

"Laura?" she asked, noticing she hadn't moved from her position angled slightly over the coma patient looking into his unsettling open eyes. "Hey," Kaitlyn said, coming closer to Laura. "Are you okay?" she asked, reaching out to touch her arm. When she did, Laura snapped up, looked out into the hallway without saying a word, and exited the hospital room.

"Rude," Kaitlyn said before moving on with her work.

Laura walked down the hospital corridor, to the nurses' station, and fought to keep herself from turning into the intensive care breakroom.

Laura scanned the room, not finding what she was looking for but also not knowing what it was she was looking for. She opened the drawers and dug around, pulling out napkins and paper plates, ketchup and hot sauce packets. She threw the items on the floor as she picked up her pace. She looked down at the mess on the floor as she made it, feeling terrible for whoever would inevitably have to clean it up. She searched through the cabinets and dropped coffee mugs that crashed to the floor in pieces. It wasn't until she saw the cake box on the counter that she relaxed, knowing what she would find inside.

Why is this happening?

She went to it, stepping on broken ceramic, squishing condiment packets that splattered yellow and red onto her white clogs. She opened the box and saw it—a large, shiny kitchen knife embedded in the remains of a birthday cake.

No.

She grasped the wooden handle and raised the knife, knowing exactly what she was going to do with it. She placed the tip under her chin and pressed. The point pierced her there, drawing a little blood, which trickled down her neck.

Please.

Her hand shook, the tremors growing with every passing second. With a series of small grunts, she shuffled her feet, moving her body closer to the table in the center of the room.

The more Laura's hand shook, the deeper the blade cut into her skin. Once she made it to the table, she raised her left hand, the one not controlling the knife, and placed it flat, palm down, on the table's surface. The jolt of the movement caused her to cry out in pain through gritted teeth as the blade slid deeper into her flesh.

Fuck you.

Squeezing her eyes shut, she sucked in a deep breath. It felt as if she were attempting to move a large boulder, but she reacted anyway; she poured all her energy into the knife-toting hand, forcing it from her chin, and then jammed the blade into the center of her splayed left hand.

CHAPTER 14

MARK

BEHIND THE CABIN door—instead of seeing the darkness outside, or his own reflection, which he guessed he might see—Mark found the interior of a home that he had never seen before.

He looked behind him at Ellie and Julia, who appeared frozen in place. Ellie had been sleeping, but Julia, who had moments ago been playing with her daughter's hair, sat still, mouth curved in a half-smile after Mark's attempt at a joke. Her hand was raised over Ellie's dark hair, which was now floating in midair. It looked like she had just let go of it as the scene paused.

Mark thought about going back to try to release them from their frozen hold, but something beckoned him forward instead. He turned toward the home before him and stepped inside.

It didn't take long to figure out where he was. A younger version of the man he'd seen in Julia and Ellie's cabin stood tall, frozen in place behind a beige couch in a living room that looked like something you would see on HGTV. The room, along with the rest of the home—what he could see of it, anyway—was almost sterile in its cleanliness.

Sitting on the couch was a frozen, terrified-looking Julia, she looked like she was trying to make herself smaller in the space she occupied. Her eyes were open, staring at what appeared to be an infant's bouncy seat placed in front of her.

The man's stance was aggressive, if that was even possible. Even the energy he gave off was violent and dark.

Mark walked closer to the scene, wondering if they would suddenly animate with his presence, but they had yet to move. He was about to place his hand on Julia's shoulder when he had a thought. He looked back at Julia and Ellie, still in place in the cabin. He went back to the door that still hung open and slammed it shut.

The *click* of the closing door acted like a play button on the family in front of him. The man raised both arms out to his sides and then let them fall.

"What am I supposed to do with this news, Julia?" said the man. "Sit back and just let it happen?"

Julia said nothing. She only cowered on the couch, never taking her eyes off the baby.

Mark assumed they couldn't see him, because neither of them acknowledged him, even though he was in their line of sight. He went to Julia, knowing there was likely nothing to be done to help her, because he had the sense that he was witnessing nothing more than an echo. A recording of a time passed.

Mark moved closer to where Julia sat, noticing a shadow on her face. He sat down next to her, hoping to get a better look. It was no shadow. It was the early, pinkish-red onset of a nasty bruise, covering the right side of her tear-slicked cheek.

Her lip on the same side was split open, a bright red line shining through otherwise healthy skin. A pit formed in Mark's stomach as Ted paced. *Maybe the worst is over now,* he thought, but he sensed this was the calm before the storm.

Just then, Ted leaned over the back of the couch, his face inches from Mark's but even closer to Julia's. If this man were real, Mark would've been able to smell his breath, which he imagined smelled sour.

"How did you do it?" Ted hissed.

"I didn't do anything, I promise," Julia muttered. "It was just an office assistant leaving a voicemail about Ellie's blood-work. I don't even know who that man is."

"So, you've said. Then, why didn't he call you Mrs. Barnet? Huh? That message started with a 'Hey, Julia?' Please tell me what kind of medical facility addresses its patients by their first name when leaving personal information on a voicemail?"

"I don't know. He was young. He probably just didn't know that he wasn't supposed to do that."

"He was young. Oh, I see, he was young," Ted said, feigning understanding. Ted moved to the other side of the couch, opposite where Mark now sat. Julia inched toward Mark, moving away from her looming husband. Helpless, Mark wanted nothing more than to protect her in that moment.

Ted settled into a comfortable casual position on the couch, arm up, elbow resting on the couch and head resting on his hand. "If you don't know him, how do you know he is young?" Ted said in a cheery voice. The juxtaposition of his tone and body position, and the anger building in the man's eyes, was all disorienting.

"I-I don't... I," Julia stammered.

"I, I, I, I," Ted said, shrugging in an affected, sarcastic manner. "You know what I think?" he said, as if they were two teenagers talking about a boy they both liked. "I think you *like* him. You know what else I think?"

Julia shook her head. Mark wasn't sure if the head shake

was her response to his question, or her begging off what was to come next.

"I think you need to be punished. But that hasn't been working for you, has it?" Ted said, pointing to Julia's swollen cheek. "I need to think of something new, and I think"—he rose to his feet—"I know what that is." He moved behind the baby's bouncy seat and, in a sweeping gesture, presented their child.

Baby Ellie.

"This thing seems to be the only thing you care about," Ted grumbled. "Am I right?"

"Please. Don't," Julia spat through her swollen lip.

"So maybe, if this is at risk, you will figure out a way to behave *like my wife*!" The last three words were so loud they startled the sleeping baby awake. Ellie fussed in her bouncer.

"Now look what you made me do," Ted said, gesturing to the whining baby.

Julia's lip quivered, and her hands balled into fists. She made a motion toward Ellie.

"Uh-uh. Don't. You. Move."

Julia looked as if an invisible arm was holding her in place as she attempted to get off the couch. "Please. Just give her to me, and I will quiet her down for you." Tears streamed down Julia's cheeks. Mark was surprised she had any left. The front of her T-shirt was soaked with mucus and blood.

"I am only going to do this once," Ted said, "and believe me, this hurts me just as much as it's going to hurt her. Maybe not as much as you, though." Ted reached into his pants pocket and pulled out a cheap BIC lighter.

Frantically, Julia threw herself into groveling. "Please, *please*, I'll do anything. Just don't hurt our baby. Hurt me; hurt me. Please hurt me."

"Quiet," he said.

And not one more word could escape her mouth, not even a sound as she watched, her eyes wild. Mark shot instinctively to his feet and went to Ellie's side to protect her, but when he tried to grab the baby, his hands wouldn't cooperate. His hands didn't go through her like a specter; they just didn't seem to work at all, like they'd forgotten how to listen to any commands from his brain. The anger boiled inside him as he watched, helpless.

Ted held up the lighter and flicked it on. He brought the flame close to Ellie's head, and she screamed at the approaching and searing heat. Before he touched the flame to her skin, though, he seemed to think better of it.

"Can't risk someone seeing this," he said, more to himself than to his wife. He threw off the small blanket that covered Ellie's legs. Julia looked frantic, as if her eyes would pop right out of her head if she fought any harder against her invisible binds, but she showed no signs of letting up.

"Son of a bitch," Ted cried, "you just have to put her in these goddamn sleepers!"

Mark saw what he was talking about. Ellie's pajamas were the kind that buttoned all the way up and covered her feet. He prayed that the act of undressing would be too much for him, that he would give up and just leave her alone for God's sake!

Ted had to extinguish his flame to remove Ellie from her clothing. In doing so, he had no choice but to grab one of her bare legs to hold up the tiny foot he'd intended to burn. Ted knelt next to her now, where he raised the leg in one hand, the lighter in the other.

With another flick of his thumb, the flame ignited. The instant it did, Ellie stopped screaming. She fell silent. Ted did nothing. He stayed in this position, the flame only inches away from Ellie's little foot as he stared blankly ahead. After a moment or two, Ted regarded the lighter with what looked like disgust. His face had somehow changed, as if all the anger and hate had drained from it and there was nothing more than exhaustion.

He let go of the button and tossed the lighter onto the coffee table that sat a few feet away. He looked back down at Ellie and redressed her, patiently closing each snap on her sleeper. When he finished, he grabbed the blanket from where he'd thrown it on the floor and covered his daughter's legs with it, tucking it gently into her sides.

He kissed his daughter on the forehead, rose to his feet, and left the room. When he did, Julia's body relaxed. She went to Ellie as quickly as she could and pulled her into her arms.

She held her as close as she could and whispered, "I'm so sorry, baby. I'm so sorry." She kissed her all over, then ran with her to the nearest hallway.

Moments later, Mark heard the familiar sound of a door closing and locking. She'd probably barricaded the door.

Mark stood alone in the living room, feeling like he wanted to cry for this family while also wanting to find Ted and put him down. He walked in the direction Ted had gone, hoping he could somehow wrap his hands around the man's throat. Past the kitchen was likely the garage—the direction Ted had gone.

Mark opened the door but found a walk-through laundry room. There, on a bench used for putting on or taking off shoes, sat Julia, with toddler-aged Ellie on her lap. Ellie embraced Julia while she rocked back and forth. Julia's shoulder looked swollen and disfigured, as if pulled out of its socket.

As Julia cried, Ellie whispered in her ear, "It's okay, Mommy. I'm going to make you feel better. I love you."

Mark let out an involuntary growl as he surged past them and through another door leading to the garage; except there was no garage, only a dock overlooking a small lake. Behind him, standing upright in the middle of the dock, was the open door, just floating there in the middle of nature.

Mark stumbled backward, momentarily disoriented at what he was seeing. Through the open door, he could still see Julia and little Ellie. He moved toward it, afraid to touch it for fear it might fall from the sky. When he'd finally gathered the nerve, he reached for the door and closed it.

Voices sounded to his left, startling him out of his astonished state. He had to work hard to stabilize himself in the space, or the disorientation would knock him right off the edge of the dock.

A few feet from Mark stood a thin, pale, balding man who looked to be a few years older than Mark. There was something familiar about his face, something about his permanent scowl. At his side was a little towheaded boy leaning his top half over the edge of the dock. He couldn't have been more than three or four years old. He wore a plain gray T-shirt and blue shorts, with a pair of worn gym shoes on his feet. Everything about him lacked the joyfulness of an average child of his age. Mark felt a twinge of sadness at the thought, but he couldn't pinpoint exactly why.

"Whoa," the pale man said, grabbing the boy by the shirt collar before he fell headfirst off the dock into the murky lake.

"You fall in there, you're gonna break your fucking neck," the man said. Mark winced at the man's language in front of the boy.

The man held the boy's collar as he half-dragged him to the end of the dock. "There you go," said the man. "If you want to fall in, do it there."

The boy gazed up at the man with wonder but said nothing.

"Don't give me that look. You were the one who seemed to think you could swim."

It had been obvious to Mark that the boy had only wanted

to see his own reflection in the water, or maybe even whatever might be below the surface, when he had leaned over the side, but this man was not smart enough to figure that out. Or maybe he was, which would've been even worse. Maybe he was just being cruel for the sake of it.

"Go on, give it a try," the man said, pointing at the water. Neither of them was wearing swimwear. It looked like they'd been taking a stroll and had happened upon this lake.

The little boy looked at the water, then back at the man Mark assumed was his father; *poor kid*, Mark thought. The boy squinted his eyes, and Mark realized he was confused about what his father was asking him to do.

"Don't play dumb with me. You think you know best? Give it a try."

The boy shook his head aggressively as tears welled up in his eyes. Then, in an instant, the man was holding the boy in the air by his shirt collar again, now stretched beyond repair, the boy's small legs dangling freely beneath him. He didn't kick or fight to get away, which led Mark to believe the boy was used to this. It made his heart heavy, even though he thought he knew who this boy might be.

Without another word, the man swung the boy back and threw him into the water. He landed with a splash and didn't come up right away. Mark panicked, searching the water for the boy.

Moments later, his head broke the surface, and he was screaming at the pitch of a seagull as he flailed and splashed and tried to keep his head above the water. His legs kicked, but his panic only drew him down deeper. He coughed and sputtered as water entered his open mouth while he screamed. His father only watched, pulling out a pack of cigarettes from his pocket and slapping it against the heel of his hand.

A woman yelled from behind Mark just as the boy's head

slid under again. "Teddy?" she called. "Where did you boys run off to?" She looked older than the man but aged through experience rather than time as if she were a lifetime smoker or sun worshiper. *She must be the boy's mother*, he thought.

The woman stepped onto the dock and walked toward the man. "Where did that boy go?" she asked again.

The man gestured to the water where bubbles surfaced. She looked at him at first with disbelief, then shock, as she realized he was not joking. The boy's head finally broke the surface again as he attempted to doggy paddle, spitting out mouthfuls and gasping for air.

"Teddy, you get back here this instant!" the woman yelled.

There was a chance, Mark thought, that this woman had honestly believed that her small son had purposely jumped into the water to be defiant, but Mark thought it was more likely that she knew exactly what would happen if she directed her anger where it belonged; it was best to direct it elsewhere. The victim was usually the best choice in these cases. As the boy eventually dog-paddled his way closer to the dock's edge, his mother reached down, grabbed his arm, and pulled him back up and out of the water, scraping his back in the process.

"What the hell were you thinking?" she shouted. "You're not getting into my car all soaking wet like that!" She stood above him, hands on her hips and not attempting to help or comfort him as he continued to cough up dirty lake water.

"I can't even look at you right now," she said finally, then stormed off.

Nearby, the man pulled out a cigarette, put it in his mouth, and grabbed a lighter from his other pocket. He lit the end of his cigarette and sucked in. "I guess you learned how to swim," the man said in an exhale of smoke.

At three, the boy already seemed to know better than to cry.

Mark closed his eyes and pinched the bridge of his nose. He wasn't sure how to feel. If this were a stranger, he would feel sad and angry at the injustice of an innocent child being raised by parents like these. But Mark knew the man this boy would become and couldn't feel sympathy for that version of him—even if he was the victim here.

Mark walked back to the door that was still floating where he'd left it on the dock. He opened the door and walked through, past Julia and Ellie in the laundry room and past the now-empty living room. He found the door that led to the cabin and took a deep breath. He turned the knob and opened it. Inside the cabin, Julia and Ellie remained frozen in the same position he'd left them.

He turned, grabbed the handle, and closed the door.

"I guess the jiggle doesn't always work," Julia said, still playing with Ellie's hair.

Mark paused, thinking. "No, I guess it doesn't."

CHAPTER 15

LAURA

LAURA SAT ON a hospital bed in the ER she was all too familiar with; the usual smell of disinfectant and plastic was surprisingly soothing to her. She tapped her feet rapidly on the floor as the doctor she had met only a few times before stitched up her wounded hand. With her other hand, she obsessively checked her phone, all while trying to wrap her mind around what the hell just happened. *How in the hell am I going to explain my way out of this?*

"Didn't think I'd be seeing you tonight," the doctor said, bringing Laura back to reality. She was new to the ER, where Laura primarily worked, so the two hadn't yet bonded. She thought her name was Taylor. Yes, it was, judging by the name tag, Dr. Anita Taylor, an unusual name for an Indian doctor. Her almost black shoulder length hair was pulled back into a half-up style, and she wore delicate gold-rimmed glasses. The woman's energy was soft and pleasant. If Laura was not mistaken, her specialty was pulmonology.

"I had a family emergency," Laura said abruptly while watching her phone to see if any of her past texts had been delivered.

"I heard," said Dr. Taylor.

"You did?" Laura said, her attention snapping back to the doctor.

"The whole hospital has. It's on the news."

"Oh, my God, what are they saying?"

"See for yourself," Dr. Taylor said, nodding toward the TV mounted in the corner. Laura fumbled behind her for the remote and turned it on. Channel 9 was the first channel she came across that was playing the news, and there it was—Ted and Julia's house cordoned off with police tape.

"Shit. Ouch!" Laura yelped at a needle-poke.

"You have to stay still while I do this," Dr. Taylor said. "You know, you are very lucky that you don't have any structural damage. This could've been much worse."

Laura nodded absently, more concerned with what the TV was saying.

"Earlier today," said the onsite newscaster, "the CEO of the medical sales staffing company Barnet Medical Group, Ted Barnet, was found unresponsive at the bottom of the stairs at his Evanston, Illinois, home. As of now, the police are not sure if the fall was an accident. Police are attempting to locate the wife of the victim, Julia Barnet, who is likely to be in the company of their eight-year-old daughter, Eleanor, for further questioning. If anyone has information on the whereabouts of the two in question, please call the Evanston, Illinois, police station at the number shown on the screen."

"Okay, that's not that bad," Laura said, her uninjured hand absentmindedly going to her mouth so she could nibble the skin at the corners of her nails.

"Are you okay?" Dr. Taylor asked.

"I mean, no, not really," Laura said, looking at her hand.

"I mean, with everything else. Can you tell me how this happened?"

"I just cut my hand."

"You did much more than that; you impaled it. I'm just having a hard time figuring out how this happened. How did the knife go through the top of your hand?"

"I was using it, and I tripped."

Dr. Taylor gave Laura a skeptical look. "Laura," she said, as she wrapped the rest of her hand. "I need you to tell me if someone did this to you. It will stay just between us. I promise."

"No. It was me. I'm just clumsy sometimes. I was going to cut some cake, and I grabbed the knife and tripped over something. I tried to catch myself with my hand, and I forgot I was holding the knife; I was lucky I didn't stab myself worse than I did." She punctuated this with a nervous laugh.

"And what happened here?" Dr. Taylor said, touching the spot now covered with a Band-Aid, under Laura's chin.

"I'm not sure how I did that. It must've been afterward; I kind of panicked trying to get the knife out of my hand."

Dr. Taylor was bobbing her head in acknowledgment but not really paying attention. Laura noticed a bit too late that the doctor had been texting someone while she had been talking.

"What are you doing? Who are you texting?" Laura said, reaching her good hand toward the doctor's cell phone. The doctor quickly backed away out of Laura's reach.

Suddenly, the curtain in the exam room flew open, and in walked two orderlies, who stood on either side of the door.

"What is this?" Laura asked.

"Security looked at the breakroom where you hurt your hand, and they thought it looked unusual, so they checked the security cameras, and they saw you breaking things and throwing things around the room."

"Okay, so I was angry. I've been through a lot today. I will pay for any damage I caused. I—"

"Listen, Laura, it's not that." Dr. Taylor paused for a moment, rolled her chair closer to where Laura sat, and whispered, "They saw you stab your own hand."

Laura's mouth dropped open, but she remained speechless. There was no way to explain this. They would think she was crazy.

"Oh God," Laura said, looking at the two men, then back to the doctor. This news would no doubt spread to the entire hospital staff; the other doctors and the nurses, her friends, they would all think she was insane.

"These men are going to take you to a room where you'll be able to get some rest," Dr. Taylor said.

"That room wouldn't happen to be in the psych ward, would it?" asked Laura.

"This is only temporary, Laura."

"Please don't do this, not now. You don't understand. I'm not crazy; the whole situation is crazy."

"I'm so sorry, Laura; this is only temporary. We only want to keep you safe," Dr. Taylor said, nodding at the two men who moved slowly toward Laura.

"Okay, okay, I won't fight you. I will come with you, I promise. But, Marco, Tommy, you know me. I work in this department, so can you please not act like you are escorting me to the nuthouse?" Laura remained still, trying to be as calm as possible. She had worked in the ER long enough to see hundreds of men and women being taken to the third floor, where she was now going, and fighting the escorts never worked.

The two men looked to the doctor, who gave them a nod. Laura felt the first spark of relief she had felt all night.

"Thank you." Laura walked toward the doorway, then stopped and turned back to Dr. Taylor. She leaned in close to the doctor, but not so close as to scare her. "Please watch the video for yourself. Ask yourself what you're *really* seeing," Laura said.

She knew better than to beg and plead with the doctor any more than she already had. Composure was the key to getting Dr. Taylor on her side.

"Take this, please," Laura said, taking the doctor's hand and placing her phone in it. "My sister and niece are in danger, and now I have no way to help them."

Dr. Taylor's brow furrowed—this was not the result she had expected.

Laura leaned in close, whispering so only Dr. Taylor could hear her: "I am not crazy, but whatever you do, don't look into Ted Barnet's eyes."

CHAPTER 16

JULIA

MARK HAD A smile on his face when he jiggled the doorknob, but when he turned back around, Julia couldn't help noticing something like shock. Had he really thought that trick was going to work again? Before she had a chance to make much more of a joke of it, she heard a muffled ring coming from Mark's back pocket.

"My phone!" Julia slid Ellie's head gently off her lap and went to him. Mark pulled the phone from his pocket and handed it to her. One after another, notification banners popped up, all from her sister.

"It's Laura." She unlocked her phone and scanned the messages. There had to be over twenty, ranging from an update on Ted's condition to her being questioned by the police.

"Something happened; he did something to her. If that son of a bitch hurt my sister…"

"But how? I thought he was in a coma?"

"He is."

"Can you call out?" Mark asked, seeming more desperate for a solution than he had been a moment ago.

Julia pressed her sister's name on her phone. "It's ringing!"

"Hello?" said a voice decidedly not her sister's.

"This is my sister's phone. Is she there?"

"Is this Julia?" asked the voice, a female with an Indian accent.

"Yes, is my sister okay?"

"Are you okay?" the voice asked. "Everyone is looking for you."

"Who is this?"

"My name is Dr. Anita Taylor. I work with your sister."

"Where is she?"

"First, can you tell me where you are?"

"My daughter and I are at the Lakeview Resort in Loomis Falls, Wisconsin. We are trapped here, and I haven't been able to get a call out to anyone. Can you please call the police?"

"Of course. While I have you, I should tell you that your sister is on a temporary psychiatric hold here at the hospital. She is safe now, but she... attempted to harm herself."

"Oh, my God, it's him. He did this to her?"

Mark stood silently beside Julia trying to decipher the conversation. Ellie began to stir on the couch.

"Do you mean your husband?" Dr. Taylor asked.

"Yes, is he still there? Is he in a coma?"

"I was just on my way to the intensive care unit to speak with our security officer. Let me check in on him. Do you think he is faking his condition?" Dr. Taylor asked, with the slightest hint of condescension. "Because I assure you, the tests they have given would prove otherwise."

"I know; it's hard to explain." Julia sighed.

Julia waited on the line, listening to Dr. Taylor's exchange with one of the nurses, but she couldn't quite decipher what was being said. Mark raised his eyebrows, clearly wanting answers, but she could only shake her head. Mark paced the room in front of the couch where Ellie thankfully slept.

"He is still here; he is getting an MRI. They said he's been having some eye movement."

"What does that mean? Does that mean he is going to wake up?"

"Not necessarily; it could mean a lot of different things, but I am not a neurologist, so I can't say for sure."

"Can I talk to my sister?" Julia asked.

"I'm sorry, but while she is on a temporary hold, she cannot be in contact with anyone but medical professionals. But I would be happy to let her know that you and your daughter are okay."

"We're not okay—"

The line went dead.

"Hello, Dr. Taylor? Hello?" She heard nothing. "Damn it!"

"You lost the call?" Mark asked.

Julia nodded. "Hopefully, she called the police."

"But what are they going to do?" Mark asked.

"I have no idea," Julia said. "But I'd take being arrested over this."

CHAPTER 17

DR. ANITA TAYLOR

DR. TAYLOR WAS STILL talking when she realized the call was lost. She tried redialing the number, but it went straight to voicemail. She caught sight of the security officer she'd spoken to earlier in the day about Laura's break room incident, so she flagged him down. He was in no hurry, but he made his way to her.

"How can I help you, Doc?" the officer asked.

"I just got off the phone with the wife of that man, Ted Barnet."

"You did?" He raised what looked like an expectant eyebrow.

"I did, and she and her daughter are at the Lakeview Resort, in a place called—"

"Loomis Falls, Wisconsin," he said, interrupting.

"Yes, how did you know?"

"They have detectives headed there now."

"Okay, good." A wave of relief washed over her, and she took what felt like her first deep breath of the night. Why was she so emotionally invested in this situation? She hardly knew Laura. She had only spoken to her a handful of times, and all the conversations had consisted of small talk. But all those conversations were also very normal, she thought.

There was no sign of the anxious woman she'd experienced tonight in the exam room. Was that why? Regardless of Anita's reasoning, she felt something in her gut, and it was much more than the tacos she'd eaten for lunch. She couldn't wait to get back to pulmonology, where it was relatively quiet.

"Did she say anything else?" the officer asked, hopeful.

"Yes, she said they are trapped there." She was about to add, "by her husband," but thought better of it. A man lying here in a coma couldn't possibly trap them.

"Trapped?"

"Yes."

"Anything else?"

"She said they could not call anyone. I'm not sure if that means there's no cell service, or if there's some other reason."

"Great, that's great. Thank you. I'll let the detectives know."

"Of course," Dr. Taylor said as the officer reached for his cell phone.

"I have one more question, if you don't mind," she said. "Is there any way I could see the security footage from earlier, when Nurse Laura had her…"

"Oh, her accident," the officer said, making air quotes with the hand not holding the phone.

"For medical reasons. We need to get her some help, obviously." Dr. Taylor was only saying this to persuade him to help her. She was beginning to think that something other than psychosis was going on here.

"I'm not supposed to," he said, looking to see who else was around. He wanted to make his phone call, and she was holding him up; Anita saw how that could work in her favor.

"I can assure you that the laws of HIPPA fully protect you," she said, "and that I cannot disclose how I came about the video, if that helps?" She knew no such thing, but he didn't know that, and that's what she was betting on.

"I have it on my phone," he said, pulling up the footage. He must've been looking at it recently, because the paused video of Laura popped up on his screen in a matter of seconds.

"I suppose you could see it for a minute."

"You can just send it to me—it'll be faster." And before she could change her mind, she was giving him her number.

"Uh, yeah, okay," he said, typing in the number as she said it. Then he looked at her once. She gave him a smile, and he pressed the send button.

"Thank you so much; make your phone call." She walked away briskly before he could second-guess his decision.

Dr. Taylor ducked into the women's washroom, unwilling to wait until she got to her office to see the video. Whatever was happening, she felt an urgency to figure it out.

She pulled up the video on her phone and watched Laura doing what the officer had said she'd done. The woman frantically searched the room, breaking items as she went before discovering the knife and grabbing it. She noticed a short, brown-haired nurse peeking out around the doorjamb; it looked as though she had attempted to enter the room but had gotten frightened and then retreated. She was probably the one who alerted security.

Laura's movement looked strange, jerky, almost like she was being attacked or yanked along. *But what would make someone want to act like they were being attacked?* Laura seemed shocked to find out there were cameras in the break room. Something just didn't feel right about this.

Without thinking, Dr. Taylor made her way to the elevator and pressed the number three button. When she reached the psychiatric ward, she asked a nurse behind the reception desk to page Dr. Sengupta. She grew impatient as she waited until he arrived.

A tall, handsome Indian man in his late twenties, dressed in gray dress pants and a light-blue fitted dress shirt that had, without a doubt, been tailored to fit his lean muscular frame, stepped up behind her. "Seriously?" he said. "You had me paged?"

"It's important. I need to speak to the patient I sent up to you earlier, the nurse."

"Nurse Mayfield?"

"Laura, yes."

"She is on a psych hold. I can't let you in there."

"I am a doctor at this hospital."

"But you're not *her* doctor. You are a pulmonologist."

"I am not joking with you. I need to speak with her. It's quite urgent. And seeing as I'm the doctor who had her placed here, I am considered part of her care team."

He held his finger over his mouth, pretending to think it over.

"Kunal, do it now, or I will tell Mother that you are dating an eighteen-year-old cafeteria worker."

"Shut up," he whispered, pulling his sister by the elbow until they were out of earshot from the nurse.

"Fine. I was going to let you see her anyway. She was asking for you. I was just messing."

Her eyebrow rose. "She asked for me?"

"Yeah, I don't know why you sent her here anyway; she seems perfectly sane and rational."

"It's a long story."

"You'll have to tell me later. I'm busy." He turned to the nurse's station. "Maria? Can you give Dr. Taylor the room card for 308, please and thank you?"

"No problem, Doctor," said the starry-eyed nurse.

Eww, Anita thought. *I know people say my brother is handsome, but... just eww.*

Anita used the plastic key card to enter room 308. It was a typical psych ward room—small, clean, and empty, save for a bed, overbed table, and a window. Laura lay in bed, staring toward the window into the darkness.

"How are you doing?" Anita asked.

Laura turned to her and sat up a bit when she noticed it was her. "As well as can be expected under these circumstances, I suppose."

"That's good."

"I don't belong in here; just ask the doctor."

"I already spoke to your doctor, and he did say something of that nature."

Laura let out a breath of relief. "That's great, so can I please leave?"

"I'm not sure how long he plans to keep you, but I came here to tell you that your sister called."

"What?" Laura shot straight up in bed now. "Why didn't you lead with that? Is she okay? Where is she?"

"She is at a resort in—"

"Wisconsin, yes, I know." Laura ran her fingers through her hair. "But is she safe?"

"Why does everyone seem to know this? Why are the police looking for her if everyone knows where she is?"

"Is she *safe?*" Laura asked.

"I don't think so; that's why I came to talk to you. I have already told the police, and they are on their way. What I am wondering is why she said something similar to what you said to me. She said, 'He did this.' I assume you're both talking about a man who is sitting in a coma in this hospital and is harmless to everyone around him. So, why do you both think he is to blame?"

"He is in a coma, but he is not harmless," Laura said.

"This is what I mean. I feel like there is something you want to say but refuse to. Just tell me the truth, and it may help you."

"I guess it doesn't matter anymore. It's not like you could have me committed again."

"Good point," Anita said, although her face did heat up at the thought. *But why?* She had no reason to be ashamed of her actions. She would've done the same whether she had known this person or not. It was possible that somewhere in her subconscious, she might actually believe that something unusual was at play here. Was that the word? No, the word was *supernatural.*

Laura sighed. "I would never have believed it until what I experienced tonight. I assume that was why my sister never mentioned any of this to me; she would've been sitting here instead of me."

Anita had a feeling this was going to be a long story, and an even longer night. Unlike her brother, who was working the night shift, her shift was over; she could've easy washed her hands of all this mess and gone home to her husband and kids and her cockapoo and cuddled up in her warm bed. Why, then, did she find herself sitting down at the end of this woman's bed, preparing herself for some outlandish story?

"Go ahead," Anita said.

Hesitantly, Laura continued, "I could never understand why my sister married him. He was an asshole from their first date. I remember her telling me right after that he was conceited and selfish. She swore she would never see him again. Then the next day he calls and asks her out again, and, to everyone's surprise, she says yes.

"The same thing happened when they got engaged, only by then she was complaining less and less about him. In fact, she wasn't saying anything negative about him ever, but she was different. She would say great things about him, but in her eyes, you could just tell that she was lying. The only time I ever felt like I could get the truth out of her was when we were drinking, or, more specifically, if Ted was drinking. He would sometimes drink to the point of passing out, and that was when we would talk honestly. She told me how awful he was and how much she regretted marrying him, but she never had a good excuse for why she didn't leave.

"Then she got pregnant, and I knew that was it. If she hadn't been stuck before, now, with a baby, he would never let her leave. Don't get me wrong, I love my niece more than anything in this world, but she became an anchor for their marriage.

"My husband and Ted have never gotten along. He was a groomsman, but that was because Ted didn't have any real friends who would stand up there for him."

Okay, so she has a controlling husband, Anita thought. *Welcome to America, or rather, welcome to Earth.* Laura's sister wasn't the first woman to live with an emotionally abusive husband, and unfortunately, she wouldn't be the last. What made this situation any different from the rest?

"I think it was Ellie's fifth birthday," Laura continued, as if Anita had psychically prompted her. "It was just the five of us—me, my husband, Julia, Ted, and Ellie, of course—at Ted and Julia's house. We had pizza and cake. Then the adults had some drinks while Ellie played with her new toys. Ted was making little offhanded comments about Evan, criticizing his job and how we didn't have kids yet; he was very passive aggressive, but that was normal when Ted had a few drinks in him.

"Evan decided he'd had enough, and went into the living room to play with Ellie. They were putting together a toy she had just received for her birthday—a princess castle or some-thing. After ten, fifteen minutes tops, here comes Ted. He plants himself on the ground right next to Evan and Ellie and starts telling him he's putting the castle together wrong. You should know that my husband is a huge self-proclaimed nerd. He has been putting model cars and planes together since he was a kid, not too much older than Ellie was at the time.

"Ted's comments were completely unjustified. But he kept it up anyway. Then he started saying that Evan was going to break the castle. 'You're going to break it, Evan. Evan, you're going to break it.' Evan just ignored it, which I think pissed Ted off even more.

"Then he got very serious and punctuated very word: 'Evan. You. Are. Going. To. Break. It.' Evan just looked at him, like he was trying to register what he was saying. Then he picked up Ellie's castle and smashed it onto the ground over and over until all the plastic pieces were cracked and bent out of shape. Ellie cried so hard as she watched him, but we were all just so shocked that we didn't know what to do. Except for Ted. He just stared at Evan with a big shit-eating grin on his face. My sister took Ellie to her room to calm her down, and Evan and I left.

"Afterward, Evan told me an urge had come over him that was too strong to resist. He said he never wanted to see Ted again, and so far, he hasn't. He apologized to Ellie and, of course, replaced her castle. He even put it together for her. But they had to come to us. Just my sister and niece, not Ted." When Laura finished her account of the ill-fated party, her whole body was trembling. Anita couldn't help but feel bad about pushing her for more information.

"That's so strange," Anita said. "I'm assuming your hus-band isn't a violent man?"

Laura shook her head. "Not at all."

"Ted sounds like an awful person," said Anita, "but that still doesn't explain why you took to harming yourself this afternoon."

"It does," Laura said. "And here comes the part that will make you want to keep me locked in here."

Anita looked at her quizzically, but not in a frustrated way. She seemed almost intrigued, and Laura took that as her cue to go on.

"For the record, I didn't believe Evan when he told me that Ted had done something to him that day at Ellie's birthday, that the staccato words he'd said to him must've hypnotized him or something. He said he had no control, and I just assumed he'd lost control... until today."

"How do you mean?"

"Ted hasn't spoken a word since his fall," Laura said.

"Right," Anita added. "He is in a coma."

"Yes. But when I was running some tests of my own, just to make sure he wasn't faking it, his eyes popped open. His dead-eyed gaze was like a tractor beam, trapping me. And when his nurse came in, she somehow broke the spell. But instead of just talking to her like I normally would've, I had this uncontrollable urge to walk out of the room. I had to look for something. I didn't know what that something was. But I knew I would do anything at all to find it. When I found the knife, I held it under my chin." Laura indicated the bandage Anita had placed there earlier.

"As soon as the tip broke my skin," Laura continued, visibly shivering, "a part of me realized what I was doing. It was like a battle inside my mind, and I fought so hard to control it." Tears slid from the corners of Laura's eyes.

"I knew I wasn't going to be able to put the knife down; there was no way—a force much stronger than me was controlling my muscles. So instead of thinking about not hurting myself, I thought about doing it in a different way, a way that wouldn't end me. And as soon as that thought popped into my head, I was able to pull it away, slam my hand into the table, and stab myself. I felt a rush of relief followed by pain. Then I lost consciousness; that must've been when security found me."

"Why didn't you tell me all of this when I first examined you?" Anita asked.

Laura gave her a look that said, *You're kidding, right?*

"Okay, I suppose I would've considered every possible explanation except your truth."

"And now?" Laura asked. Her eyes burned into Anita's.

"I will not say," Anita began, "that I believe that your brother-in-law can control others with magical hypnotic mind control..."

Laura's hopeful gaze diminished.

"But I will admit that I don't believe that you were fully in control of what happened in that break room."

Laura exhaled. "That's more than I expected. Thank you."

Anita nodded and gently patted Laura's leg.

"So, what now?" Laura asked uncertainly.

"Now, I need to do some more digging." Anita moved closer to where Laura sat in her bed and reached back to adjust her pillows. "Let me just fix these for you."

Though Anita prided herself on her bedside manner, she wouldn't normally fluff her patients' pillows.

"Let me know if you think of anything else," Anita whispered.

"And don't let my brother find that."

Laura narrowed her eyes at Anita, but she turned away and headed for the door. Anita looked back just in time to see Laura reach under her pillow and grab her cell phone.

CHAPTER 18

JULIA

"I SHOULD TELL you something," Mark said. Before Julia could respond, though, Ellie, who'd been sleeping, began stirring on the couch.

"Shoot, I must've woken her," Julia said, rushing to her daughter's side. She sat down next to her daughter and rubbed her head, hoping it would help get her back to sleep.

"Shhhh," Julia whispered. "It's okay; go back to sleep. Mama's here."

Ellie rolled onto her side to face Mark and stared at him. "Is this the guy you tried to murder me for?" Ellie said.

"What did you say?" Julia asked, sure she'd misheard her daughter.

"You heard me."

"Ellie?" Julia said, admonishing her daughter.

Mark turned to look at Ellie, noticing an expression on her face he had not seen before. Hatred.

Ellie rose to a sitting position. "Your precious little angel isn't here right now."

Julia took a deep breath and then exhaled before saying

what she knew was true but didn't want to admit—not to Mark, not to herself, not to anyone.

"Ted?"

"Ding, ding, ding! What do we have for her, Johnny?"

"What the fuck is this?" Mark asked, searching both their faces for clues, no longer worried about his language in front of a child. Because this was no child, not anymore.

"Isn't that something I should be asking?" Ellie/Ted said. She got up from her seat on the couch and walked slowly toward Mark.

"Ellie, baby," Julia said, panic rising, "if you're in there, it's time to come back now. I know you are stronger than he is."

"If I want to, I will keep her locked in a box in my head forever."

"She's your daughter," Julia said. "Why would you do that to her? I know you love her. You have never laid a finger on her."

"How could I, Julia? Every time I touched the kid, I turned to Jello. But this… this is different. She was asleep. She never even saw me coming. And to be quite honest, any bit of love I had left for her vanished when she pushed me down those stairs."

Julia could see the look of confusion in Mark's eyes. And instead of trying to plead with her "daughter," she went right to him.

"Ellie didn't do anything," she said to Mark. "It was me. Ted and I got into an argument, and he started getting physical. I got him to the edge of our staircase and pushed him. That's why we came here. And now you know everything."

Mark remembered the staircase she was talking about when he walked through the front door, into what he now guessed was Ellie's memory. *Was Ellie using all her energy to show me her memory?* Mark wondered. *Is that how this bastard get into her head?*

"Hmm," Ellie/Ted said. "The logistics don't work, though, do they? You see, Marky Boy, when I was so savagely thrown down the stairs, this little lady right here had an electric cord wrapped around her neck, with the other end tied to our bedroom doorknob." Ellie/Ted laughed. It was a gleeful sound, one reserved for the likes of Christmas morning. The sound gave Julia the chills.

"So, there is no way that she could've pushed me."

"No, that's not—" Julia tried to argue, but Ted cut her off.

"It had to have been our little angel."

"I guess you gave up on trying to convince me you were a victim in all of this?" Mark said.

"That was too much work. It took too much energy. Just like the two geezers that own this place. They were fighters."

"Were?" Mark said, his hands closing into fists. Not that he had any intention of punching a little girl. He wasn't even sure if Ted could feel pain through Ellie's body. Julia rushed to his side, if only to prevent him from hurting her daughter.

"I need a drink," Ellie/Ted remarked. Still using Ellie's body, he walked into the kitchen and opened the fridge. When he found nothing there, he went to the cupboard. He reached up, opened the cabinet door, and instantly realized he couldn't reach anything inside.

"Fuck," he said, slamming her small fists on the countertop.

Julia glanced at Mark, who gave her a shrug in return. Then they both watched as Ellie/Ted found a kitchen chair and dragged it over to the counter. He didn't have the strength to carry it over, so it scraped the floor as he went. He slammed the chair as hard as an eight-year-old could against the lower cabinets.

Seeing such anger and frustration coming from her

daughter was confounding to Julia. Ellie was the most patient kid she had ever met, and Julia found it hard to hold herself back from simply helping with the chair, but she restrained herself, her logic, at least temporarily, winning out over her empathy.

Ellie/Ted stepped onto the chair and began searching through the cabinets. When she still didn't find what she was looking for, she turned around with a big, unnatural smile spreading across her face.

"I just remembered something," Ellie/Ted said in a sing-song voice. "When I was playing Marky Boy earlier this evening, there was quite the setup; it was like a pharmacy over there. A regular Dr. Kevorkian."

Ellie's pajama-clad body skipped toward the front door of the cabin and opened it. Mark took on a catlike stance ready to pounce, but Julia stopped him before he could go for Ted. Julia shook her head vigorously, knowing the power Ted had over herself and others. More than anything, her body remembered the pain it had felt over the years, not only at Ted's hands, but at her own, when Ted had decided she needed to teach herself a lesson.

She knew her husband better than she'd ever wanted to, and most of the time, appeasement was the only option. Mark raised his hands in frustration, obviously not understanding why she didn't just let him tackle the monster inside her daughter's tiny frame. It would've been easy, or so he assumed. But she pressed his arm down, attempting to relax his tension, and followed behind Ellie/Ted. Julia didn't know what she expected to see beyond the front door, but she also didn't care.

They followed Ellie/Ted outside. The outside was just… outside. But they knew better than to expect things to be normal. There was nothing normal about any of this, but as they walked, they could hear the night animals and insects chattering. Julia touched her own arm as she felt a breeze pass over it. It *felt* real.

Ellie/Ted walked to the front door of Mark's cabin and, without hesitation, turned the knob and entered. Julia followed, but Mark stopped her and whispered, "I don't think he can control anything else when he's inside her."

The realization flooded Julia's eyes, and she just nodded. They both stepped inside the cabin.

Ellie/Ted had already found the bottle of Jack Daniel's and was holding it with two hands. "Here's what we're going to do. I'm going to ask you some questions, and if I don't like your answers, I'm going to take a drink." Ellie/Ted set down the bottle and attempted to open it, but found he didn't have the finger dexterity he once had.

"Open it," Ted said to Julia.

"Ted, can I please just talk to Ellie and make sure that she is okay?"

"No, she's sleeping. Open it."

"Ted, Ellie's body can't handle alcohol like you can. It could kill her."

"Then I guess you'd better hope I like your answers. Now sit down."

Julia nodded to Mark to play along. She wasn't sure what Ted could do to Ellie, but she wasn't willing to risk finding out. She just hoped that Mark understood what her nods meant. He seemed to, at least, because when she nodded, he took a seat at the kitchen table along with her. Ted used Ellie's small arm to place the bottle of Jack Daniel's in the center of the table. Mark watched as he tried to reach the center and saw him kneeling on the dining chair to do so. At that moment, Mark's eyes lit up as an idea came to him.

"How long have you and Ellie planned on murdering me?" Ted asked.

"We didn't," said Julia. "How could we? You knew everything we did. Everything we thought."

"You gave me that much credit? I can't read minds, you stupid slut. I can only control them."

Mark glanced at the figure standing behind Ellie/Ted. It was Izzy, holding herself up at the kitchen counter and staring at the Jack Daniel's bottle. Her eyes flicked to Mark.

Ted pushed himself up on Ellie's knees again and grabbed the bottle from the center of the table. She pulled the bottleneck to her lips, and just as she tipped it back, Mark shot up and snatched the bottle from her grasp. He pulled the bottle up over the girl's head and held it just out of her reach. Ted growled in Ellie's sweet voice.

The girl leapt from her chair and clawed at Mark, who tried to push her off with one hand without hurting her.

"A little help here!" he cried.

Julia snapped out of her terrified reverie. "What should I do?" she asked as Mark slapped the girl's hands away from his arm where she was attempting to scratch him.

"Just grab her!"

And Julia did. She came up from behind her daughter's body and grasped her in a bear hug, pinning her arms to the sides.

"Let me go!" Ellie screamed.

And Julia looked as though she might. Mark saw her failing resolve and warned her. "That is not your daughter. That is your devil."

Julia squeezed tighter, and Ellie cried.

"Mommy?" Ellie said, in the highest, sweetest voice possible. "What are you doing, Mommy? Why are you hurting me? Don't you love me anymore?"

Tears fell from Julia's eyes, but she maintained her hold.

"We have to tie him up with something," Mark said.

"Here, let me hold him, and you find something." They did a quick switch, and now Mark was behind the girl, holding her arms down.

"Don't hurt her, please," Julia pleaded.

"I won't! Just go!" he shouted.

Julia scanned the room for some kind of rope or something they could use to hold Ted in place. *That's not my baby,* she thought. *My baby is sleeping. Sleeping. That's it.* She ran toward the bed and began tearing the covers off. She pulled the sheets from the bed and grabbed two of the pillows.

"Is she going to take a nap?" Mark said, still struggling to keep Ellie/Ted still. Ted spat every obscenity at them while struggling against the restraints. If the situation hadn't been so tense, Julia would've laughed out loud at the ridiculousness of it. Julia grabbed a pillow and pulled off the case.

Ellie/Ted looked into Julia's eyes. "Let. Me. Go."

Julia looked right back into hers and said simply, "No."

An exuberant burst of energy came over her. It was the first time she had ever said no to this man. And even though Ted occupying her daughter's body stole some of the satisfaction away, it was still a remarkably freeing feeling. She wanted to repeat it—no, no, no, no. She wanted to dance around singing it, but she didn't have time, so she settled for the look Ted was giving her. It was utter dismay, and it was spectacular.

She rolled the pillowcase and tied it around her daughter's mouth, knotting it at the back of her head. "Set her down in the chair," Julia said, and then she dropped the pillows and began rolling the sheets. Mark settled the girl's body in the kitchen chair, working against her violent squirming. Julia grabbed a pillow and put it behind her back, then placed one lengthwise against her torso. She then wrapped the rolled sheet around the pillow in front and around the chair in back and tied it into a knot. They could both see that she was figuring out how to squeeze her hands up through the makeshift bonds, so Mark grabbed them and held them together in her lap while Julia wrapped another sheet around them.

"I was thinking electrical cords, but I guess this works," Mark said.

"She's still my baby," Julia said, and Mark acknowledged this with a slight nod.

"Okay," Julia said. "Now what?"

CHAPTER 19

ELLIE

At first, Ellie could only see blackness. When she realized she couldn't move, her breath came in short, quick gasps. Her limbs were curled, and she couldn't stretch out. She screamed and kicked; her heart felt like it would beat out of her chest, and finally, light filtered through the darkness.

Then suddenly, her sky opened. The woman stood above her, reaching out an open hand. Ellie didn't hesitate. She grabbed the woman's hand and pulled herself up and out of... a box. She'd been in some kind of box—though it was more like a trunk, like the ones from old movies, in which women carried their belongings onto some luxury cruise liner.

"Thank you," she said to the woman, searching her surroundings while attempting to slow her breathing.

"You're very welcome," the woman said.

Ellie stumbled back at the sound of her voice; hearing it for the first time sent a strange mix of emotions through her. She felt at home, almost like she had when she'd found her mother earlier in the night, only different. But she also felt fear.

She'd seen the woman so many times before; for as long

as she could remember, she'd always been there. Part of her thought that maybe this woman was her conscience, but deep down she knew the woman was a ghost, which could only mean one thing.

"Am I dead?" Ellie asked hesitantly.

The woman smiled. "Oh, my goodness, no, sweetheart. You are alive, I promise."

"Where are we? How did I get here?"

"That's an excellent question, but I don't want to scare you. I will tell you that you are safe. I will make sure of that."

"I know," Ellie said, studying her. "You always have."

Ellie looked around at what seemed to be a garage. An old car sat in the center, and tools hung on the walls and lay on a large workbench. The floor was stained with what looked like rust. There was a calendar on the wall. Ellie went to it. Old and covered in dust, it featured a picture of the Virgin Mary and was currently open to August of 1997.

"This is my grandpa's garage, isn't it?" Ellie asked.

The woman nodded.

"I never met him. He died before I was born. My dad told me he used to work on cars."

"That's right."

From beyond a nearby closed door, a voice boomed: "Get your ass in that garage right now, goddammit!"

"Come quickly," the woman whispered, guiding Ellie to a spot behind the car. They both crouched down and peeked around the side of the car as a balding man in overalls walked into the garage, dragging something behind him.

"Stand up, you little shit!" he shouted. From beneath the car, Ellie could see that it was a young boy, no older than she was now. He tried to scramble to his feet, but the man pulling on his shirt kept knocking him back down while simultaneously shouting at him to stand. It made no logical sense, and

Ellie wanted to shout back at him, but the woman discouraged her with a slow shake of the head.

The door flew open again, and this time, another woman walked into the room.

"What did he do this time?" the woman asked.

"Why don't you go back to your booze and let me handle the boy," said the man.

"Oh, fuck you. 'Cause you're a fucking saint!" she slurred.

"It's one in the afternoon, Veronika; isn't it time to crack open another bottle?"

"Just don't leave marks this time, or DCF will be on our asses again."

"Let me do my fucking job!"

And with that, the woman left, slamming the door behind her. The boy looked as if he were about to fall over. You could see he had already taken quite a beating. The balding man unfolded a metal chair and threw the boy onto it.

"Now, you're going to tell me exactly what happened at camp today."

"I already d-did," the boy stuttered.

The man didn't like the answer he got, so without a word, he grabbed the boy's hand, rested it flat on the worktable, and held it there. With his other hand, he drew back a hammer, which he slammed onto the boy's hand, all but destroying his pinky finger. The boy screamed and sobbed, mucus running down his face.

Ellie buried her face in the woman's chest, trying her hardest not to make a sound.

"Let's try that again," the man said. The boy was now sobbing, unable to catch his breath.

"Please, no!" the boy cried through halted breaths.

"Did you have anything to do with that boy drowning?"

The boy just bit his lip and shook his head. The balding

man drew back the hammer again, but before he could slam it down, the boy cried out, "Yes! I did! I did! I told him to go into the water, and he did! And I told him not to come back up!"

The balding man dropped the hammer onto the worktable, walked to the other side of the garage, and began rummaging through something. Ellie felt a rush of relief that the boy would be okay. He'd told the truth, and her mother always said, "I won't be mad as long as you tell the truth." Ellie looked back at the boy, who remained seated, whimpering and clutching his hand. When the man started back toward the boy, Ellie could see the boy's face change: It went from pained to terrified.

"We have to help him," Ellie whispered to the woman and tried to move away from her, but the woman grabbed her gently by the shoulders and brought her back down to her side.

"It's too late," she whispered. "This is a memory you are watching, but I'm uncertain what will happen if they see you."

The pain in Ellie's eyes seemed to break the woman's heart, but she held her close anyway.

The tall man set down a metal box with knobs and dials on the front. He plugged a cord that ran from the back of the box into a wall outlet and plugged two more pieces into the box itself. The two pieces looked a little like metal flashlights.

Before the boy could register anything more than his own pain, the man placed the two flashlights up to the boy's temples on either side of his head. A low buzzing sound issued from the machine as the boy's eyes rolled back into his head, and his whole body vibrated. The boy's crotch and pant leg darkened with urine. The man saw this, a look of disgust registering on his face, but he still refused to let up.

With a spark and a pop, the lights in the garage went out. The man let go of the boy's head, which the flashlights were holding in place, and the boy slipped off his chair and onto the ground. The boy lay inches away from Ellie and the woman, his face upturned in their direction but eyes closed. Seeing him gave Ellie a sick feeling in her stomach, and there were so many reasons for it, but she wasn't yet able to sort through them.

The woman from inside the house rushed through the garage door once again, screaming, "What the hell are you doing out here? I was in the middle of my programs!"

The boy's eyes opened and looked straight at Ellie. She jumped back in shock, but the boy looked like he wanted to say something to her, so she scooted just an inch closer so she could hear him. To Ellie it sounded like, "Esa fraida wider."

"What does that mean?"

But instead of responding, the boy's eyes rolled back once again as he convulsed. Foam collected at the sides of his mouth.

"Oh, my God!" the balding man's wife yelled, rushing to the boy's side. "What the fuck did you do to him?" She shook the boy to wake him. "Teddy! Teddy! Quit fuckin' around, Teddy, wake up!" She slapped his face even though it was obvious to Ellie that he was having a seizure. Ellie covered her ears, closed her eyes tight, and rocked herself until all the sound drifted away.

When she finally opened her eyes, she was alone with the woman. She sat in silence for a moment—still seated behind the old car, the garage otherwise empty. When she felt ready to talk, she did.

"That was my father, wasn't it?" Ellie asked as tears streamed down her cheeks.

The woman nodded solemnly.

"And those two horrible people were… my grandparents?"

"Yes," the woman said.

"Why are we here?"

"He trapped you here, and I came to help you. He doesn't

know that I'm here or that you can get out of that," the woman said, pointing at the trunk in the corner.

"Why does it matter?"

"I don't think he wants anyone seeing these memories, so it's important that he doesn't find out. Okay?"

"Okay," Ellie said, hugging the woman, who then kissed her on the forehead.

"There are some memories that I really don't want you to see. And I think that box can also be used as a doorway. If you go back inside, you may be able to find your way back."

Ellie glared at the box, remembering how it felt to wake up inside of it, alone, trapped, terrified. She shook her head.

"No... I can't go in there again. I won't," Ellie said as she cried into the woman's chest.

"I have always loved you," the woman said, cupping Ellie's head in her hands and turning her wet face to hers.

"I have always loved you too," Ellie whimpered.

"Your mother loves you, too, and right now she is probably terrified wondering where you are. Am I right?"

Ellie nodded in agreement.

"I think she has been scared enough today, don't you?"

She nodded again, although she didn't want to, because she knew what it meant. It meant that she would be getting back in that box.

Ellie stepped back into the trunk and lowered herself down into it. The woman began to close the lid, but Ellie stopped her. "I'm scared."

"I know, my love, but you are also brave." She closed the lid. "And this will all be over soon."

CHAPTER 20

DR. ANITA TAYLOR

"HELLO AGAIN, DOCTOR, long time no see," said Ted's on-duty nurse from the whiteboard in his room.

"I told a family member I would check in on him," Anita said. "How is he doing?"

"That's sweet of you. Well, he just got back from his MRI, and they ended up giving him a small dose of Ativan. Apparently, he was having a series of small seizures that they wouldn't even have seen if it weren't for the imaging, so thank God for minor miracles, am I right?"

"You are. How long ago did he have the Ativan?"

"It's been about thirty minutes. They kept him in recovery just to monitor him afterward, but not too long. I have to do my rounds, so if you need anything, give me a shout."

"Thank you." Anita then waited for the nurse to leave Ted's room before moving any closer to him.

"Hello, Ted, is anyone home?" She placed her fingers around his wrist to check his pulse. "My name is Dr. Taylor, and I just wanted to check a few things." She grabbed her stethoscope from around her neck and used it to listen to Ted's heart. "I am not going to hurt you."

She continued her exam, placing her stethoscope back around her neck, and grabbed a penlight from her lab coat pocket. She leaned over and opened his eyelids one at a time, flicking her penlight to and away from his pupils. As she expected, left eye, no change. Right eye—she jumped back, dropping her penlight to the ground. "It can't be."

Anita bent toward the floor, not wanting to take her eyes off Ted, though she couldn't see where her light had landed. It had somehow rolled all the way underneath Ted's bed.

She got down on her belly, stretched her arm as far as she could, and finally grasped the penlight. She pulled herself up on all fours and made her way to standing, only to drop the penlight again.

Ted was sitting upright in his hospital bed. His right eye was open and staring directly at her. His left eye fell lazily to one side, as if its owner had no control over it. Anita gasped and stumbled back, tripping over the chair behind her. Ted turned his head to look around the room, seeming to take everything in with his one eye.

"Is this a hospital?" Ted asked.

"I'm going to get your doctor," Anita said, trying not to stumble over anything else.

She made it halfway to the door before Ted spoke again: "Auntie Laura? Are you here?"

Laura came out *Waura*. The slurred, childlike words stopped Anita in her tracks.

"What did you say?"

"Is my Auntie Laura here?" Ted's face looked as though it were melting as the words dribbled out. "She works at a hospital. Can you get her, please? We need her help."

Every sane part of Anita's brain begged her to run screaming through this hospital up to her brother's floor to check herself in. But the bigger, more curious part of her decided to wait, to try and see what the hell was happening here.

"Who is 'we'?" she asked, taking a step toward him.

Ted looked at Anita, turning his head as if he were a puppet. It reminded Anita of a movie she and her brother used to watch about two guys carrying a dead body around, which other people thought was alive.

"Me, Ellie," Ted said, giving Anita a smile that sent shivers down her spine.

"And my mom, and this guy named Mark who is trying to help us," Ted said. "Where did you come from? We were at a cabin in Wisconsin somewhere. I can't remember what it's called, but the name has 'lake' in it. Are you a doctor?"

"Yes, I am, and I'm a friend of your Aunt Laura's. Tell me, Ellie, how can I help?"

"I don't know how I got here. I was asleep, and then I was in a box and then a garage, and now I woke up here. I can't seem to get back to myself. I'm really scared, and I don't know where I am; and I don't know how this happened... and I feel weird."

"It's okay; why don't you lie down and just relax." Anita wasn't sure if it was more for the girl she was supposedly speaking to or for herself. This day was getting stranger and stranger.

"It's going to be all right, Ellie," she said. "I'm going to help you, okay?"

The Ted/Ellie thing nodded its head.

"I don't want to scare you," Anita continued, "but I want you to know that this time, you woke up in your," she swallowed attempting to quell her dry throat, "your father's body. Your father is in what we call a coma, so he can't move or talk or do much of anything. That is why it is quite shocking to find you like this. And I cannot even believe what I am saying to you right now."

Anita rubbed her eyes with the heels of her hands.

Ellie attempted to raise Ted's head and look down at the arms attached to her. It was a struggle, but she was panicking now, which made it even harder to control the body's movements.

Anita rushed to her side to help her lift the head. Ellie used Ted's good eye to look down at herself. She saw the hair covering her forearms and began to sob.

"Shhhhhh," Anita said, attempting to cradle Ted's head, but it was like holding deadweight, so she laid it back down on the pillow. She settled for rubbing her head, just as she did with her own daughters to get them to sleep. Anita couldn't help but think how strange this would look if anyone were to walk in.

"But if I am here… where is my dad?" Ellie asked as she attempted to control her sobs.

"I'm going to try to find out," Anita said, reaching into her coat pocket and pulling out her cell phone. "Damn it. Sorry. I forgot to store your mother's phone number in my cell."

"It's okay, I know it." Ellie recited the number through shuddering breaths. Anita typed it in and heard it ringing on the other end.

A frantic-sounding woman picked up on the other end. "Hello?"

"Hello, is this Julia?"

"Yes, it is! Please, I need your help!"

"Julia, this is Dr. Taylor again. Um, I don't know how to say this, but, well, I think I may have your daughter here."

There was a pause on the line.

"Ellie?" She was practically screaming now. "How? Is she okay?"

"Yes… Well, again, I'm not sure exactly how to say this…"

"How do you mean she's there? How do you know?"

"She told me. She just gave me your phone number."

Anita could hear someone talking in the background; the words were mumbled, but it sounded like a man's voice. Then she heard Julia say, "Oh, my God! It can't be!"

"Hello?" Anita said meekly, trying to work her way back into the conversation.

"Um... did she... uh... did she wake up in my husband's body?" Julia said tentatively.

"Okay, I guess I *do* know how to say it," Anita said. "My daughter woke up, too, only it's not her; it's Ted." Anita snorted. "I'm so sorry. This is all just very weird. Would you like to talk to your whatever?"

"Yes, please!"

Anita handed Ted/Ellie her cell phone, now pretty sure she had completely lost it, though surprisingly not caring so much.

"Mom," Ellie said in Ted's voice.

"Yes, baby, it's me."

"Mommy, I'm so sorry. I don't know how this happened. I just want to come back."

Anita laughed again at the word *Mommy* coming out of this grown man's mouth, with his deep yet childish voice. She couldn't help but listen in, and she didn't feel ashamed of her intrusion—this was something impossible, and here she was witnessing it.

"I know, baby, I know," Julia said. "I'm going to get you back, okay? We're going to find a way."

There was a knock on Ted's door, followed by Ted's nurse saying, "Knock, knock," to greet them.

Anita grabbed the phone from Ted/Ellie and bent down to him. "You must stay perfectly quiet and still. Pretend you are sleeping." Ellie closed Ted's eyes and lay still. Anita raised her phone to her ear and began talking loudly. "Yes, I'm with him right now. No, I do not have any updates for you right now, but I'm sure once the doctor gets the results of the MRI, he will give you a call."

The nurse walked in quietly so as not to disturb the conversation.

"Uh-huh, of course. It's my pleasure. I'll let your sister know, and I'll get back to you as soon as I hear anything."

Anita tried to ignore the sound of Julia yelling on the other end of the line, begging her not to hang up the phone, pleading with her to stay with her daughter, even threatening her life if she didn't comply. Anita understood; she was a mother, too, but what other choice did she have?

"Yes, talk soon," Anita said, hanging up the phone.

"Was that the family?" Ted's nurse asked.

"Yes, extended sister type situation." The nurse looked confused, but Anita just continued, "Is Mister, um, Ted due for any more tests this evening?"

"No… His job is just to rest up for the rest of the night."

"Great, I'm sure that will help." Anita didn't mean for her comment to come off sarcastic, but once it was out, it was already too late. "Can I just have a moment? His family asked me to give him a message, in private. Then I'll get out of your hair."

"Of course. I'll just come back in a few minutes."

"Thank you. Thanks so much."

Anita waited for the nurse to leave the room, then rushed to Ted's side. "Ellie?" she whispered in Ted's ear. "It's me, Dr. Taylor. If you're still there and you can hear me, nod twice."

Ted's head whipped up and down twice.

"Jesus, let's not take his head off, okay?"

"I'm sorry, it's hard to control," Ellie whispered from the side of Ted's mouth.

"It's okay. Listen, I have to go."

"What? No, you can't leave me here like this."

"I have to go; otherwise, they'll think something is up."

"Something *is* up!" Ellie whispered loudly. "Maybe they can help us."

"No, Ellie, you can't think that way. The truth is, nobody is going to believe you, and I don't want you stuck in a comatose body for the rest of your life. I'm going to find a solution for you. But I need you to stay as quiet and still as possible. Okay? I mean it. If one person besides me or your Aunt Laura comes in here, they cannot see you move or make a sound."

"Okay," Ellie said with a sigh.

"I will tell the nurse not to bother you if she doesn't have to, but if she does, not a peep. Understood?"

"Can you at least… um… "

"What is it?"

"Turn on the TV?"

"How do you expect me to explain why I'm leaving a TV on for a coma patient?"

"I dunno, say I always really liked TV."

A little flustered, Anita said, "Quiet, okay? I'll be back soon."

Anita ran into Ted's nurse on her way out.

"Have a good night, Doctor."

"Thank you, you too. Quickly, before I go, the family has requested that Ted not be disturbed too much more tonight, if at all possible. I guess they really believe the rest will help."

"Okaaay," she said, drawing out the word a little too long. "I'll try not to disturb him."

She was trying to be nice, but Anita could tell she thought the request was ridiculous. She should've worked harder to befriend this woman, if only for her own benefit.

"Doctor? Is that the TV I hear?" the nurse asked, pointing toward Ted's room.

"Yeah… um… he always really liked it."

∽

Anita tried not to burst through the elevator doors when she reached the floor of the psych ward, but her pace was quicker than usual. As her mind raced while she decided what she was going to tell Laura, or her brother for that matter, she almost missed the scene playing out before her.

Standing at the nurses' station was an agitated man, gesturing wildly at the nurse on front desk duty. Up ahead, she saw her brother rushing to meet them. Approaching, she could hear what the man was saying.

"Listen, my wife went to work this afternoon, at this hospital, in fact, and hours later, I get a call saying she has been admitted to the psych ward? I mean, this call woke me up in the middle of the night with no explanation. And now you're telling me I'm not allowed to speak to my wife? Am I getting this right?"

"I'm sorry, sir, but our policy states—"

"I don't care about your policy. I care about my *wife*!"

"I'll handle this, Marcie," Kunal said, guiding the nurse out of what he perceived as harm's way. "I am Dr. Sengupta. Your wife is in my care this evening. How can I help?"

"Mr. Mayfield?" Anita said before the man could reply.

"Yes," he responded, turning to her.

"Hello, my name is Dr. Taylor. I am the doctor who admitted your wife this evening." Anita reached out her hand, and, to her surprise, the man reached back to shake it. He glanced back and forth, from her to her brother, not knowing who to address first. Anita was sure her brother would have words with her later for cutting him off like that.

"I believe this has all been a misunderstanding, and I would like to get it straightened out for you."

"Will you excuse us for one moment, Mr. Mayfield?" Kunal said. He used his patented elbow-guiding move on his sister to pull her out of earshot of his patient's husband.

"You can't just tell people that," he said, whispering loudly. "Sorry, I accidentally had your wife committed, is grounds for a lawsuit."

"I'm sorry, but something is going on, and it's more important than hospital policies."

"More important than losing your license?" Kunal asked.

"I don't think it will come to that. When you hear what I have to say, you will understand. Just please, we all need to talk to Laura."

"Well, gee, as long as the rest of the hospital's policies are out the window, let's go have a party with a psych patient on suicide watch."

"Great, thank you," Anita said as she walked back toward Laura's husband.

"That was called sarcasm!" Kunal shouted.

CHAPTER 21

JULIA AND MARK

JULIA LET OUT a guttural noise that sounded like a growl, or an animal in pain. She ended the phone call and took more than a few deep breaths.

Thoughts raced through her head, and she had trouble keeping them straight. She glanced over at Mark and realized that she probably looked manic. In a way, she was. How was she supposed to do her most important job, protecting her daughter, from hundreds of miles away? She found it difficult to direct any rage at Ted when he sat in her beautiful daughter's body, so she didn't know where to expel her pent-up energy. Then it came to her: Mark.

Looking at him, really focusing only on him, helped to slowly channel her rage into something else. Gratitude. And from the look on his face, he was getting the message. Julia was still amazed at how she could express so much with just a look, because she often needed to convey emotions this way with her daughter. It was borne of necessity.

"Thank you," Julia said.

Mark, taking a moment, straightened up and nodded.

"You're welcome. Thanks for the help." She gave a nod of

acknowledgment. Then they both looked at him/her writhing in the binds.

"So, what now?" Mark asked.

Julia walked over to the table, grabbed the open bottle of Jack Daniel's, and took a swig. She set the bottle back down and walked to the monster of a man occupying her daughter's body. She held her fingers up in the shape of a cross and spoke: "The power of Christ compels you!" When nothing happened, she dropped her hands, shook her head, and said, "Your guess is as good as mine."

"Funny," Mark said dryly. "Now, should we talk to it, or him? What do we even call it?" Mark asked.

"I wouldn't. You'd be shocked to know what that bastard can make you do. Why do you think we were stuck with him for so long?"

"I know," Mark said.

She looked at him sideways. "How? How could you possibly know?"

"Something happened to me at your cabin. Time must've stopped or something, I'm not sure, but when I tried the door, it opened for me... into what I can only guess was your house, and I walked into what I think was a memory. One of Ellie's. And then one of his." He pointed at Ellie/Ted. "I saw what he is capable of, and it was... scary."

"Oh, my God. Did Ellie do that? Did she project her memories?" Julia asked.

"I think so."

"I didn't know she could do that," Julia said.

"I think there may be a lot you don't know about what she can do," Mark said. "She herself may not even know. She was sleeping when it happened, so maybe it wasn't under her control."

"And that's also when he found her, isn't it?"

"I don't know, but I would guess yes. I also don't think we should be talking about this in front of him."

Just then, Mark noticed that Ellie/Ted was no longer struggling in his binds but listening intently.

"You're right." Mark thought for a moment, then said, "Paper. Maybe I can find some around here somewhere?"

"Wait," Julia said, "my phone." She grabbed it out of her pocket, pulled something up, and began typing, then handed Mark the phone.

"What model is this?" he said, looking at it like it had sprouted wings.

"I don't know, whatever the last one was. Read it."

The screen read: *We can write to each other on this so he can't hear us.*

"How do I…?"

He fumbled with the phone. She took it from him, touched the screen, and the keyboard popped up. She handed it back to him, and he poked at the letters. After what seemed much too long to Julia, he handed the phone back to her.

What do you think would happen if we tried the door?

She looked at Mark and shrugged. Mark was the first to move, and Julia followed close behind. He gave her a "get ready" kind of look before turning the knob on the front door, which swung open.

What they found on the other side surprised them both.

It was the area just outside Mark's cabin. Crickets sang, a strong breeze whirled leaves across the ground, and the huge full moon lit up the night sky. Instead of stepping outside, Julia reached for the knob and closed the door once again. Mark shrugged.

Julia started typing on her phone, then handed the phone to Mark.

I can't leave without her.

Mark pointed to himself and then to the door.

Julia took the phone back and wrote: *Is it a good idea to separate?*

Mark held both hands up and shrugged. Just when Julia started typing something else, the phone in her hand rang. She answered it immediately.

"Hello?"

"Hello, Julia, this is Dr. Taylor."

"Oh, my God; is everything okay? Ellie—"

"Ellie is fine, well, as fine as she can be, I suppose. I'm with your brother-in-law. We're going to speak to your sister now."

"Wait, Evan is there? Is Laura okay? Going where? Where are you? Did you leave Ellie?"

"I couldn't stay in the room any longer. Your husband is a coma patient. I had no reason to stay in his room, but she is going to be fine. She knows to stay quiet. Has there been any changes on your end?"

"Well, I am talking to you, so that's huge, and things..." Julia glanced at Mark, her eyes asking if she should continue with Ted listening. Mark moved to Ellie/Ted's side and stuck one index finger in each of her ears, then sang as loud as he could. The only thing he could think of was the song Patrick Swayze sang in the movie *Ghost* to annoy Whoopi Goldberg's character into helping him. Out came, "I'm Henry the eighth, I am!"

Julia moved to the opposite end of the cabin, her free hand covering her other ear. "It seems like when Ted is here in Ellie's body that he can't control anything else, but I'm not sure if he realizes that, or if he just doesn't care."

"Okay, that's good. Now we just have to think of a way to get them switched back."

"I also think that all of this happened while Ellie was asleep," Julia said.

"Hm, okay," Dr. Taylor said. "I had a thought, but I'm not sure if it means anything. Shortly before Ellie woke up here, Ted's doctor had given him Ativan to stop seizure activity. I wonder if that had something to do with him being able to jump or travel into Ellie's body?"

"So, what do you think that means? When it wears off, will he go back to normal?"

"I have no clue. I'm just pretending I'm in a sci-fi movie right now in order to protect my sanity. It would make just as much sense if monkeys flew out of my butt right now."

"Okay," Julia said, trying to keep calm herself. She had experienced some insane shit over the years, but this really tipped the impossibility scales. But right now, all Julia could think of was the fact that this woman, this perfect stranger in a science-based field no less, the last person she would expect to believe her, was going along with this insanity without question. Could this really be true, or was it another trick? Anything was possible at this point, but Julia didn't have any other choice but to trust her. *Ellie always says she has a guardian angel. Maybe she's right. Please, God, let her be right.*

"Okay, that's all I have for now. If you think of anything else, text me; that way, you don't have to keep listening to that annoying song," Dr. Taylor said.

"Thanks. I will. And Dr. Taylor, I just wanted to say, um… well, thank you."

"You're welcome."

"Oh, no…" Dr. Taylor said suddenly.

Julia went cold. "What? What is it?"

"I forgot. There are two detectives on their way to you."

"Here? Now?" Her initial reaction was fear; this was exactly what they were running from, but was it? What danger was more present? Police and the possibility of jail time and Ellie ending up in foster care? But she wouldn't, because Laura would take her; and she loved her Aunt Laura and Uncle Evan. Right now, Ted was the immediate threat, and maybe, if they were lucky, someone would come to the rescue.

"Yes, they headed that way over an hour ago. And they are not concerned about helping you, according to your sister," Dr. Taylor said.

"Why didn't you say anything sooner?"

"I'm sorry. I was a little busy helping your recently possessed sister and having a conversation with the soul of your daughter speaking through your husband."

"Shit, shit, I know you're right. I'm sorry; that was out of line. It's been a long night. But wait... did you say possessed?"

"I am going to find a way to help you and your family, Julia, I promise, but right now I have to go."

"Oh, okay, thank you, Doctor. Thank you so much."

"I think it's okay if you call me Anita now."

"Anita. I don't know how to thank you."

"Do it over a drink. We're all going to need one at the end of this."

Once Julia hung up the phone, she had to tap Mark to snap him out of singing.

"Sorry," Mark said. "I was getting into it."

"I could tell," Julia said, then realized he was doing her a favor and softened her tone. "I always loved that movie."

"So did Izzy." A ghost of a smile crossed his lips. "She was crazy for Swayze."

"We have a problem," Julia said, and Ellie/Ted started up again, trying to get words out while shifting in his binds. They could tell he was spitting muffled obscenities into his gag.

Mark pointed to the phone, suggesting they continue typing their conversation, but Julia shook her head.

"We're running out of time." She led him over toward a far corner of the cabin. "The police are on their way."

"Oh, thank God," Mark said. "Finally."

"It's not a good thing, Mark. What happens if they take me away? What happens to Ellie? She will either be stuck inside Ted's body in a coma, or she'll wake up in her own body, alone and scared in the back of some police car." Tears welled up in her eyes as she considered the possibilities.

"Okay, okay," Mark said, slipping his arm around Julia's shoulder. He'd felt hesitant to touch her until now. He wasn't sure why. Maybe it was out of respect for personal space, or because he didn't want to make her feel uncomfortable. But deep down, Mark knew it was his own fear keeping him distant. What if he liked the way she felt in his arms? How would Izzy feel about that? How would he feel about it?

He had already opened his heart too much, and Ellie had managed to slip inside. He wasn't sure if it happened because of her special gift, or if it was because of his newfound ability to give and accept love—something he'd sworn only months ago he would never do again.

Mark decided that this woman had had enough, and if his embrace could give her any relief, it was worth the risk. She had already been stronger than he could have ever imagined, but he guessed a decade of fear would thicken anyone's skin.

He thought the hug would calm her, but instead, it appeared to open some hidden space deep inside. The well opened, and she sobbed into his chest. He felt her back hitch as she tried to take in a breath. He rubbed her back in circles like he had when Izzy would get sick, vomiting into a trash can after chemo, but to his surprise, he did not cry. The only thing he could think of was that, subconsciously, he had missed being strong for someone else. This small realization gave him the strength he thought they all needed to survive this night. At least for a little while.

CHAPTER 22

KUNAL

KUNAL, ANITA, AND Evan walked into Laura's private room together. Evan rushed to where his wife sat in a chair by the window. If the chair hadn't been screwed into the ground to prevent patients from throwing it, it might have toppled over.

"Baby, are you okay?" Evan said, holding Laura by the face and kissing her, not giving her a chance to answer him.

She let him get his hugs in before attempting to respond. "I'm okay, I promise."

"That does not look okay," he said, gesturing to her injured hand.

"Oh, that," she said. "Ask Dr. Taylor. It could've been much worse."

"It was almost like someone knew what they were doing," Anita added.

"Okay, so I see you're injured, but that still doesn't explain why you're in a psych ward."

Anita looked at Laura, then at her brother, and, with a long exhale, told the whole unbelievable story.

Once she was done, Laura looked resigned, Evan sympathetic, and Kunal on the verge of explosive laughter.

"Did you do all of this on my behalf?" Kunal asked, looking around the room. "Are we on *Scare Tactics*? Are there cameras here somewhere? Are these people actors?"

Kunal's laugh didn't falter until he recognized everyone else's grim expressions.

"I already figured it out," he said. "You can all stop now."

"Please… please don't tell me that this is a real shared delusion?"

"It's not a delusion, Kunal; that's why I wanted all of you here. This is really happening," Anita said. "And we don't have much time."

"So, you what? Want me to figure out a way to get an eight-year-old girl out of a comatose man's body?"

Anita nodded solemnly, knowing it was going to take more than this to convince her brother.

"And you two, you're sitting there acting like this is just another day in the park," Kunal said, looking at Laura and Evan.

"I think the phrase is a *walk* in the park, Doctor," Evan said, and Laura put her hand on his and shook her head.

"I think you all belong here. That's what I think. Especially you." Kunal indicated his sister. "The woman who, at six, convinced her four-year-old brother that Santa and the tooth fairy didn't exist."

"I understand, Kunal. I really do, and as hard as it was then to convince you, which I know now was a shitty thing to do, this will be even harder. I need you— No, an innocent little girl, who may still believe in Santa, needs you to ignore your instincts and just go along with this. We need your help."

Kunal gave an incredulous laugh. "And how exactly can I help this 'girl'? Should I psychoanalyze her? Would that help?"

Anita's face lit up. "Actually, yes. Do you still do dream analysis and astral projection stuff?"

"Astral projection is something I am working to debunk, and you know that."

"But you know a lot about it, don't you?"

"I know that it's bullshit."

All Anita needed to do was give him her "impatient big sister" look.

Kunal rolled his eyes. "Yes, fine. I know a lot about it."

"Perfect." She looked at Laura. "Then I'll only need two more favors."

⨍

The four unusual suspects looked as if they were about to get caught robbing a bank as they stepped off the elevator. Kunal walked up to the nurses' station as Anita, Laura, and Evan followed behind.

"Hi, I just spoke with Dr. Thompson, and he said he was going to call in and let you know we were coming?" Kunal said, glancing at her chest, but just to get a better look at her name tag. *Sara.*

He waited for a moment, hoping something in her expression or features would register familiarity.

He was pretty sure he had made out with this nurse at last year's holiday party, so if Dr. Thompson hadn't yet made the call, that might be their in. Or it could have the opposite effect, depending on how she'd felt about that night.

The last thing he wanted was to start a scene for something so ridiculous, but he hadn't needed to worry. Once his words registered, her mouth turned up into a smile, and he remembered why they had made out in the first place. Those lips.

"Yes, Dr. Sengupta?" she asked, with no hint of familiarity whatsoever.

"Yes, that's me," he said awkwardly.

"You can go on in."

"Thank you; we'll try to keep quiet," he added.

"Not necessary. These are all coma patients," she whispered. With a slyer tone, she added, "If something woke one up, we would thank you."

He laughed and said, "I guess you're right," but this interaction had thrown him off. Did she really not remember him? He remembered their night as pretty passionate. Was he so forgettable? He remembered pretending not to remember someone before, just to avoid the awkwardness of turning them down. Was this how they felt?

Kunal was still living in his own thoughts when his sister nudged him. They stood at the door to Ted's room, hesitant to step inside until Anita made the first move.

Ted's body lay in the same position—flat on his back, his arms at his sides.

Kunal watched as his sister approached the man. She leaned down and whispered something. Then she shook the man's shoulder. Nothing. His sister looked nervous, like she was just realizing she might have gotten it wrong.

"Ellie," she said—louder this time. "Ellie? It's me, Dr. Taylor. You don't have to pretend anymore. It's okay."

Still nothing.

Kunal shifted uncomfortably. He couldn't believe he had let his sister drag him into this. Not to mention calling Ted's doctor at home and waking him to get permission to bring Ted's sister-in-law in to visit. She was never going to live this down.

"Laura," Anita said. "Maybe if you try, you can get her to wake up or come out. Whatever it is that she does."

"I can try," Laura said, taking Anita's place next to Ted's bed.

"Um... Ellie?" She looked around the room, then chuckled anxiously at the ridiculousness of what she was doing. "Ellie, baby, it's me, Auntie Laura. I have Uncle Evan here with me, and we want to talk to you. Can you come back, please, baby?"

"Okay," Kunal said, clapping his hands together. "Have we all had our fun? Can we head back upstairs now, please?"

"Ellie!" she said firmly, just below shouting. "If you can hear me, it's very important that you come back to us right now!"

"Maybe they switched back already. Let me try to call Julia," Anita said, picking up her cell and making the call.

Kunal turned toward the door. "That's it. I'm going back to the psych ward where things are normal."

"Listen, man, I know this all sounds nuts, but would you mind just hanging out a bit longer?" Evan asked. "I appreciate that this is all messed up, but you're already here."

Kunal realized he was acting just as he had when he and Anita were children, those times when she would try her hardest to convince him of something, and he would just walk away, not wanting to deal with it.

But he wasn't a child anymore. And more than anything, he didn't want to look like one, not even to these people he'd just met. He couldn't run away from the things he was afraid of, and he couldn't ignore people to get himself out of uncomfortable situations. It was time to grow up, so he would stay, at least until the end of the phone call.

"Julia, has anything changed? Have they switched back?" Anita covered the phone's microphone and whispered, "She sounds like she has been crying."

Anita listened for a while, then said, "She's going to check."

Laura continued to shake Ted's body and call for her niece while they waited. Finally, Julia came back to the line. And Anita shook her head.

"It's okay, Julia, please calm down. She is probably just sleeping. Yes, we are going to get her back. Just wait for us to call back." Anita was about to hang up when she paused in thought. She turned the phone on speaker and held it closer to Ted's head.

"Julia, are you still there?" Anita asked.

"Yes, I'm here."

"I want you to call out to your daughter."

A beat passed, and Anita was about to tell her again when, through tears, Julia called to her daughter: "Ellie, sweetheart. I love you so much, and I miss you. I promise I will see you soon, but you have to come back. Do you understand? Ellie? Ellie!"

They waited, watching Ted's body closely as Julia continued to yell for her daughter from the other end of the line.

Then Ted's right eye popped open.

"Ellie? Is that you?" Anita asked.

Kunal looked on in horror, waiting for a response.

"Mom?" Ted/Ellie's voice grunted out.

"Yes, baby, it's me. I'm on the phone."

"Auntie Laura? Uncle Evan? What are you doing here?" Ellie asked.

Kunal stepped toward Ted's body to get a closer look at the mouth that was mumbling words. The body then scooted itself up on floppy limbs, head lolling from side to side.

"It really is like fucking *Weekend at Bernie's*," Kunal muttered.

Anita nodded. And nobody mentioned his language in front of an eight-year-old girl, because none of them could wrap their minds around what they were seeing.

"Who are you?" Ellie asked out of the corner of Ted's mouth, his single eye looking directly at Kunal.

"This is my brother, Kunal. He is here to help you too," Anita said.

"Ellie," said Julia's voice on the other end. "I need you to do whatever these people tell you, okay? They are going to help get you back to me. Do you understand?"

Ted's head nodded.

"She can't hear you nod sweetheart," Laura said.

A very kid thing to do, Kunal thought.

"Okay, Mommy," said Ellie.

"I love you forever, baby," Julia said.

"I love you forever too."

"We will call you back," Anita said, hanging up the phone.

"Ellie," Anita said, and Ted's head snapped toward her. In a movie, Kunal thought idly, it would've made a gross crunching sound.

Anita stepped closer to Ted's bedside to speak to Ellie. "Where were you just now? Why couldn't you talk to us when we were calling?"

Evan could see Ted's body struggling to get comfortable, so he went to adjust the pillows. Kunal liked him more for this. It also made him wonder if they, him and Laura, had kids of their own, something he hadn't considered when admitting her for a psych hold. Not that it was something he would've taken into consideration when deciding if a hold was necessary, unless the patient was a danger to his or her child.

As Kunal's mind wandered, he realized he was actually considering this grown man, scooting forward on pillows, to be an actual child.

Once "Ellie" got into a comfortable position, she was ready to share.

"Before I came here the first time, I was in another place," Ellie said. "When I got bored waiting for Dr. Taylor to come back, I fell asleep. I thought I could get back to my mom, but instead, I went back to the other place. Then, when I heard my mom calling, I got back in the box. Then I just woke up here."

Anita looked at Laura for answers but received only a shrug and a head shake in response.

"Can you tell us what the other place looks like?" Anita asked.

"It's like a garage," Ellie said.

"Okay," Anita said, still waiting for any of this to trigger something in the child's family. "Can you tell us more about it? Is anyone else there? Is this a real place?"

"I think it's my father's memories," Ellie said. "He is there, but he is young, like my age, and his parents are there too. He can see me, but they can't."

Kunal threw his hands in the air, shocked that the people in this room were seriously considering any of this.

"Is there anything else you can tell us about this garage or your father, Ellie?" Anita asked, ignoring her brother's visible reaction.

Tears began forming only in Ted's right eye, now displaying plainly visible fear.

"It's okay, you can tell us," Anita said, crouching down to Ellie's level and grabbing a hand that she wasn't quite sure the girl could even feel.

"They tortured him there," Ellie said, "sometimes with a box thing with wires attached to it, but mostly with water."

"Who tortures him?"

"His parents, my grandparents, I guess. I never met them in real life. They died before I was born."

"All right, thank you, Ellie, and I'm sorry you had to see that."

Evan moved closer to Ted/Ellie's side and placed a comforting hand on her shoulder.

Anita went to her brother and pulled him out of earshot of the others. Kunal opened his mouth to protest, but his sister cut him off.

"I don't really care what you believe right now. I need you to react as though you believe all of this is true, and once it is all over, you can question everything you ever thought to be true in this world. Can you do that? Please."

"I… I just."

"Pretend we're in one of those movies we grew up watching. The ones where we would yell at the screen and tell them what they *should* be doing. Regardless of what you think, be the smart guy in the story."

Kunal huffed and rolled his eyes, shifting from one expensive loafered foot to the other before finally saying, "Fine. If I were in this fantasy world, I would say that the place she is talking about is somewhere deep in Ted's subconscious mind. She is trapped, either in his body or in his mind, and she can't figure out how to get anywhere else."

"Okay, how do we help her figure out how to get back to her own body?"

Kunal took a moment to consider this before answering. "Can I talk to her?" asked Kunal.

"Go ahead," she said with a condescending tone.

"Jesus, I don't know. I've never spoken to a girl trapped in her father's body before. Cut me some slack."

"I'm sorry; it's okay. You can talk to her. Just be nice."

Kunal inhaled and approached Ted/Ellie's bedside. "Hi, Ellie. Can I ask you a question?"

Ted's head nodded slowly.

Kunal shook his head. He was still having trouble processing the idea of speaking with a girl trapped in her father's body.

"Ellie, when you go to the other place that you talked about, is there a way that you get there? Like a door, or an opening of some kind? Or do you just wake up there?"

Ellie thought for a moment, then got excited when she remembered. "It's a box!" she shouted, a little too loudly.

Laura looked to the door, expecting a nurse to check on the commotion. She leaned down and whispered to Ellie, "You must keep it down just a little, sweetie. We want them to think that you are still asleep, okay?"

Ted's head nodded, and Ellie whispered, "Sworry."

"It's okay," said Kunal. "What kind of box is it?"

"It's a big, like, suitcase box thing. The woman called it something, but I can't remember."

"Like a suitcase that you can fit into?" Kunal asked.

"Yeah, and it has straps on it."

"A trunk maybe?"

"Yes! That's it; that's what she called it. I can come back here when I get inside and close the lid."

"That's great," Kunal said.

"What woman, Ellie?" Laura asked. "Are you talking about your dad's mom?"

Ellie shook Ted's head.

"The other woman, the one who helps me sometimes. But this time, she talked to me."

"Do you know who she is?"

"No, but she feels like a mom. I have always seen her. Especially when things are scary."

"A spirit guide, maybe?" Kunal said, but more to Laura than anyone else. He couldn't quite believe he was speaking to a patient, one who had been committed to his unit only hours ago, as if they were suddenly peers.

"That could be helpful," he said.

"Is this the woman that you told me about?" Evan interjected. "The one who helps when your dad scares you?"

Ellie nodded, looking at her uncle.

"Okay, Ellie, I have one more question for you. When you woke up for the first time in that place, was it after you'd fallen asleep in your regular body?"

"Yes, I was lying on the couch at the cabin, and my mom was rubbing my head. It always makes me fall asleep."

"Then I think," Kunal said, "I know what we have to do."

CHAPTER 23

MARK

"AND HOW EXACTLY do I do that?" Julia asked.

Mark couldn't hear the other end of Julia's phone conversation, but he could see in her face she'd received some positive news. He moved behind Ellie/Ted's chair and stuck a finger from each hand into Ellie's ears. Her body struggled against him, but since she was bound and diminished in strength, she quickly gave up and settled in. Mark considered the irony of Ted leaving one comatose body, only to inhabit one now bound and gagged.

"Okay, I'll call you right back," Julia said into the phone and ended the call.

"I have to talk to you," she said to Mark.

"Okay." He looked around, as if the room would give him some type of sign of how to accomplish that task.

"Come to the bathroom with me," he said, and she followed.

Before they stepped into the small room, Mark shouted to Ellie/Ted, "Don't try anything stupid!"

They closed the door most of the way, leaving only a crack.

"We have to get him to sleep," Julia whispered. "They're going to do the same with Ellie. Dr. Taylor's brother is teaching her astral projection or at least trying to."

"Okay," Mark said with a quick frown, "but how do we get him to go to sleep—sing him a lullaby?"

"I have no clue. Any ideas?"

"He seems to like alcohol a lot. We could get him drunk enough to pass out."

"I don't want to poison my daughter's body with alcohol if I don't absolutely have to."

A realization struck Mark. "You might not have to."

He left the bathroom, went straight for the pill bottles on the kitchen table, and searched them until he found the one he was looking for. He grabbed it triumphantly and handed it to Julia. Julia read the label. Sadness crossed her face, soon followed by a look of determination that made Mark proud.

"I need to go outside to call Anita," she said. "Can you stay here with him?"

Mark nodded and sent her on her way.

"I have diazepam," Julia said into the phone after Anita picked up.

"How did you get ahold of diazepam?" Anita asked.

"It's a long story. Will it work?"

"Yes, it should, but only give him five milligrams to start. We have no way of knowing whether a drug-induced state will create the proper sleep state for astral travel. It's the same on my end, but we have no other choice besides waiting until they fall asleep naturally, and since Ellie just woke up, I don't see that happening soon."

"If we have detectives coming here now, we can't wait. We have to at least try."

"Okay, let's do it."

"One more thing, Doctor... I'm sorry, Anita."

"What is it?"

"When Ted was in a coma, he could somehow control things over here; he kept us trapped. Who's to say that won't happen again once we get him to sleep?"

Anita gave a shuddering breath. "I think that's just a risk we're going to have to take."

"Can I talk to her first?" Julia asked. "Just for a minute."

"Of course."

"Mommy?" Ellie said through Ted's deep and garbled voice.

Julia winced at the sound of the word "mommy" coming from Ted's voice. He had mocked her so many times with almost that exact tone. It made her skin crawl to hear it, which made her feel instantly guilty. This was her daughter; she just had to keep reminding herself of that.

"Hi, baby, do you understand everything they are telling you over there? What you're going to have to do?"

"I think so. I know I have to go to sleep, and then I'll go back to my body, but I'm not sure how yet. Dr. Taylor's brother is teaching me."

"Good. I know you can do this, baby. I can't wait to see you and give you a great big hug. I miss you so much." Julia struggled to hold back the tears. She didn't want Ellie to know how scared she was. If she started crying, she would get congested; it happened every time, and Ellie could always tell. It happened too often. An eight-year-old should never be so familiar with her mother's voice after crying. More than anything, she needed her daughter to be brave, and that would entail Julia setting the example.

"I miss you too, but, Mommy, I'm really scared." Ted's voice quavered.

"I know you are, baby. I am too. But we have both been through worse. And do you know what that means?"

"What?"

"It means that this is going to be a piece of cake. You are the bravest, smartest, and most powerful person I have ever known. You're going to do great."

"Okay, Mommy. I'll try my best."

Julia's sinuses tingled, and she knew she couldn't hold back the tears much longer. "I love you forever."

"I love you forever and ever," Ellie said.

"Hey now, that's not fair," Julia said with a cough to clear her throat, and Ellie giggled in Ted's voice.

"Sleep tight, my love," Julia said and ended the call. Before she went back inside, she let the dam burst.

She gave herself some time to let it all out before she had to force herself to pack it all away again. One by one, she packed away the anger, the fear, the frustration, and the sorrow. Then she stood firm and wiped her face clean.

When she pushed the door open, she half expected to see an entirely different cabin, maybe even a different country. What she found instead was an empty chair, with strings of bed sheets draped over it, cascading to the floor, surrounded by two pillows.

A crash drew her attention away from the empty chair. Shifting her gaze, she saw Mark and Ellie/Ted circling the kitchen table playing a game of cat and mouse. Ted, using Ellie's small hands, grabbed whatever he could get his hands on—a napkin holder, a small ceramic soap dispenser, and salt and pepper shakers—and threw them in Mark's direction. He managed to dodge them all.

"How did this happen?" Julia asked.

"I don't know; one minute we were sitting there, and the next he was up and running for the door. I managed to catch him before he got outside, and now this!"

"Can't you just tackle him like you did last time?" Julia

said, shouting over the crashing. A spoon flew past her head, missing her by centimeters, then knife after knife.

"I didn't want to hurt Ellie," Mark said.

"She'll heal; just get him."

"Got it," Mark said and quickly rounded the table, but before Mark could make his grab, Ellie/Ted took a steak knife and held it to Ellie's throat.

"Make a move and I'll slit her fucking throat," Ted said in Ellie's sweet innocent voice.

"Ted, please. That's our baby."

"Oh, please, this is *your* baby. You know this kid wants nothing to do with me. She tried to kill me, so why shouldn't I do the same?"

Shaking, Julia asked, "What is it you want?"

"What I want? What I *want*? Well, what I want isn't going to happen, is it? Because my body is stuck in a coma in a hospital bed right now. So, I have to take the next best thing."

"Wait," Mark said, frozen in place, hands raised in a surrendering position. "Why don't we all just calm down and discuss this. I'm sure we can come up with some kind of compromise."

"I don't think so," Ted said. "I'm done compromising with this bitch."

"What are you going to do? You're going to kill the body you're inhabiting, or what, kill us?"

"Please don't give him any ideas, Mark," Julia said out of the corner of her mouth.

"Then what?" Mark said. "The police are on their way. They will find you here covered in blood with our bodies at your feet, and they will take you away. They will charge you with the attempted murder of your father, and the murder of your mother and a stranger. Or you can tell them the truth and just end up in some institution for the next ten years. Sounds like a great life."

"No better or worse than the one I have thanks to them," Ted said, motioning toward Julia.

"Or you could take me!" Mark said, stopping Ted in his tracks.

"You don't have what we have. You don't have the power it takes—"

"Don't I? I bet you have no idea that my dead wife is standing beside you right now."

"Is she? Isn't that interesting." Ellie/Ted stepped closer. "But I'm afraid seeing dead people just makes you a crazy person," Ted said and lunged again.

"What about the lake?" Mark shouted. "Your father teaching you to swim." With the latter word, he used finger quotes. "How would I know about that? How would I know about Ellie's power over you, even when she was a baby?"

This caught Ted's attention. His posture relaxed as he listened to Mark speak.

"The police will be here soon, so you have a choice: You can live out this ridiculous revenge fantasy in a child's body and end up in juvie for years. Or you can let them live. Give Ellie her body back and take mine."

"No!" Julia said. "I won't let you do that."

"You don't have a choice."

"Go on," Ted said, still resting the knife blade against Ellie's chin.

"I was going to kill myself anyway," Mark said. "You know that. I have nothing left to live for. I left a note at my home. Whoever finds it will suspect I ended things. You can go on living my life."

"You expect me to believe that you'd be willing to live out

the remainder of my life, even though I'm in a coma, for her? Wow, Julia, you must've shown this fucker a good time."

Ellie's posture and mannerisms had changed so much that Julia almost didn't recognize her as her daughter. She strutted around like her husband had since the fateful day she'd met him, and Julia wondered if it was even possible for the two of them to switch back. Yet Ellie was still alive, albeit in this bastard's body. Could she live that way forever? The thought made her sick, but at the very least, she would still be alive.

"You don't have to do this," Julia said.

"I do. This is what I deserve."

"How could you say that? You're a good man. You helped us, and you didn't have to."

Mark realized he'd never spoken the words aloud: "I killed my wife and my baby."

"Ha! I knew it! I was right," Ted said.

"Mark, your wife had cancer," said Julia. "No one would blame you for giving extra meds at the end. I promise. My sister works at a hospital; it's completely—"

Still glaring at Ellie/Ted, Mark said, "That's not what I mean. I never did that."

"What, then?" Julia asked. "What could you possibly have done that was so bad?"

⚘

Mark sat in the foam- and vinyl-padded wooden chair, his elbows on his knees and his head in his hands. If he'd known for sure he was alone, he would've wept openly, because he was having a hell of a time holding back.

He could feel the presence of a man taking a seat across from him. He raised his wrecked face to look at the man, who nodded at him. Mark reciprocated.

"You doing all right?" the man asked.

"Uh, yeah." Mark was surprised by the man's forwardness. Most guys his age would do whatever it took to ignore the nearby distressed man.

Maybe the man's brazenness opened Mark up to what the man had to say, or maybe Mark hadn't realized how cathartic it would feel to lay his burden down on someone—anyone—else.

"You can tell me about it," said the man. "I'm a medical professional, if that helps."

Mark took a better look at the man in his full suit and shiny black shoes. Next to him sat a black rolling carry-on sized suitcase. Medical sales, *Mark thought, not sure that counted as a medical professional.*

"I'd rather not talk about it. Thank you for asking, though."

"Tell me."

Mark couldn't explain why, but he had the sudden urge to tell this stranger everything he had just experienced in the adjacent room.

"My wife and I have been trying to have kids for over two years. We tried everything. We were just about to start looking at surrogate options when my wife started feeling terrible. She was exhausted all the time and so sick that she couldn't keep anything down. We took a test, and it was positive."

"That sounds like a good thing," the man said. "If you had been trying for so long."

"It was. We were thrilled. We went to our first appointment, got the blood test, and saw the baby, just a little speck, but it's our little speck, the little speck that we have wanted for so long."

"I am failing to see the issue here, man."

"Her blood test came back with elevated white blood cells, so the doctor wanted to run some more tests. We just got the results. The exhaustion and sickness were not just from the baby. My wife has aggressive breast cancer."

The man blinked. "Shit."

"We were just told that treatment in the first trimester could kill the baby, but without treatment, they don't know how fast the cancer will progress. I couldn't stay in there. I couldn't even be strong for my wife. And she is the one going through all of this."

"Don't factor yourself out of this. She has the physical symptoms, but you wanted that baby just as much as she did. You have every right to feel how you do."

"I want the baby, but I can't live without my wife."

"So don't live without either of them," the man said.

Mark gave a short laugh. "If you can tell me how, I will do it in a heartbeat."

"Don't do the treatment. Most cancer patients go into remission during pregnancy. Postpone treatment and have the baby. Then, once she delivers, she can start her treatment. If she is in remission, you don't have to worry about the cancer spreading during that time."

Was this really an option? Mark thought he vaguely remembered hearing something like this before, but could it be true? Is this what the doctor was telling his wife right now, something he was too chickenshit to stay and listen to?

"This is a real possibility?" Mark asked.

"Hell yes, it is, without a doubt. Ask anyone."

"I have to get back in there," Mark said, tears now filling his eyes for a different reason. "Thank you." He stood and moved toward the man to shake his hand.

The man stood, too, feeding off Mark's excitement. Mark turned the handshake into a hug and thanked the man a few more times for good measure, then raced back through the doors. Once Mark rejoined Izzy, he did indeed learn that some women can enter a remission phase during pregnancy, but the doctor did reiterate the fact that she would in no way recommend trusting in that outcome. She told them it was a crapshoot. Still, the seed had been planted, and the possibility of Mark having both his wife and their baby was too strong to deny.

When Izzy's appointment was over, they went to the front desk to check out. There was the man, saying his goodbyes to the nurse on staff. Mark went up to him to thank him one more time.

"You were right," Mark said. "The doctor did say that some women go into remission during pregnancy."

"There ya go, my man," the man said, slapping Mark on the back.

"Thank you so much. You do not know what you have done for us."

"My pleasure. And hey, what are you hoping for? Boy or girl?"

"Daddy's little girl, Ellie." Mark raised his hand, fingers crossed.

"Listen," the man said, whispering to Mark. "Don't. Let her. Convince you otherwise."

Mark studied the man. "I won't."

"Ellie is a really good name, by the way."

"Thanks," Mark said, taking Izzy's hand and leaving the office.

CHAPTER 24

MARK

"I CONVINCED HER to hold out on treatment, even though she wasn't sure it was a good idea. I was positive that it was all going to work out."

Julia looked over at Ellie/Ted as Mark spoke, then back to Mark, in complete silence.

"Izzy made it to twenty-two weeks. We found out that we were having a girl, Ellie." Mark gestured toward Ellie. "We were already calling her by name. She went into labor and delivered the baby. Stillborn. I just couldn't figure out why... until we discovered Izzy had not been in remission. She was feeling so much better in those first months that we just assumed everything was going as planned. We were both afraid of the risk imaging would have on the baby, so we opted out of any scans during her pregnancy. Her cancer had spread and advanced to stage four. By that time, it was really too late for the treatment to do anything but make her sick and miserable.

"We tried anyway. She lasted four more months. Around the same time, our baby was supposed to have been born. I buried her with our Ellie's ashes and began planning my exit."

"Mark, I am so sorry, but that still wasn't your fault. There was no way you could've known."

"I could've listened to the doctor instead of some medical sales rep, for one."

Julia took another look at Ellie/Ted, now smirking.

"When did you say this was?" Julia asked.

"It's been nine months since I lost Izzy—so a year and a half or so."

Julia let out a sigh of relief. The scene felt all too familiar: a sales rep, the urge to tell a stranger everything. But the timeline didn't add up. Ted did visit medical offices when he started as a rep, but that was back before Ellie was born, when the two first got married. He quickly gave up office sales when his business took off.

Julia supposed it was possible that someone else had similar powers of persuasion, but it was more likely that Mark just wanted his wife and baby so badly that he wasn't about to let anything convince him otherwise. The power of a medical professional's word must've been enough.

"Are we going to do this?" Ellie/Ted said. "Or are we going to have a blubberfest?"

"We're doing it," Mark said. "But first, I want one last drink. Julia, do you mind?"

"I'll get it," she said, not even hesitating.

"Pour me one too," Ellie/Ted said. "I think we should celebrate."

"You don't know how it will affect her," Mark said. "Her body, I mean."

"If I'm in it. It's *my body*. Plus, I created it. I can destroy it if I want to. Give me the fucking drink."

Mark went to the kitchen table and sat down, hoping his body blocked Ted's view of Julia as she poured the drinks.

Ellie/Ted sat across from him, placing the knife down on the table.

"So," Mark said, "how do we do it? Switch, I mean."

"That, I'm not sure. I know that when I was in a coma, I could do all kinds of things, as you well know."

Mark wished he could turn around to convey to Julia what he was thinking: *We cannot let this man get into my body.*

"And Ellie was asleep when you... well, possessed her, I suppose," Mark asked.

Julia brought three glasses of whiskey to the table and passed them out.

"How did you find her?" Julia asked. "How did you find us?"

"Ellie and I have something you will never have—a psychic connection," Ellie/Ted said. "It's like a beacon that gives off a light, and her light is so bright it was the first thing I found in the dark."

"So, we just need to go to sleep?" Mark asked, picking up his glass of whiskey.

Ellie/Ted looked from Mark to Julia, pausing before his response. He picked up his own glass and moved to take a sip, then stopped.

"Pretty much. Whatever my loving wife put in this drink should help." Julia's eyes jumped around, not sure where to land without giving away her guilt.

"How long does it take a fully functioning person to pour whiskey into a glass?" Ted asked. "Not as long as it does to dissolve pills in it, I'm guessing. Now that I think about it, you're doing me a favor. Why don't you go ahead and hand your boyfriend some of those pills so we can get busy."

"Ted, I—"

"Hand. Him. The. Pills."

This time was different. She did stand up and reach into

her pocket. She grabbed a handful of loose pills she had placed there moments earlier. She looked at them there in her hand. The ability to actually *decide* had been returned to her after so many years, and she wanted to sit in it, to feel the wheels in her brain turning.

"It's all right; he's right. We both need to be asleep for this," Mark said, extending his hand to her. Julia turned her hand over and dropped the pills into Mark's hand.

"There is one problem, though," Mark said. "The police could walk in here at any minute. What happens if we haven't, well, you know, switched?"

"I guess they'll be taking a catatonic eight-year-old off to juvie," Ellie/Ted said.

"No!" Julia shouted, and Mark could see the satisfaction on Ellie/Ted's face at Julia's distress.

"I won't take these pills unless you can guarantee that won't happen," Mark said.

"Oh, no? How much do you want to bet? I'll bet you the soul of one little girl that I can make you take those pills."

"Ted, please!" Julia cried. "If you have ever cared for me, or for Ellie, don't do this."

"Put. The. Pills. In. Your. Mouth. Mark," Ted said without hesitation.

Mark opened the hand cupping the pills and looked at them. He remembered doing the same thing repeatedly as he doled them out to his wife before bed. Next, he glanced up at Ted, who sat staring at him through eyes that were no longer Ellie's.

He looked at Izzy, too, as she leaned against the chair, struggling to hold herself up. She reached one hand to her head, pulling off the scarf that covered what was left of her beautiful, wrecked hair, long golden strands coming with it.

"Tell him to go fuck himself, baby," Izzy said.

Mark, without a hint of struggle on his face, looked at Ted. "My wife says you should go fuck yourself."

The arrogance that clung steadily to Ellie/Ted's face disappeared. Mark could tell that Ted wasn't used to feeling this way. He wondered if, since he was a child, there had ever been a moment another person had defied him. He could see the rage building inside of Ellie's small body, too small to even contain it, when headlights flashed through the kitchen window.

Julia shot up and glanced outside. "Cops are here!"

"We have to do this now," Ted said. "I'll take care of the cops."

"How do you plan on doing that?" Julia asked. "As we all just saw, your... skills aren't as powerful as you thought."

Wow, Julia thought. Had she just spoken to her husband that way? She had never dared to take such a tone with him before. Maybe it was Ellie's smaller body. Or maybe it was Ted's failed attempt to force Mark to take the pills. Either way, she felt a flutter of excitement and determination.

"Remember my little trick with the doors?" Ellie/Ted said.

"Do it," Mark said.

Julia peeked out of the window once more, careful not to show her full face in case they were looking in the cabin's direction.

"They're going to the office. That should buy us some time."

"You know what you're doing with these pills?" Ted asked.

"My sister told me how many to give you."

"Your sister? Now that's interesting. I'm surprised she can hold a phone after what I did to her."

Julia's face fell. "What did you do to her?"

Ted grinned his Cheshire cat smile and said nothing. Julia went for him, but Mark jumped up to stop her.

"We don't have time for this," he said. Mark took Ted's glass and slammed it down in front of him. "Drink."

"If you poisoned this drink, I swear to you that your little girl will live the rest of her life trapped in a box, in a place you will never find her."

Mark glanced in Julia's direction. His eyes said, *Your call.*

"Drink it," Julia spat. Ted tipped the glass back and downed it in one swallow.

"I hope you've taken care of yourself," Ted said to Mark. "I don't want to have to reverse any of your bad habits."

Mark clenched his jaw, understanding that this man wasn't worth the effort. Ellie/Ted got up from his chair, went to the queen-sized bed that Mark had shared with Izzy so many times before, and crawled under the covers. Mark and Julia stood watch at the kitchen window.

"Can we trust him to do what he says he will?" Mark asked.

With minor hesitation, Julia said, "Absolutely not."

CHAPTER 25

TEAM ELLIE

"Do you remember what it felt like when you fell asleep and went to the other place?" Kunal asked Ellie. "The garage you told us about?"

As best she could, she nodded her father's lolling head. His brain still couldn't tell his body what to do or how to do it. It took Ellie all of her will to control the man's broken body, now resting on the hospital bed, his head on the pillow that her Uncle Evan had cared enough about to fluff for her. The thought made her want to cry.

"I think so," she said before the tears could fall.

"Okay. Do you remember exactly what you were thinking about before you fell asleep last time?"

"I wanted to talk to the lady. I thought maybe she could help me."

"Good, that's good. So, you thought of her, and that thought brought you to the garage place, where she last was, right?"

"Yeah, she was there."

"Do you remember feeling at all like you were floating? Or

169

seeing your body, or your father's body in this case, beneath you as you floated above?"

"No. I just went to sleep, and I woke up in the box, er, trunk thing."

Kunal nodded, still confused about where he found himself. He was still trying to process that he was looking at an adult male who had the definite speech pattern of a child, but who also shouldn't be capable of speech at all. Only a few hours ago, Kunal had trusted in the sanity of his universe, its reliable lack of what his mother would call "oddities." Now, here he was with his formally rationalist sister, teaching a possessed man how to travel to another astral plane. If he hadn't been terrified of the dangers of drugs for most of his life, thanks to warnings from his parents, he would swear he was tripping on something.

"It seems like this trunk may be some kind of portal to other places," he said, choosing his words carefully.

"Anita. Do you remember when Nani used to tell us about the 'City of Nine Gates'?"

Anita sat in her memories for a moment, then looked up at her brother.

"Oh, my goodness, yes! I had forgotten all about those stories."

"Okay," Laura said, anxiously pacing the room. "Elaborate, please."

"It's been a long time," Anita said, "but if I remember correctly, it had to do with the body's orifices being a portal to other spiritual realms."

"Orifices?" Evan asked, sounding disgusted.

"Eyes, ears, nostrils, mouth, and the, ah… Well, you know the other ones," Kunal said.

Evan nodded, putting a hand up as if to say, *Say no more.*

"So, you're saying Ellie is using one of the nine portals when she's in a human body?" Kunal asked his sister.

"That makes sense, but what about when she is in the box? There is no human body to travel with," she said.

"Maybe the box is like a dwar, one that Ted unknowingly created in his mind," Kunal said, speaking more excitedly than he had since all of this started.

"But what is a—" Laura began, but Evan stopped her.

"Maybe they should just explain all of this to us later."

"It basically means *portal*," Anita added quickly.

"Okay, that makes sense," Laura said. "As much as something can make sense right now."

"Ellie," Kunal said, directing his attention back to the girl in a grown man's body, who now not only looked terrified but also confused. "I believe that if you think hard enough about someplace, then the trunk may have the power to bring you there. Does that make sense?"

Ellie didn't answer him right away. Kunal was just about to ask again when she finally spoke up. "Like the wardrobe in Narnia?"

"Exactly like that! Only, you have the power to control where it takes you." Kunal felt a sudden urge to connect with the girl in some way. He grabbed the man's hand, now resting on the bed, and held it in his own.

"Ellie," he said firmly, "if you listen to anything I tell you right now, listen to this. You have the power. You are in control. You can do anything you decide you want to do. Do you understand?"

Ellie blinked her eyes hard, and that was when they all discovered that Ted's body was capable of producing tears. "Can I have a hug?" Ellie asked before she even realized she was going to. Kunal didn't hesitate. Anita caught the tail end of her brother's hug, and she instantly knew that they had won him over. Part of her felt like they were kids again, working together for a common good, but instead of convincing their parents to take them to Disney World, they were convincing a little girl to trust in her own abilities. The thought warmed her heart, made her realize how much she'd missed him in recent years when their busy lives had pulled them apart.

Anita approached them. She wanted to give them privacy but also understood the urgency of what they were trying to achieve.

"Are you ready, Ellie?" Anita asked.

"I think so," Ellie said.

"I'm going to give you some medicine that will make you fall asleep," Anita said.

"What if I can't find my way back to my mom?" Ellie asked.

Kunal and Anita shared a quick glance before Kunal spoke up. "The medicine will wear off, and you will wake up. It will either be back with your mom or here with us, but you will make it. I promise."

Just as Anita reached for the vial in her lab coat pocket, her cell phone rang, and she fished it out instead.

It was Julia.

Anita answered with, "Are you okay?"

"Yes, he's out, but there's a problem," Julia said.

"The police are there?" Anita added.

"Well, a couple of problems. We've convinced Ted to help us with the police."

"Uh-huh," Anita said, unsure of how to react to this news and if she should even tell the others.

"But he'll screw us over," Julia said.

"Without a doubt," Anita said, smiling for the sake of the others, especially Laura. "What does that mean?"

"Mark wants to help get Ellie back. He just needs some

more information, including where to find her and the details of the room where Ted's body is resting."

"Okay," Anita said, still racking her brain for a way to keep this information from a select few people in the room. None of them had time to think, though, only time for action. "Okay," she said again, this time resigned to telling them.

"I'm going to put you on speaker." Anita did just that and then explained what Julia had just told her, taking only a second to stop Laura before she objected. "I know that all of this is terrible for so many reasons, but we don't have time to worry about that now. Kunal, quickly explain to Julia and Mark what you told Ellie, and then, Ellie, sweetheart, I need you to explain what the garage looks like."

They both did what they were told without hesitation.

Then suddenly, Kunal slapped his palm to his forehead. "What is this, the nineties? We can just take a picture of the room and text it to you."

His statement was met with silence on the other end.

"Julia?" Anita asked, assuming they'd lost the connection. "Please tell me we haven't lost service."

"No," Julia said. "But we might; now that Ted is out, there is no telling what he could do. He could cut us off again."

"Then we will do it quickly!" Kunal said, grabbing his own cell phone from his pocket to snap the photo.

Kunal took a few pictures from multiple angles, then used AirDrop to send them to his sister.

"Julia, I'm sending them to you now. Good luck."

"Thank you. Ellie, Mark is going to come and help you get back, okay, baby?"

"Okay."

"I love you more than anything in this whole stupid world, baby. I'll see you in just a bit." Ellie giggled, which made everyone in the room teary-eyed.

"I love you too, Mommy. And Mark?"

"Yes?" he responded, with an anxious clearing of his throat.

"Thank you." It didn't come out as a passing thank you, as if someone had just passed her the salt at the dinner table. Ellie's thank you said something more than anyone in the room could possibly know or ever understand.

"You are very welcome," Mark said. "See you soon."

CHAPTER 26

TED

HE HOVERED OVER the officers, watching as they knocked ceaselessly on the front door of the Langsteds' home. *They must've already tried the office*, Ted thought. He wasn't hovering above the two men, as a disembodied spirit would. His apparition wasn't visible to anyone at all, but his essence, his being, surrounded them.

In that moment, he decided he would be everywhere at once.

Ted was outside with the police officers. He was in the bedroom of the impossibly soundly sleeping Mary Beth and Dave Langsted. He was in the cabin of his scheming, traitorous bitch of a wife with her confounding new lover. He was in the town of Loomis Falls, spreading himself thin as he covered Main Street: the bar, the gas station, the post office, the laundromat, the cafe, the newspaper, the police station.

Interesting, he thought.

He could see the inner workings of the lumber mill and those within working the midnight shift. He saw into an apartment building and homes, viewing snippets of the lives playing out there, and he felt powerful. Ted wasn't sure if he wanted to be trapped inside any physical body, but something told him he could not go on forever this way. What if he dispersed himself too thin, across the town, the state, the country, and on and on? What if he drifted into space—evaporated?

The thought scared him. Floating into space alone forever, maybe he had already become too thin, too large even to hold himself together. He also realized that, in existing this way, he had less control. Now that he was seeing everything, he was actually in control of nothing, and that wouldn't do. There would be time, he thought as his gaze grew narrower. Once he was in his new body, he could practice, grow his powers.

His view shrank as he wished it to. No more homes, no more mill. He could live another forty years in Mark's body if he took care of himself. The police station, the post office. But why only forty years? Now Main Street and back to the resort. Ellie had at least seventy more years ahead of her. Seventy more years. And to be young again…

Ted was now back inside the Langsteds' bedroom before he shifted outside again to the front door where the officers discussed their next move. He could feel his power once again, his control. He would take his daughter, but she was still his daughter, and because of that, he would give her Mark's body. Why not let her live? It was the least he could do for his own flesh and blood. But first he had to make sure that she and her bitch mother weren't hauled off to jail.

CHAPTER 27

DETECTIVES MASON AND PHILLIPS

A CHILL RAN down the back of Detective Phillips's neck, and he shuddered.

"You okay?" Mason asked.

"Yeah, someone just walked over my grave," Phillips said.

"What?"

"It's just a thing you say when you get a chill and feel uneasy. You've never heard it before?"

"No. Sounds kind of morbid," Mason said.

Phillips only shrugged in response.

"Let's see if anyone answers at the cabins before we call in for the search warrant," Mason said.

Phillip nodded, but as he walked toward the cabins, something struck him: a virtually uncontrollable urge to check the Langsteds' door one more time. He turned back to the door and reached for the handle.

"Come on," Mason said, already walking away.

Phillips jiggled the handle a few times before turning and

opening it. He looked back at Mason, who watched the door as it swung open.

"Exigent circumstances?" Phillips asked.

"Looks like it to me," Mason added. Both drew their weapons before calling out.

"Police!" Mason called. "Is anyone here? We are entering the premises. If anyone is home and able, we need you to come out with your hands up!"

The officers stepped inside the house. Behind them, the door slammed closed. Phillips leapt for the handle, pulling at it.

"It's locked."

"Come on, let's keep going."

They entered what looked like a darkened foyer; they searched the corners. It was clear. Mason found a light switch and flicked it on. An overhead light lit the room of the old house. The house appeared unchanged since its construction, and it smelled of must and well water. The room was small, and now that it was lit, it seemed more like a breezeway, with a door leading into the main house. Mason gestured for Phillips to open it, and he did.

They repeated their mantra, stepping into the next room. As they walked inside, they seemed to forget their protocol and police safety training. Their weapons dropped to their sides as their eyes searched the room glowing with early morning light. Confused, they both turned back to the entry door—which was no longer there.

Another door had replaced it, an expensive, ornate one. The home looked nothing like the old farmhouse they had just walked into. The decor was traditional, with wainscoting on the walls and crown molding on the ceiling. A professional decorator had been hired for the job, no doubt, but the home decor, although nice, was not what dumbfounded the two detectives—it was the daylight shining in through every window they could see, including the sidelight next to the front door that hadn't been there moments ago.

"Phillips, what time is it?" asked Mason.

Phillips raised the hand not holding his gun, pulled his suit jacket sleeve away from his wristwatch, and looked. "It's three o'clock in the morning," he said, still in shock.

"Wasn't it dark outside when we walked into this room?" Mason asked.

"Yes, it was." The detectives looked at each other, then back at the door they hadn't just walked through. Phillips tried the door handle, but it didn't budge.

"What the fuck is going on here?" Phillips asked, not expecting a reply.

"Let's keep checking," Mason said. Remembering his gun, he raised it and continued his search. "Police! If anyone is home, come out with your hands raised!"

Mason rounded the corner of the entryway first, then called for his partner to come quick. Phillips hadn't expected to find his partner on the floor of a powder room, kneeling next to a woman's bloodied body. Mason checked her pulse, careful not to touch the blood but failing because of the sheer amount of it. He shook his head.

"Mrs. Langsted?" Phillips asked.

"I'm guessing."

"And where is Mr. Langsted?"

"Let's find him."

They continued searching the rest of the house and found no trace of Dave Langstead. They were in what appeared to be another woman's bedroom on the upper floor of the house when they heard the banging on the front door, along with what sounded like a man shouting.

"Marcia! Marcia, open up!" *Bang, bang, bang!* The man

kept banging on the door with his fists, over and over. "Are you okay? I heard something! Marcia, if you don't open up, I'm calling the police!"

Bang, bang, bang!

Phillips and Mason rushed down the staircase to the front door and pulled it open. Instead of finding a distraught man calling out from the front porch, they saw something too unbelievable to comprehend. The door opened to a kitchen of an entirely different house, where a man stood frozen in a disheveled sheriff's uniform, face-to-face with what appeared to be the dripping wet corpse of a long-dead man. His putrid skin oozed with pus, seeming to melt off him. Globs of a slimy substance dropped heavily onto the linoleum floor as he swayed. The smell of rotting flesh and sewer water hit both men at once.

"Fucking hell," Mason whimpered. Both the man and the corpse turned to look at the detectives loitering in the nonexistent doorway. Phillips grabbed Mason and pulled him back before slamming the door closed.

"Are we dead?" Mason asked. "Did we die?"

"I don't know. I don't know. I don't know," Phillips said, grabbing at his hair as he paced. He went back to the door and grabbed the handle again. Mason grabbed his arm before he could open it again.

"I can't," he stammered. "I can't see that again."

"I don't think we will," Phillips said. He closed his eyes, took a deep breath, and pulled the door open again.

This time, the door opened to reveal an old farmhouse living room. This home was more of what they thought the Langsteds' home would look like.

"Are we back?" asked Mason, as if his partner would have that information any more than he would. There was a couch in front of where they stood, and the figure lying on it stirred, disturbing the surrounding pile of empty beer cans, which crashed to the floor.

"What the—?" the man said, half asleep. He looked to be in his early thirties and clearly out of shape.

"Is that you, fucker?" He was not only drunk, but agitated and reaching for something on the floor next to him. He was likely searching for a gun, one he couldn't seem to find. The men didn't give him time. They slammed the door closed again.

"Let's try a different door," Phillips said. Mason just stood there, eyes wide as if he'd just seen a ghost. He was clearly in shock, but instead of trying to convince his partner to come with him, Phillips just moved on.

He entered the kitchen, saw a back door, and went to it, stepping over a spilled container of coffee creamer. He pulled the back door open, revealing what looked like a cheap, old motel room. There were two queen beds in the middle of the room. A woman lay sleeping on the floral-patterned bedspread.

On the bed nearest him was a boy, who was thin and frail and looked to be about twelve years of age. The boy raised up onto his elbows and saw Phillips standing in the doorway. He swung his feet over the edge of the bed and attempted to stand. When his bare foot hit the thin carpeted floor, Phillips swore he could hear the bones breaking inside of it. The boy fell and caught himself with the other foot, which also made a horrid snapping sound. This time, instead of just the foot bones breaking, Phillips could see the tibia of the boy's shin crack in half, the jagged edge of the bone showing just under the skin of his leg, looking like a bag of broken sticks.

The boy continued toward him as the bones of both his legs continued to break and deform. He fell to the ground, and the sound of what had to have been the boy's pelvis cracking in half threatened to fully empty Phillips's stomach.

The last thing he saw as he closed the door was the boy reaching toward him from the floor of that motel room, his small shoulder dislocating in the process.

Phillips rushed back through the kitchen, slipping on the coffee creamer but catching himself on the kitchen counter before collapsing. He made it to the living room in time to hear more banging on the front door, then what sounded like an axe being slammed into it. *They're breaking the door down,* he thought.

Who?

He grabbed Mason by the arm and dragged him up the staircase, which was no easy feat. They went back inside the dead woman's room and closed the bedroom door. Opening the closet door, Phillips found only clothes, a discovery that brought him both relief and frustration.

"How do these goddamn doors work?" he cried.

Whoever was breaking down the door now appeared to be inside the house. It sounded like multiple people, in fact. He wasn't willing to wait and find out what deadly, undead, or monstrous things would soon find them. He pulled open the bedroom door again, and when he saw what looked like a warehouse on the other side, he yanked his partner through and slammed the door closed behind them.

CHAPTER 28

TEAM ELLIE

"I'm scared," Ellie said to Kunal. She wasn't sure why it was him she told that to, but she knew she liked him. It didn't hurt that he was handsome, but she also liked his energy; he was funny and fun to be around.

Although she knew she was in her father's broken body, inside, she was still Ellie, and her eight-year-old self was having a hard time understanding why everyone except for her Uncle Evan was so standoffish toward her. Her Aunt Laura had always showered her with hugs and tickles, but now, in the time that she needed it most, when she was more scared than ever before, she did not receive any affection.

She tried so hard to raise her father's hand to anyone who would take it, but all she got was a small finger twitch—not nearly enough for anyone to see. But he did. *Kunal* did. The one person who'd walked into this room not willing to believe any of their wild story saw it. He saw her and rushed to her side. Kunal took Ellie's father's large hand in his own and squeezed it tight. Evan noticed and rushed to bring him a chair so he could sit next to her.

"Thank you," Kunal said, and Evan nodded.

"Listen to me, Ellie," he continued. "You're the strongest, most powerful kid I have ever met, and I've met a lot of kids. I mean, I am a doctor, come on."

Ellie giggled and squeezed his hand tight, letting him know she didn't want him to let go.

"This is all going to be over soon. And once it is, I'm going to take you out to my favorite ice cream place in the city. And I'll buy you the biggest rainbow ice cream cone they make. I may even let my sister tag along." He nodded in her direction. "Does that sound good?"

Ellie made her father's face smile, but it looked more like a grimace of pain. She then nodded his head as vigorously as she could.

"Okay, then, hop to it. I'm craving some ice cream."

"Okay," she said. "I'm ready." Anita looked on, surprised at how good her little brother was with children, especially in this unique situation. She never imagined him as a father, but she guessed he'd make a damn good one. At that moment, she almost stopped seeing him as an immature, goofy, thirteen-year-old boy. Almost. Kunal cleared his throat, looking at her, and she remembered she had a job to do. She grabbed the vial from her pocket, but a sound from the door made her shove it back inside.

"Why is this door closed?" Nurse Sara said, opening the door to Ted's room.

Kunal jumped up from his seat, hoping the nurse hadn't seen him holding the hand of this coma patient because he had no good, rational reason to be doing so.

"Hi. We're almost finished here. Just discussing some private, um… confidential things with my patient here." He gestured to who he thought was Laura, but who turned out to be Evan. He noticed his mistake and fixed his error. The nurse looked back and forth from Evan to Laura, then back at Kunal.

"I'm sorry, but—" Sara said, but Kunal cut her off, guiding her back to the door with a hand on the small of her back.

"No, I'm sorry to be taking up so much of your patient's time, but as you stated, these are coma patients, so they have a lot of time."

"I just think it's an odd time to meet one of your patients," Sara said. "And I'm sorry to say, Doctor, but what I overheard of your conversation sounds strange to me."

"This is a new experimental role-playing technique that is—"

This time it was Kunal who was cut off by his sister.

"That's confidential. You know, HIPPA and all of that, but we will be done soon, I promise." Anita rushed Sara out the door and closed it behind her.

"Why did you do that?" he whispered aggressively to his sister. "Don't you know better than to be rude to nurses? We need her on our side."

"I'm sorry, but we don't have time to sweet-talk the nurse. We have to do this before it's too late."

Kunal held his hand out to Anita. "Give me the syringe."

"Why? I can do it."

"She likes me better," he said, unwilling to deny it.

Anita handed over the medicine and syringe. Kunal inserted the syringe into Ted's IV port and pressed down the plunger.

"Okay, it's done," Kunal said, and walked toward the Sharps container on the wall.

"Wait, don't throw that away; recap it," Anita said.

"That's so dangerous," Kunal said.

"More or less dangerous than administering undocumented medicine to a coma patient that is not your patient and leaving evidence behind?"

"Shit, you're right." He handed her both items. Anita

shook her head, carefully capped the needle, and put it and the vial back in her coat pocket.

"Ellie," Kunal said, shaking her—or her father's—shoulder. (This would never *not* be insane to him.)

"She's out."

"Now what?" Laura asked.

"Now we wait," said Anita.

"Here?" Evan asked.

"Absolutely not," Nurse Sara said, her tone sterner now. "I've called Dr. Thompson, and he is on his way."

Kunal gave Anita a look that read, *Look what you did.* Anita could only shrug. They'd been having silent conversations like this since they were kids, trying to keep things from their parents. They'd learned to say a thousand things with just one look. Anita's shrug said, *I had no choice.* But with decisions come consequences, and these would not be good for either of them.

"Sara, please call him back and tell him it was a false alarm," Kanal begged. "We are all done here. We're leaving, all of us."

"You'll have to take it up with Dr. Thompson when he gets here," she said, crossing her arms over her chest.

"Sara, please. If you call Dr. Thompson here in the middle of the night for a false alarm, the only person he'll be angry with is you, because we will already be gone by the time he gets here. Sara, you know I'm right." She huffed a little but still didn't give in.

"Wait a second. Isn't Dr. Thompson scheduled for surgery in the morning? From what I understand, neurosurgery isn't something you should do when you're sleep-deprived."

She looked at each of them one by one, then uncrossed her arms. "Shit. I need to call him back." They all exhaled a sigh of relief. "You all need to be out of here by the time I get off of the phone." And with that, she rushed out the door.

"We are all leaving right now," Kunal said, giving one of his thousand-word looks to Evan, who still stood in the corner near Ted's bedside.

Evan knew right away that this look meant everyone except for him. He was one of those people you could meet a handful of times and still never seem to remember. A few times, Kunal had forgotten the man had even been in the room. Not that he wasn't good-looking; he was fine, average height, average looks, average everything. He was also very mild-mannered, which is what made him perfectly forgettable.

Kunal knew that if the three of them walked out of the room together, Nurse Sara would not notice there'd once been four. Hell, he even wondered if his own wife would notice that she'd left him behind. For all their sakes, he hoped she didn't—at least not until they got into the elevator.

Evan gave Kanal a nod, then floated his way further into the corner of the room. He looked around for places he could hide if the need arose. There were a few possibilities, and he made sure he was situated where those places would be easy to get to in a pinch. For once in his life, he was thrilled to be who he was.

Anita walked next to Laura, and Kunal trailed behind them. Before leaving the room, he hit the light switch on the wall, slipping Ted's room into darkness—or at least as much darkness as a hospital room could get, which was never enough for the patients who actually wanted to get some sleep. But if the room looked dark, it might also look empty, so it was worth a try.

They passed by the nurses' station, where Ted's apologetic nurse, Sara, was on the phone with a seemingly angry Dr. Thompson. He gave a quick wave, making sure she saw them leave. She returned his wave with a scowl and a head shake—just fine.

They made it all the way to the elevator and up two floors before Laura realized she'd forgotten something.

"Evan!"

Kunal couldn't help but chuckle at the *Home Alone*-like moment. He explained the unspoken deal he'd made with her husband, putting her mind at ease. That was until he reminded her she was, in fact, still on a psychiatric hold.

CHAPTER 29

ELLIE

Kunal's face was the last she saw before slipping under. It was his aura that she carried with her into the box. Had it not been him, she wasn't sure she would've had the strength to enter this place again, this place filled with so much pain.

When she opened her eyes, she expected the darkness, just like the last time. She hoped the woman would be there to help her again. She wanted her to be there, but the last time she saw her, there'd been a feeling emanating from her. Not fear, exactly. Ellie couldn't put the feeling into words. If she had a thesaurus, maybe. Her Uncle Evan had taught her how to use one on his phone once, during a game of Mad Libs. She was still trying to grasp the word when a sliver of light appeared in front of her. It was the woman, and as soon as their eyes met, Ellie knew the word: desperation.

"Come quickly," the woman whispered, reaching for Ellie's hand and pulling her out of the trunk. Once she was out, Ellie could see why—the garage was already occupied, but this time it was not only her father and grandfather. Another man was there as well.

The man had receding brown hair. He was of average

height and had an enormous belly. Aunt Laura called them "heart attack bellies" because of something about the fat surrounding the heart. He was wearing a short leather jacket with a colorful sweater underneath, and he had a gold chain around his thick neck. On his fingers were multiple gold rings. The smell of tobacco smoke and cologne permeated the air.

The woman pulled her back to their previous spot behind the old car. She saw the horse symbol on the back and the word *Mustang*, and she wished she had noticed it before so she could've told Mr. Mark about it, but there was no use worrying about it now.

Ellie could hear the man speaking to her grandfather, but she couldn't make out the words. It seemed like the man was giving him instructions. She tried peeking around the side of the car to get a closer look, but the women grabbed her, pulled her back, and shook her head.

Ellie hadn't needed to get any closer, because just then, the voices rose, louder.

"I won't *do* it anymore! Not for him and not for anyone!" The voice belonged to Ellie's father, though he seemed older and more confident than the last time she'd seen him here.

"Don't make me beat you in front of our guest, boy," her grandfather said, through what sounded like gritted teeth.

"You. Will. Not. Hurt. Me," Ted said, in the same staccato fashion she had heard so many times before.

Ellie, though, feared what was to come next, because it was just then that a realization came to her: Ellie's father had never hurt her physically, and he was never able to control her with his words like he had with her mother. It wasn't that Ellie was special or that he had some hidden love for her. Her father didn't have power over blood relations.

She heard the *zip* of a belt being rapidly removed, and then she heard the *swish* of it whipping through the air and the *crack* as it hit her father's skin. The clinking of metal filled the air as the buckle-end of her grandfather's belt struck her father's flesh. As much as she hated the man her father was, this was only a boy, nothing more than a scared boy.

The boy's screams rang out, then stopped. Now she heard water splashing onto the concrete floor. This time, she had to see. She pulled away from the woman's grasp and peeked her head around the side of the Mustang, where she saw her father's legs flailing out behind him as her grandfather held his head down in a washtub filled with water.

After what seemed like forever, he pulled her father's head out of the water and threw him to the ground. He coughed and choked, and when he got it all out, he begged. "No more water, please!" the boy cried. "I'll do it. I'll do anything you ask, just not the water again, please!"

The two men laughed.

"That's what I thought you'd say," her grandfather said. It made Ellie sick to see the joy his son's pain brought him, but, she supposed, like father, like son. As they say.

Her father lay dripping wet on the concrete, still trying to suck in air, when he turned his gaze to her. He looked at her, startling her, then clearly said, "Not the water, anything but water." Then, as if it had never happened, he went back to lying with his head on the floor gasping for air. Ellie shot back to her spot next to the woman, and the room went silent. After a few moments, the woman rose. "It's over now. You don't have to hide." Ellie stood up on wobbly legs and looked around the room. She was right. They were alone in the garage with no evidence that anything had just taken place.

"I don't understand," Ellie said to the woman. "I thought the last time my grandfather was trying to get him to stop using his powers?"

"He was, and he did. Until he and your grandmother

realized that not only were they not affected by his control, but they could profit from it. And that's exactly what they did."

"So, they tortured him into it?"

"It seems that way. There may have been some good in your father at one time, but they destroyed that years ago."

"It's so sad. Maybe he could've done good things with it."

"Maybe, but what matters now is that you are safe," the woman said, wrapping Ellie in her arms. Ellie hugged her back but didn't leave it at that.

"But I'm not safe," she said, pulling out of their hug. "Not yet. I'm still trapped here. I need to get back to my mom, back to my body."

The woman hushed Ellie as she embraced her once again. "Shh, it's okay. It will all be okay. You can stay here with me." Ellie couldn't deny the love she had for the woman who had been with her for her entire life. She felt at home in her arms, but it was not enough; and this time, she pulled away hard.

"What do you mean?" said Ellie. "We can't stay here in this garage. We have to get home, back to my mom."

The woman's face faltered. "I don't know how to say this, but there is no way back. Your father made sure of that. This is the box he plans to keep you in. But even though we are trapped, we are still together. We will make the best of it, I promise. I will tell you stories and teach you things. I can comb your hair." She reached out and petted Ellie's long brown hair. Ellie grabbed her hair from the woman's fingers, ripping some of it out in the process.

"No! I'm leaving! I don't want to stay here with you! My friend is coming to save me; he is going to bring me back! He promised he would! He *promised*!"

Ellie wept. She curled herself up into a ball on the ground. The woman went to her at first, afraid to touch her, then laid her hand on her and stroked her back.

"My little nugget," she said. The woman had called her that since the day she was born all those years ago, but this was the first time Ellie could hear her or communicate with her. Yet somehow, the familiarity of the nickname comforted her, and her weeping slowed, along with her heaving breaths.

"He promised," Ellie said. "He promised he would come for me."

CHAPTER 30

MASON AND PHILLIPS

THE TWO MEN stood in the middle of what appeared to be a warehouse. On closer inspection, though, it turned out to be a lumber mill.

They looked back to where they'd just entered the building. The entryway was no longer there, so there was no option of going back through it if they wanted to.

They still carried their guns but held them more like security blankets than the symbols of fear they once were.

Beneath the potent scent of wood lingered another odor—a metallic one, all too familiar. It was not the smell of decay, but of blood freshly drawn and spilled.

They searched for the source, and it didn't take long. The machines in the mill were still running, as if their minders had abandoned them mid-shift. The disturbing truth was that the men and women who worked those machines hadn't left at all. They were still there, parts of them at least, strewn everywhere. Not on the saws, conveyor belts, or debarkers, as you would imagine, but all over the floor at the workers' stations, as if they had fallen apart where they stood.

They saw arms separated from shoulders and pieces of feet

missing from legs that were also missing from torsos. It was a massacre. Seeing the worst of it, Mason, the lead detective, the man Detective Phillips respected most and tried like hell to emulate, began to cry.

Phillips wasn't sure what to do. He had never seen a grown man blubbering before, and he wasn't sure how to comfort him. He looked around for a place he could take the man away from all the gore to save what was left of his sanity. Whatever had done this to these people had clearly done it recently, and Phillips didn't care to know what or who it was.

He found a private handicapped bathroom, then grabbed Mason by the shoulders and guided him there, reminding him he was okay, that he was going to be okay.

Phillips threw open the door, expecting to find another strange house or maybe a restaurant—even a goddamn funeral home would've been better than this place. But instead of a new place, he found a bathroom. Resting on the handicap accessible toilet sat a man attempting to hold in his own intestines.

"Help me," he said, blood spurting from his mouth. When he tried to move, his entrails bulged through his splayed fingers.

"What the fuck; what the fuck," Phillips repeated, and the men backed out of the bathroom, slipping on puddles of blood as they moved. The dying man shouldn't have been something to fear, but here in this place, in this strange world, the sight terrified them. They ran through the carnage until they came to a door labeled with their salvation: Exit. They pressed their bodies against the metal push bar and ejected themselves outside.

They now stood in a dimly lit hallway. This was not an extension of the lumber mill. The hallway had doors on either side, with nameplates on the wall next to them. It resembled a hospital, only more residential. Phillips winced at the smell—a medical-grade disinfectant to cover feces and the musty scent of the elderly—which indicated their location.

This had to be a nursing home. Much less scary than their last pit stop, and for that, he was marginally grateful. Mason did not look well; his skin had turned pale and waxy, and his body appeared to be almost vibrating. Phillips feared that if he stopped to rest or even attempted to help him, his mind and body would similarly deteriorate. It was why he had become a detective in the first place; he was great under pressure. It was the times when the pressure finally released that scared him.

Maybe this place is just a place, he thought. Maybe they wouldn't open any doors for a while, just in case.

CHAPTER 31

MARK

HE USED THE front door, the same one he'd used when he was transported into Ellie's memory, or at least what he thought was her memory. The door opened into the same place: the Barnet's home. But instead of walking into the family drama of before, the room was quiet. Mark made his way into the living room and found the family there, frozen in place—Julia cowering on the couch, a tear frozen to her cheek. Ellie's mouth was open mid-cry. Ted stood sentry over them.

Mark scanned the scene before him, waiting for something to happen, for life to erupt into the frozen figures there. Nothing. He sat on the couch next to Julia, touching her shoulder. Her shoulder felt like that of any other living being. Heat emanated from her, yet when he shook her body, not a hair moved. He walked over to baby Ellie, feeling the wetness on her cheeks as she slept. He circled Ted, wanting nothing more than to beat the man to death right there. It would be like shooting a man in the back, yes, but he didn't care.

Mark paced the living room, trying to recall what he was missing.

"A box, a box," he repeated.

"I will trap her in a box," he remembered.

"I will keep her in a box in my head."

"No," Mark said.

"That can't work."

It wouldn't be stranger than anything else that has happened today, Mark thought, and he walked behind the couch to where Ted stood for the second time today. He touched the man's back, which also felt solid.

Mark wasn't at all sure how any of this worked. A large part of him still suspected he was having a very detailed dream. Or maybe he'd taken those pills after all, and this represented the last electric burst of his synapses. It didn't matter, because he was here now. He closed his eyes and thought of the place Ellie had described to him, and then he opened them and reached toward the back of Ted's head.

Instead of grasping hair, Mark's hands moved through the back of Ted's head as if the man were a ghost. Then, instead of his hand passing straight through Ted's head and through his face, his knuckle bumped into something cold and hard. He felt around and grasped the object in his hand.

"No," Mark said. "It can't be."

He turned the doorknob inside of Ted's head, and a light emanated through the spot where Mark's hand rested. He was forced to squint his eyes as the light grew brighter and more expansive, flooding the room. The light enveloped him completely, shining so brightly that he had to cover his eyes even though they were shut tight. Just when Mark thought he could no longer handle the light, it dimmed.

Mark removed his hands from his eyes and opened them, still squinting against what was now a different light—the light of day. Once his eyes had finally adjusted, he could see that he stood on the driveway of a small brick bungalow. Ahead of him was an open garage; inside was the old red car Ellie had described. He took a deep breath and walked toward it.

Mark heard the crying, but it wasn't what first grabbed his attention; instead, he knew he'd found her when he saw the head of golden curls sticking up behind the car's back end. They were as familiar as his own body was to him. Mark shook his head, knowing his eyes must be deceiving him, tricking him. A cruel trick.

He rounded the corner to find Ellie crumpled on the garage floor, crying with her head in the lap of a woman.

Mark knew what this was. The last time he saw Izzy, back at the cabin, she had seemed stronger, her hair fuller, her voice a bit stronger. But this? This was Izzy. This was Izzy at her healthiest. Before cancer stole her vitality. Was he capable of creating this version of her in his own mind?

It had been so long since he'd experienced her this way that it didn't seem possible now. Mark was so entranced with this version of his Izzy that he didn't even register the fact that Ellie was, in fact, in contact with her. Izzy ran her fingers through the girl's hair as she sobbed. Before he could wrap his mind around it, Izzy turned her hazel eyes to him. Her smile cracked his heart in two.

Tears dropped from his eyes, landing on Ellie's pajama pants. She stirred, rose up, and turned toward him. That same light, the one he had just seen in Izzy's eyes, lit up Ellie's. She scrambled to her feet and jumped into his arms. "I knew you would come!"

Tears burst out of Mark's eyes as he crouched down to embrace her. Her force knocked him back onto the floor. "I told her you promised, and that I believed you and that you wouldn't lie!"

Her whole body held him tight in a massive bear hug. His

mouth hung open in shock as he squeezed her back, his hand grasping the back of her head and stroking it as Izzy had done.

"I got you. I got you," he whispered to her.

He didn't take his eyes off Izzy as she got to her feet. She had on a sundress that didn't look familiar to him, and he wondered how he could've dreamed it up.

Mark pulled Ellie out at arm's length so he could look her in the eye.

"Are you okay?"

Ellie nodded. "My other mom was here with me."

They both rose to their feet, Mark not taking his eyes off Izzy. "Your other mom?" he asked.

Ellie went to Izzy, taking her hand. "She was my mom before my mom was. I lived in her tummy first. She has been with me for as long as I can remember, but here I can touch her, see?" Ellie lifted Izzy's arm and moved her own hand across it, showing Mark that she was just as real as they were.

That Ellie could not only see Izzy but speak to her and touch her was so unbelievable that Mark almost missed what she was telling him. Ellie looked back and forth at the two people standing beside her, confused about the way they were looking at each other.

"Are you really here?" Mark asked, choking back tears.

"I am. We are," she said, caressing his face. He grasped her hand and kissed it all over; he rubbed her skin on his lips and breathed her in. The scent and the feel of her skin against his was something he never thought he would experience again.

"How? How is this possible?"

"I've always been with you," she said. "You just weren't ready to see me. All you could see was the monster you created out of all the trauma. But I've been there, waiting, and when I wasn't with you, I was with her."

"How did you find her?" Mark asked, rubbing Ellie's hair as she clung to his side.

"I don't know. All I remember is the pain of losing our baby, then the pain of leaving you, then just pain. And then there I was, and there she was, and I just knew she was our baby. I had an overwhelming need to protect her from something, so I stayed. Then one day, she saw me, and my heart felt full again. I've watched and protected her the best I could. I followed her here, and I could feel her and speak to her, and she could speak to me. That bastard was trying to trap her here."

"I don't understand any of this," Mark said, looking at Ellie, then back to Izzy, even more confused than he had been. *What is she saying? The soul, the spirit, of our daughter never truly died? That* she... Mark rubbed his eyes vigorously, as if it would help his brain make more sense of this. *That she transferred instead, that she leaped into Julia's womb?* It was all so insane; how was he expected to believe this?

"It's our daughter, our Ellie," Izzy said, grasping the girl's hand. There was a place inside of Mark's soul that knew this to be unequivocally true; it was something he had known, no matter how impossible it seemed, from the moment he'd met the girl.

"How is any of this possible?" he asked.

"It's a gift, and God knows we deserve it," Izzy said.

"Is it true, Mr. Mark? Are you my first daddy?" Ellie asked.

Mark looked at Ellie, at her eyes in particular. The girl's features were those of her mother, Julia, but her eyes... her eyes were undoubtedly Izzy's. He wondered if he'd noticed it all along. Was this the reason he was willing to delay his inevitable fate, to help her and her mother?

"Yes, I believe it is," he said, pulling them both into him. It was the first time Mark had felt whole in a long, long time.

CHAPTER 32

MASON, PHILLIPS, AND TED

TED WATCHED AS the two men wandered the Golden Oak Rest Home halls. It wasn't too hard to create a loop for the men to walk through—soon, they would find the hallway neverending. He had placed them in the traumatic moments in time, in a town that seemed to have endless trauma.

But Ted, as clever as he knew himself to be, was running out of ways to distract them from their original goal. Ted was even having trouble remembering why he was doing this. Who exactly was he helping with this? And how would he sustain the help? Now that Ted had a moment to think about his options, what did he care if his bitch wife and kid got hauled away for his attempted murder? If he had access to lover boy's body, he could walk away free and clear from all of it, and they could fend for themselves.

He just needed enough time to ensure his vessel was free and Julia wasn't attempting to sabotage him. The problem was that he would have to focus on multiple tasks at once. Or would he? One of the men already seemed to be losing it. Ted thought maybe there was a way to use that to his advantage.

Phillips was so busy dragging Mason through the hallway

that he hadn't noticed they'd passed the same door at least four times. Once he finally noticed, though, his anger only had one place to go: his partner.

"What the fuck, man! Will you do anything to help or just let me drag you around like a useless zombie!"

Mason turned his dead-eyed gaze to Phillips.

"What the fuck are you staring at?" Phillips asked.

"What did you say?" Mason slurred as if he'd had a few too many.

"I said I'm going to gut you."

Mason swallowed hard, confused about his partner's sudden aggressiveness.

"I said I'm going to slit your throat the first chance I get." Mason looked down at his hands and noticed he still held his gun; now, he raised it up high and pointed it at Phillips's head.

"Whoa, man! I didn't say anything!" Phillips held up his hands.

All Mason heard was, "I'm going to kill you slowly." He cocked the gun.

"Toss your gun and open that door," Mason said, pointing at the door behind Phillips in the hallway.

"Mason, what are you—"

Just then, Mason lashed out with the butt of his gun, attempting to strike Phillips in the head but slamming it into his shoulder instead.

He did as he was told, stammering as he pleaded for Mason to calm down, but when Phillips saw the tremor in Mason's hand, he decided quiet was best.

The door opened into what appeared to be an office with a front desk, a few chairs, and not much else. Phillips took his eyes off Mason's gun for only a moment to look out the window.

"I think we're back at the resort; this looks like the office, doesn't it?" Phillips said, noticing the trees outside the front window.

Mason heard, "This looks like a great place to end your life."

"Sit down, you piece of shit!" Mason said, gesturing his gun toward the chair. He searched around the office as Phillips did as he was told. He opened the drawers and emptied them, locating a roll of duct tape.

"Please don't do this," Phillips pleaded as he watched Mason tear off strips of the tape with his teeth.

"I'll come for your family next; I'll rip your daughter's arms off," was all Mason needed to hear before placing the tape over Phillips's mouth. He then tied his arms behind his back and his ankles to the chair. One could barely see the man's clothes through the duct tape when he was done. Phillips writhed and shook beneath the tape, and Mason looked upon him seemingly pitiless. Once he was satisfied with his work, he sat in the chair next to Phillips, relaxed his body, and stared blankly ahead. If Phillips had been paying attention, he would've noticed that Mason looked like his batteries had just run out.

CHAPTER 33

MARK

THEY TOOK THE time they desperately needed. They held each other and cried, finding it difficult to believe they were all together, but Mark hadn't forgotten what he was there for, nor the time crunch they were under.

"We have to figure out a way to get you back," Mark said to Ellie. Izzy's face fell at this revelation.

"Get back?" Izzy asked, tilting her head to one side. Mark had seen her do it a thousand times, so he knew she was genuinely confused. The void of sadness grew within him.

"We have to get Ellie back to her mother before—" Mark paused, wondering if Ellie needed to know what had been going on back at the cabin or not. He decided she did not.

"I just have to get her back soon."

"We're all here together, finally. And you want to leave?" Izzy looked panic-stricken.

"We can't stay here in this garage forever," Mark said.

"Why? Why can't we? What else is there?" Izzy was getting upset, and it was the last thing in this universe Mark wanted, but he could also see that her reactions were beginning to scare

Ellie. Mark didn't want Ellie's only memories with Izzy to be tainted by fear.

"Hey, hey," Mark said, going to her and taking her in his arms. "She is just a little girl. She has her entire life ahead of her. We can't expect her to spend it here just because we want to be with her. I need to get her back to her mother."

Izzy broke away from Mark's embrace and ran to Ellie, grasping her from behind. "I *am* her mother!"

Mark looked at the fear in Ellie's eyes and wondered how much more the girl could handle.

"Of course you are, Izz; nobody's denying that." Just then, the door from the house to the garage flew open. Izzy pulled Ellie back behind the car, and Mark followed. They sat as quietly as possible as the scene played out beside them.

"What did you do? What the fuck did you do?" someone said. Mark snuck his head around the side of the car to see. He couldn't make out the faces from the way they were turned, but he could see that the slimmer, younger-looking man of the two was covered in blood.

"They're going to come after us, you stupid fuck!" said the older man. He looked familiar to Mark, and he quickly realized that this was a slightly older version of the man he had seen on the dock earlier in the evening, which meant the younger one was Ted, and the older, his father.

Ted shook his head. "No, they won't. They're all dead."

Ted's father ripped at whatever hair he had left as he paced around.

"That's not all of them! That's not all there is! There is always someone higher up, more powerful. Do you think they will let you get away with this? They are going to come here and murder all of us! These guys don't mess around; they just handle it! What the fuck were you thinking?"

"I was thinking they would take it out on you," Ted said,

and his father slapped him hard in the face with the back of his hand.

"And your fucking mother, too, genius!"

Ted lifted his bloodied face to his father. "Two for one."

Ted's father's panic turned to murderous rage, and he lunged for his son. "Save me a spot in hell, you son of a bitch!"

The two men panted and groaned as they struggled, knocking tools from the workbench to the floor and spilling unfinished bottles of beer. An electric buzzing filled the space, and Mark remembered seeing a table saw when he'd entered the garage. The buzzing sound changed to a whirring, and Mark clasped his hands over Ellie's ears, protecting her from what he was sure they were about to hear. He realized he should've covered her eyes when the first spatter of blood whipped across the wall in front of them. Some blood hit Mark's cheek, and he flinched and turned away, still sheltering Ellie with his arms.

At last, the wet whirring sound ended, but Mark was still too frozen to risk sneaking a look. Izzy, Mark, and Ellie sat huddled together as Mark tried to avoid staining Ellie's hair with splattered blood.

Once he'd built up enough courage, he left Ellie in Izzy's arms and shifted to the edge of a car to assess the danger.

Ted stood, wiping his face with a rag. Next to him, his father was lying over the table saw, nearly decapitated.

Bile rose in Mark's throat as he took in the scene in front of him. The door to the house swung open.

"What the hell is going on in here?" a woman's voice shouted. She must've seen the blood then, because she drew in a deep breath and let out a horrible, tortured bellow.

"Frank! Oh, my God! What the fuck did you do?"

Ted took in his surroundings, and his gaze landed on the hammer on the workbench next to him; it was also covered in blood. He grabbed it and went for her, his sneakers slipping in the blood as he did, giving her just enough time to run back into the house and slam the door behind her, but not enough time to lock it. He ripped the door open and slammed it behind him.

Mark turned back to his unconventional family. "We have to get out of here now!"

He stood quickly, trying in the process to drag Izzy and Ellie to their feet. He couldn't understand why they weren't more panicked. Hadn't they at least heard what had just happened? His legs shook, but Ellie and Izzy seemed almost resigned.

"Don't look over there," he said.

"It's okay," Izzy said calmy.

"What? There is *nothing* okay with this. We have to get out of here!"

"No, we don't. It's okay; it's not real," she said, taking his hand. Mark shook his head, and she pulled him closer. "It was real at one time. But what we're watching is nothing more than a memory."

Mark shook his head again. He wiped at his cheek, at the spatter of the dead man's blood. "Does this look fake to you?" he said, holding out his hand to her, but there was nothing there. He tried rubbing it again, but once again it came back clean.

"It can't be," Mark said, his head on a swivel. The dead man was no longer dangling from the table saw, and the blood spatter was gone, along with the smears on the floor from where the young man had slipped. The hammer was back where it had been when Mark walked in. The shock of what he had just experienced caused a delay in his understanding, but eventually, he realized that this was no different from the memory that had brought him to them in the first place. Ellie's memory.

"Fine, but regardless, she can't stay here." He pulled Izzy further away, out of earshot from Ellie, and whispered, "Do you think it's safer for her to stay here? For her to experience these horrible things?"

"I have protected her from the worst, and now you can too. They don't last long, only a few minutes."

Mark hugged his wife because he couldn't bear arguing with her when he'd finally gotten her back. He kissed her face all over and placed his forehead against hers.

"I love you more than I have ever loved anyone or anything. You know that, right?"

Izzy nodded her head and recited their favorite line from their favorite movie.

"And I you." Mark huffed a laugh, shook his head with a smile, and kissed her. Tears fell from both of their cheeks as they did. He felt his own, but he also felt hers. They were real, and they were beautiful. As much as Mark wanted it to be true, until that moment, he had not been sure that this was the real Izzy. Hearing the *Braveheart* quote sealed the deal.

"Baby," he whispered to her. "If you were Ellie, and you had a choice to be alive and live a full life or be here, which would you choose? And please think about it before you answer. Think about her." He guided their gazes to their daughter. Tears continued to fall on Izzy's pink, healthy cheeks, but now they didn't seem like tears of joy—once again, they seemed more like tears of sadness and loss.

"You have me, baby," he said, "and you will never lose me again, I promise you."

He expected a kiss, or at least a nod. He did not expect her to pull away as she did.

"Not while he is still there," she said. "I will not let her go back if he can still hurt her."

Mark didn't need to say anything; he knew she was right. If Ted was still alive, in whatever body he chose to live in now that his own had been irreparably damaged, Ellie and Julia would never be safe—the man's pride would never let them go.

I wonder what would happen, Mark thought, *if his body died before he could make it into mine. Or, God forbid, anyone else's.*

"I may have an idea," Mark said. "Ellie, I need you to stay here with Izzy for a little longer."

"I'm coming with you—you came for me. I have to go back with you." Ellie spoke fast, and Mark could tell she was beginning to panic. He couldn't blame her. She had no way of knowing if he would come back for her. Her fear kept her trapped in this place. And no matter who he was to her, she had no real reason to trust him.

Mark knelt on the ground before her to look into her eyes. "I know this is scary, and you've had to deal with so much more than you should've tonight. But we don't want you to just be safe for now; we want you and your mom to be safe forever. I am going to try to make that happen. Can I ask you to trust me one more time?"

Ellie turned her head away, as if it were the last thing she wanted to agree to.

"Hey, I found you, just as I said I would. Didn't I?"

Ellie nodded her head but couldn't stop the sniffles and the flow of tears.

"I need you to trust that I will do that again. Okay?"

She didn't want to, but she nodded again.

"Okay," Mark said, nodding with her. "Can I have a hug?"

She fell into his arms.

He had no intention of pulling away from her first, so he

waited until she began to release him on her own before he let her go. If this were the last time he would get to hug her, he wanted to be sure the release was on her terms. If he could teach his daughter one thing, it would be that she had a right to choose when something was over.

"Are you going to kill my dad?" Ellie asked.

Mark wasn't sure how to answer her question. Even with all that had happened, Ted was still her father, but he was also a monster, and she was fully aware of it. Ellie herself might have attempted the same thing only hours ago, if Ted was to be believed.

"I think it may be the only way to keep you safe," Mark said.

"He doesn't like water. He told me that when I was watching one of his memories. I'm a really good swimmer. I can hold my breath for almost a minute."

Mark nodded. He didn't have time to unpack any of what she had just said, but if he knew her, he knew that bit of information would be helpful at some point tonight.

"I'll be right back."

"Now," he said to Izzy. "How do I get to the hospital?"

CHAPTER 34

MASON AND TED

ONCE, MASON AND his wife had seen a hypnotist perform at a theme park, during which the man had somehow convinced a group of six people to walk around a stage, clucking and flapping their arms like chickens. With a snap of his fingers, they paused and looked around at each other, confused about how they'd gotten there.

Mason felt the same way when he awoke from his trance-like state. The only difference: Mason knew how he'd gotten there, and what he had done.

Phillips sat beside him, taped so tightly to the chair that his skin bulged beneath the duct tape. His eyes were closed. Inspecting him further, Mason realized why. He just wanted him to stop saying those horrible things. To stop threatening him and his family. He just needed him to be quiet for a moment so he could think.

What Mason hadn't realized in his haste was that he had taped not only his partner's mouth, but also his nose.

"No, no, no, no," he said, rushing to Phillips's side, trying like hell to get a grip on the tape around the man's face. Finally, he managed to rip it off.

"Come on, Dan; come on, wake up." He patted his partner's face, then slapped him harder and then harder still, but Daniel Phillips's head just lulled to one side or the other.

"Fuck!" He checked Phillips's neck for a pulse. He couldn't feel anything, but he was never great at the medical stuff. He turned away, hoping that his sense of touch would be heightened if he weren't looking for the faintest hint of a pulse in Dan's neck. In the process, he saw his bent-over reflection in the dark window—which stood up without him moving.

It made no sense. He hadn't moved, yet his reflection had, and there it stood, smiling back at him.

"Look what you did," his reflection said. *"You're going to go to prison. How many men do you think you put in there? You're going to be a fan favorite."*

His reflection paused for a second, as if thinking. *"That is, unless you tell them what really happened. Then maybe you'll get lucky. Perhaps they'll just stick you in the loony bin. They'll load you up on pills, and you can shuffle around in your slippers all day, telling everyone about the doors to other worlds."*

The real Mason shook his head, refusing to admit what he was seeing or hearing. He ripped at the tape around Phillips's arms and legs. Maybe if he could get him on the ground, there would still be time for CPR. But there was so much tape. He searched around the office and finally found some scissors as the voice in his head droned on:

"Richard McNulty, remember him? He was the guy who cut his wife into little pieces and added her to his morning smoothies. Wasn't it your testimony that put him in the nuthouse? That would be a fun guy to get to know."

"Shut up!" Mason screamed, spit and sweat flying as he untangled the last of the duct tape. He pulled Phillips to the floor and began chest compressions. He could no longer see his reflection, as they were behind the front desk of the resort's front office, but he could still hear him just fine.

"Or maybe," the voice continued, *"none of this is real, and you're in your bed at home trying to bring your pillow back to life?"*

Mason kept at it, compressing Phillips's heart.

"Okay, okay, enough of that. I will tell you one thing that is true. This guy right here suspected you were a dirty cop. He's got a file the size of the Bible on you. He even gave a copy to one of his CIs just in case something happened to him."

"That's not true," Mason said, still doing compressions.

"Oh, no? Remember that little party you had at your place? Did you ever check your electronics for bugs? I bet you didn't." The voice took on a singsong cadence.

Mason had no memory of the party. He wasn't the partying type, but as quickly as he could deny the thought, a new memory sparked in his mind, back when he'd had a few of the guys over from work. They'd been headed to the basement to play some pool, but Phillips had lingered back in the living room.

"You coming, man?" Mason called to him.

"Yeah, just a sec. I'm just going to use the bathroom."

Mason remembered thinking it was strange, as there was a new bathroom in the basement. He blinked back to the present, the vision of Phillips sprawled under him, motionless and pale. "But I don't even have a basement," Mason said to himself in the window.

"But you remember it, don't you?"

"I do. Fuck." He stopped his compressions and looked down at his partner, as still as the floor he lay upon.

"What am I going to do?"

"Just explain it all to your boss. He'll understand," said the voice.

The real Mason stood to look at his reflection, and there he stood, with a big, shit-eating grin plastered on his face.

Mason looked down at his partner and began to cry. He raised his head to look at the window, and instead of seeing himself standing where he had been, the scene had changed. The desk was no longer in front of him. Now he saw only two chairs, one empty and one filled with his own lifeless body. Behind him, splattered on the wall, were the contents of his head.

Ted—or what was formerly known as Ted—waited outside for a few moments. He didn't care to see the actual deed; he just loved the orchestration. It was taking longer than expected, though. Just as he was about to turn back to the office, he heard it.

Bang!

"The end," Ted said, then realized he still had to make sure the old couple hadn't woken from the sound of the gunshot. Ted had polished his skills in the last hour. In the beginning, it took time to focus on his intentions and the intended outcome, but after some mental trial and error, he could now simply think of the couple's bedroom and there he would be.

He knew what he was about to do would take all his attention, so he would have to do something else to ensure the couple stayed asleep. He was right: The couple had been startled awake. The old man reached for his glasses on his bedside table, still dressed in his bellhop costume from earlier in the night, which made Ted laugh. He liked these two, and he decided not to kill them after all. Instead, he stood next to a flustered Dave and whispered in his ear: "You will go to sleep. You will stay asleep. Until someone shouts your last name."

Then he went to Mary Beth's side of the bed and told her the same thing. Dave put his glasses back on the nightstand table, and they both crawled into bed and fell back asleep.

Ted hadn't entered the deal with his wife and Mark faithfully. He knew they would attempt something to stop him, but in his time away from his body, Ted had also... expanded his operations. So he was confident he could handle anything in his way.

He watched Julia as she peeked out of the cabin window, no doubt having heard the gunshot. Ellie's body lay still on the bed, breathing but empty. And when Julia realized she wouldn't see anything in the darkness, her mother's instinct told her to protect her child. She went to Ellie's body and placed her hands on her shoulder and back.

He felt not one ounce of love for his wife, and he wondered if he'd ever held love in his heart for her, or anyone, really. He thought he could have loved his child if he hadn't resented her so much. He had no control over her, just like his parents, and if he couldn't control her, that could only mean one thing: She would learn to control him, and if what he suspected was right, she had inherited at least some of his abilities. Why, then, did he not have access to that ability when he occupied her body? Because such power wasn't attached to the body but controlled by the mind.

He could kill her. But if her spirit or essence, or whatever the hell it was, wasn't inside of her body, she would undoubtedly live on. She may even find her way to another body, one in which she could use her ability. Ted suspected it might take time, but with enough practice, he could do the same. Julia had been easy to control, especially after he was able to use their daughter as leverage. Her sister Laura, however, had a stronger will, but with time, Ted was sure he could break down just about anyone.

Now, possession—this was new. He wasn't even sure exactly how it worked. Ellie's mind had been somewhere else when he found her body, or vessel, as he now came to think of it, but she was also special. What about Mark? Was it even possible for his mind to empty completely, to make the space needed? And how long would it last? *There will be time to worry about all of it*, he thought.

As Ted watched Julia, he felt an overwhelming desire to torture her as he had earlier in the night—or, more accurately, as he had with the cops next door. But he knew that Ellie and her companion might be back at any moment.

CHAPTER 35

JULIA

SHE KNEW SHE'D just heard a gunshot, the shooter clearly close by. Her hands rested gently on her daughter, protecting her but also checking for signs she was still breathing. Ellie's body gently rose and fell, and Julia could almost convince herself that her little girl was just sleeping.

Julia's cell phone rang from inside her pocket, and she fumbled to get it out. "Hello?" she answered, not even checking to see who was calling.

"Jules?" It was Evan.

Why is it Evan? What happened to my sister that she wouldn't be calling herself? "Evan, what happened? What's wrong?"

"Nothing, everything's fine," Evan whispered.

"Why are you whispering?"

"They kicked everyone out of Ted's room, but I stayed behind to keep watch. Nobody has noticed me so far. Listen, your friend Mark was just here."

Julia's mind automatically tried to rationalize what Evan was saying. *Mark? How?* Then she remembered that the situation they were in was anything but rational. Questioning any of it would do no good. She listened to what Evan had to say.

"He wanted me to let you know he found Ellie, and she is safe."

"Oh, thank God," Julia exhaled. "Where are they? Are they coming back?"

"Not yet—hold on, stay very quiet," Evan whispered, even quieter than before, and Julia realized what a precarious position Evan had put himself in for them. Her heart swelled for this man, who was not a blood relation but was willing to do so much for her and her daughter. She was so grateful that her sister had found him.

She heard a nurse enter the room and start speaking to Ted as if he were a child. Machines beeped and whirred in the background for a few minutes, then nothing.

"Evan," Julia whispered, not wanting the sound of her voice to give away his hiding place, but also eager to hear what was going on. After another minute or so, she could hear the rustling of a curtain.

"She's gone. We should be okay for a little while now," he said, still whispering, though he was a little less cautious about it.

"What did he want you to tell me, Evan?"

"He said that it's not safe for Ellie to return while Ted is still there. He has a plan. He's going to come back on his own first. He told me to update you on what's going on at my end."

"Jesus, okay. Thank you."

"No problem."

"Evan, no, I mean it. Thank you for doing this," she said, her voice breaking.

"Anything. Anytime," he said sincerely. "Get rid of that bastard."

Still hunched over the kitchen table, Mark's body began to move.

"Oh, Evan, he's coming back—talk soon!" And with that, she hung up the phone.

"You're back," she said. "I just talked to Evan. Is Ellie really okay?"

Mark nodded his groggy head. "She's fine."

"Thank God. So, what's the plan?"

"Give me just a second. I feel kind of woozy," Mark said, attempting to stand. "This doesn't feel right."

"The drugs are still in your system," Julia said, jumping in quickly to help him as he fell back into the chair. She held his arm and braced him as he stood.

"It's okay, take it slow," she said.

"Any signs of Ted?"

"No, but I heard a gunshot, so I wouldn't be surprised if he were behind it. I don't want to rush you, but Evan said you had some kind of plan?"

"I think I need to sit down," Mark said, leaning his weight toward the couch. Julia helped him lower his body so he could sit.

"I need something to drink," Mark said.

"But we need to—"

"Get me a drink… please."

Without another word, Julia walked to the kitchen. Then she turned back to him and asked, "What would you like to drink?"

"Whiskey."

She went to the kitchen, grabbed the bottle and some glasses, and poured. She brought the glass back to Mark and handed it to him. He took a long drink, looked at the glass, then looked at her.

"Give me your phone," Mark said.

Julia reached into her pocket, grabbed her cell phone, and handed it over to him.

"Sit."

She did.

CHAPTER 36

MARK

MARK HADN'T NEEDED to go to sleep; he just closed Ted's eyes, and the bright light brought him back into Ellie's memory. He wasn't sure how exactly, only that he'd thought hard about the feeling of the door handle he'd found in the back of Ted's head, along with the light that had helped him travel to the garage to find Ellie.

As he stood behind Ted's illusion, he wondered if this path was even necessary. If he thought hard enough about a place, would he be able to take himself there?

Mark closed his eyes again and thought as hard as he could about the cabin in which he'd left Julia. He also thought of his own body and what it might feel like to reenter it. He opened his eyes again, only to find himself still standing behind Ted. Instead of wasting more time trying, Mark went to the door that had initially brought him to this place. He opened the door, then closed it behind him, expecting to find his body slumped over the kitchen table where he had left it.

What he found instead was disorienting. Julia sat on the couch with her back straight, staring ahead at nothing. Next to her sat his own body, wide awake, with a glass of whiskey in hand.

He thought for a moment that they could see him, but Julia wasn't looking at anything in particular, and he was sure that Ted, who had to be inside Mark's body, would have reacted had he seen him walk through the door.

This was not an ideal situation, especially because it seemed like Julia was back under his control, but what mattered now was that Ellie was still safe, and Ted was still here. If he had fled, he would've been lost to them. But why was Ted still here? He had his body. Why wait around? Maybe he had decided that his freedom was not enough. Maybe he intended to take his family with him.

"Shit!" Mark said aloud to no one. "Now what?"

He could take over Ellie's body and hide, but there was no guarantee he'd be able to get back out. If she were to wake up, Ted would catch her anyway, and then who knew what he would do to her. As demonstrated in the scene in that garage, Ted was not a man to be underestimated. He thought about the couple that Ted had brutally murdered. His parents, no less. They hadn't seemed like upstanding people, but they still didn't deserve to be butchered by their own son. They should've gotten the chance to grow older like the Langsteds.

Dave and Mary Beth, Mark wondered, had Ted done something to them? If they were alive, would he be able to occupy one of their bodies? If they were sleeping, he thought there was a chance. Mark at least knew one thing for sure. The only way out of this was to kill Ted, which meant he would have to kill himself. It had been his goal for this evening anyway.

He turned toward the front door again, but before he opened it, he thought hard about where he wanted it to lead. He took a deep breath, and whether it was with his mind or his actual hand, he wasn't sure, but he turned the handle. The door opened to the outside, where the darkness now faded to a gray dawn.

The first thing Mark noticed was the police car parked in front of the office. His hope swelled, then rapidly deflated when he realized that, short of shooting Ted in Mark's body, there wasn't much the police could do. Also... would that be so bad? If it meant helping Ellie and her mom live a safe, happy life, it was a trade-off Mark was more than willing to make, even if it meant Mark would end up being the bad guy in this night's story.

Drawing closer to the office, he saw the light inside was on. Hopeful, Mark tried picking up his pace to a jog but realized he wasn't really walking, just moving in the direction he told himself to.

Entering the office, he noticed red paint splattered on the back wall of the office. *No,* he thought with growing horror. *Not paint.*

It was blood, blood and brain matter. Mark winced, not believing what he was about to do. He walked behind the front desk to find two police officers; one lay splayed out on a chair in front of the bloodied wall. The other lay on the floor at his feet.

Mark couldn't see the weapon that had caused the damage. Whoever had caused this may have taken it, even though this looked like a murder-suicide.

Mark didn't want to go near the body, but he had to know if Ted was now armed with a gun. Dealing with surprises had lost its luster hours ago.

He went to the dead man's side, attempting to look at the surrounding floor, and the man shifted in his seat. There was a wet slopping sound as a flap of the man's scalp hit the floor beside him. Mark felt like fainting—something he wasn't sure was even possible in this state. He bent over, wondering if throwing up was also a possibility, when he saw the tiniest bit of movement in the second man's shirt. Could he be breathing?

He put his hand on the man's chest, and although he wasn't sure how he was doing it, he felt the warmth of the man beneath his hand. There *was* movement, albeit faint. He sucked in a breath. This man was alive.

As far as bodies go, a trained police officer was a much better choice than an elderly man. But Mark wasn't sure how to go about occupying his body. He had done it with Ted's body in the hospital, but he had help, or guidance at least. He hoped the man was just unconscious, and not so injured that, once he made it inside, his body might be just as hard to control as Ted's had been. Getting out of Ted's body had been easy—the drugs were still in effect, and that must've been one reason it had been so hard to move or talk while he was in it. He wasn't sure how he would leave this man's body, but he would worry about that when the time came.

It couldn't possibly work like it did in the movies, could it? In *Ghost*, Patrick Swayze sat atop Whoopi Goldberg to take over her body. Could it be that simple? He decided that option would be Plan B.

First, he would close his eyes and focus his mind's eye on the man. He wasn't sure if anything was happening, but when he squinted one eye open, he found himself looking at the blood-spattered ceiling—which meant it had worked.

Mark sat up in Phillips's body. He stretched out his long limbs to get a feel for them. This man had to be at least six-foot-four, making him taller than Mark, who was only five-nine. It was something he'd have to get used to fast.

Mark scrambled to find the weapons he knew the men must have had. He spotted one gun on the floor a few feet away and grabbed it. Then he searched the room for another weapon. He found it in the waistband of the dead man, not holstered, which was strange.

"What happened here?" he asked in his now-unfamiliar voice. He held both guns in his hands, not knowing how to use them. *What are the odds of me getting off a straight shot with one of these? What are the odds of someone taking these from me and using them on myself or someone else? Pretty good*, he thought. *Not worth the risk.*

This isn't a firefight anyway. It's a mind game.

Mark took the guns outside with him, walked a few hundred feet to the lake's edge, and threw them one at a time into the lake.

Mark made his way to his cabin, and as he was about to knock on the front door, he realized he had no plan. What he did have was a new body with a new identity. He glanced in the direction of the detectives' car, wondering which one of them held the keys. Checking his pockets, he was relieved to know that he wouldn't have to dig in the dead man's pockets after all.

After a slight detour to the now-unlocked police car, Mark returned to the front door of his once-favorite cabin. He knocked on the door and pulled out the wallet from his pocket; it held the detective's badge and ID. He read it as the door swung open.

Julia stood at the open cabin door with a strange smile that didn't quite reach her eyes. "Can I help you?" she asked.

"I'm looking for Julia and Ellie…" Mark paused when he realized he had never learned their last name. He trailed off, hoping she would save him.

"That's me and my daughter; she's sleeping," Julia said with a robotic cadence.

"My name is Detective Phillips, and I will need you and

your daughter to come with me back to the station. There is reason to believe you both may be in danger."

"Oh no," Julia said without a hint of surprise.

Mark leaned forward and, under his breath, said, "Go get Ellie, Julia. Carry her to the car right now."

"That's not going to happen," a voice said from behind Julia. A figure walked up, putting his arm around Julia's shoulders. It was like looking in a twisted mirror to see himself with his arm around her, with an overconfident stance, and with those eyes. Ted's eyes. Mark hadn't expected it to be so jarring, seeing himself in this way, but he was stunned into silence for a moment.

"Can you tell me what this is all about, Officer?" Mark didn't like the way Ted emphasized the word *officer*. He must've known the detective's condition before he showed up at the cabin's door. Hell, the bastard was probably responsible for it. So, why was he playing this game?

"This woman and her daughter need to come with me to the station," Mark said.

"Is that right?" Ted said. "And which station would that be?" Ted folded one arm across his chest and rested the other fist under his chin, giving an exaggerated, confused look.

"I don't think I got your name," Mark said.

"I don't think I gave it," Ted said with a smile. Mark hadn't known it was possible to hate his own smile, but in this moment, he wanted to punch himself in the face.

"Please step aside, sir," said Mark, "it's of the utmost importance that these two come with me."

"'It's of the utmost importance'?" Ted mimicked, then shoved him like a schoolyard bully.

"You know what I find funny, Officer?" Ted spat. "That not fifteen minutes ago, you were half dead inside that front office over there. And now, miraculously, here you are, ready to take everyone to the station."

"Not everyone," Mark said. "Bring Ellie to the car, Julia."

"Go sit. Your ass. On the couch. Julia," Ted said. Julia walked over to the couch, turned around, and sat down.

Julia said Ted was controlling, but Mark hadn't imagined anything to this extent. From her examples, it was clear Ted was a master manipulator, but to put her in this kind of state, one almost like deep hypnosis? It was more than any human should be able to do.

"Now what, lover boy?" Ted said with a laugh. "Please tell me this was not your plan. Just come in here and ask her to leave with you? Did you honestly think that would work?"

As Ted laughed—a tinny, alien noise Mark couldn't believe came from his own throat—Mark reached into his pocket and retrieved the police-issued taser he'd found in the police car's center console. He pressed the buttons, and two prongs with wires attached shot out of the handheld device, inserting themselves into the skin of Ted/Mark's forehead. Mark squeezed the trigger on the device and didn't let go until Ted/Mark was on the floor unconscious.

Mark assumed that once Ted was unconscious, Julia would snap out of whatever trance she was in. Yet she sat still, glassy-eyed.

He moved closer to where she sat, still holding the taser, finger resting above the trigger. He waved a hand in front of her face. Nothing. He snapped his fingers, but they made no sound. He tried again, but again, nothing. Was this guy unable to snap his fingers? *Is that even possible if I know how?* But Detective Phillips's fingers were long and didn't fit together quite right to make a snapping sound.

He grabbed Julia by the shoulder with one big hand and shook her. Once he stopped, she just moved back into place.

"Fuck!" he said and raised a hand to slap her. He couldn't do it. He had never slapped a woman in his life, and this man's body was large. He could really do some damage if he wasn't careful. He pulled back again and let his hand hit her face, but it was so light she hardly moved.

"Damn it! Just do it!" Channeling self-directed anger, he slapped her hard. She fell sideways on the couch and sat up as if spring-loaded, her cheek turning redder by the minute.

Ted/Mark's body stirred on the ground, so he pulled the trigger again. The body twitched, then fell flat once again.

Mark decided that if he couldn't get Julia to help, he had to immobilize Ted himself. He pulled a kitchen chair over to the man, just as he had done earlier with Ellie's body. He found the makeshift ties they had created still wrapped around the chair spindles. Mark was not a large man; he liked to think of himself as average, but he still weighed much more than Ellie, so he worried about being able to drag his body up into the chair.

He reached under his body's arms and pulled up. It was much easier than he had expected. Then he remembered he was in the big man's body and was grateful for the hours the man must've spent at the gym.

Once he got Ted/Mark into the seat, he tied his wrists behind him. It wasn't as easy as it had been earlier; the wrists he was tying were much bigger than Ellie's. Mark could only pray they would hold as well until he could find something stronger to use. He grabbed a kitchen rag from the sink and stuffed it in Ted's mouth, hesitating only a moment to think about the bacteria on the rag. Even though Ted was in his body, any present germs would affect him eventually. Mark, however, didn't have time to worry about that now.

He needed to secure Ted before he woke up, only he didn't have anything long enough to wrap around his head to keep the gag in place. *Duct tape would be helpful right now,* he thought, before remembering that he'd left a lot of it strewn on the floor of the office after discovering the detectives. Mark wondered if he could get away with not gagging him, but then remembered how he'd just ordered Julia to sit down. Unless he couldn't talk, it would be easy for him to get her to untie him.

Mark took his belt off, planning to secure it around Ted/Mark's head to keep the gag inside. He realized, though, that he would have to make another notch in the belt to secure it. He bent over to rebuckle his belt, and as he did, his tie kept getting in the way; twice, he had to move it before finally throwing it over his shoulder to see the belt holes. *Why does anyone wear these stupid things anyway?* With a shake of his head at his own stupidity, Mark quickly untied his tie, then wrapped it around Ted/Mark's mouth, holding the washcloth in place. Then he tied it tight at the back of his head.

Once Ted/Mark's legs were secure, he tried one more time to rouse Julia from her trance. He thought about taking her with him, or loading her and Ellie in the police car, but what if he woke up and got loose before then? He also worried about taking Ellie's body out of this cabin. When she did make it home, she would come back to the place she last remembered being, and if she did that and her body was missing, he wasn't sure what would happen to Ellie. He surmised he could get there and back quickly enough.

With one more look back, he walked out, leaving Ellie, her mother, and an unconscious monster behind.

CHAPTER 37

ANITA, LAURA, AND KUNAL

THE GOONIES, AS Kunal affectionately called their little group once (the name didn't stick), were waiting out time in his office. He'd nodded off only a few minutes after resting his head on his desk. Anita lay across two less than comfortable hospital chairs, trying like hell to fight off the sleep that had been threatening her since her adrenaline had worn off. Laura paced the office, chewing the sides of the fingers on her good hand, glancing every few seconds at the phone on Kunal's desk now plugged into his charger.

"I can't do it!" Laura shouted, startling Anita awake. "I can't just sit here and do nothing. I need to help my sister and my niece."

"First," Anita said, getting more upright in the chair. "You haven't slept in how many hours?"

Laura tutted, as if that were a nonissue.

"And second, you cannot legally leave this hospital for seventy-two hours."

"Have we not all determined that I did not do this to myself?" Laura asked, pointing to her injured hand.

"We have, but good luck explaining that to anyone that matters," Anita said.

Laura incredulously pointed at Kunal, drooling on his desk calendar.

"He doesn't look to be in any shape to discharge you."

"So, I just have to sit here and hope they don't die?" Laura asked.

Anita shrugged, too tired to do anything else.

"You know," Laura said, "regardless of what happens to Ted tonight, my sister could be in a lot of trouble—and even more so if he dies."

"Do you think she had anything to do with it?" Anita asked.

Laura didn't answer right away. She was hesitant to say what she truly felt, though Anita and her brother had more than earned her trust.

"This place isn't bugged, is it?" she said, only half joking.

Anita gave a small laugh and shook her head.

"I would be so proud of her if she did. No one deserves it more than Ted. But I don't think she would've."

"No?" Anita asked.

"No. She wouldn't do anything to risk losing Ellie. Never."

"And Ellie? Could she have done it?"

"I hope she did," Laura said.

Anita made a hum sound that sounded like a laugh.

"I'm not joking. I hope she shoved him down those goddamn stairs as hard as she could."

"I wasn't laughing. I was thinking about you asking if the office was bugged, like we're the FBI in the fifties."

Laura laughed half-heartedly, then suddenly stopped. "Wait a minute, that just reminded me of something—a comment that Julia made one night a few months back. I told her she should just have an affair when Ted was at work. I know, it was not my proudest moment. It was what she said after. She said she could never do that; he's probably got hidden cameras everywhere. Afterward, she freaked out, realizing that if he did have hidden cameras, he would hear us talking about him. That was the last time we hung out at her house because she believed he might."

"Don't you think the police would've found cameras if there were any to find?" Anita asked.

"Not if they don't know to look for them. They are so busy worrying about blaming my sister that they may not even look at anything else."

"So, what can we do?"

Laura frowned. "I'm not sure. I'm sure it's still an active crime scene. Right?"

"If this were a movie, it would be, but this is real life. What do you think the odds are of someone walking into that house right now undetected? I bet one of us could walk in there right now, make a meal, take a shower, and no one would even know."

"But if we found one and gave it to them, wouldn't we be charged with tampering with evidence or something like that? Entering an active crime scene, maybe?"

"That depends on the outcome," Anita said, sitting up straighter in her seat, this line of thinking waking her up. "If we found a camera, were able to review it, and found something that incriminates Julia or Ellie, we could just destroy it and no one would ever know. If we find something that clears them, the cops would likely be so embarrassed that they hadn't found it, they would 'forget' that we broke the law."

"Why are you talking like this is something we are actually going to do?" Laura asked.

Anita shrugged and raised her eyebrows high.

"Will he let me go?" Laura asked, gesturing at Kunal.

"No, but he can't stop me, especially because he is unconscious right now."

"I can't let you take that risk for my family. You hardly know us."

"I think this night has brought us closer than most, don't you? Plus, I will not go through all this only to let an innocent woman go to prison."

"You can't drive anywhere right now. You're exhausted."

"That's what Uber is for. Plus, they won't be able to identify me by my vehicle. It's the perfect plan. I'll even have him drop me off down the block, just in case. I just have to get into the house."

"I can help with that," Laura said, reaching into her pocket and pulling out the key.

CHAPTER 38

ELLIE

SOMETHING DIDN'T FEEL right, and if Ellie had learned anything in her eight years of living, it was to trust her instincts, because she had good ones.

"I have to help him. I think he's in trouble."

"He's fine," Izzy said from the floor beside Ellie.

"But what if he gets hurt, and I could've done something?"

"He won't, I promise. He can't."

"What do you mean?" Ellie asked.

"Just that he needs to help you, so he won't let anything bad happen," Izzy said, pulling Ellie into another hug.

Ellie knew adults well enough to know that this "other mom" wasn't telling her the whole truth, but she also knew better than to dig any deeper. When Ellie first believed she was stuck here, she happily hugged her other mom. She felt safe in her arms, but now she felt trapped by them.

She pulled away from Izzy gently, so as not to upset her, and looked her in the eye. "You can come with me. We can help him together."

"I can't. I can't leave this place, and neither should you, not until it's safe."

"Why can't you leave?" Ellie asked, growing frustrated and even a little scared. Was Izzy even going to allow her to leave? Ever?

"All this time I haven't been able to speak to you or hold you in my arms. If I leave now, I don't know where I may end up, or if I'll ever see you again. I can't take that risk."

"You're just scared. I was too, but you helped me, remember? You helped me get out, and I found my way back."

Izzy shook her head in response.

"But what if my mother gets hurt?" Ellie said. "What if she dies?"

"Then you have me, and I will always protect you, just like I always have." Izzy tried pulling Ellie to her, but she broke away.

"No!" Ellie cried. "I don't want to stay here with you! I don't want to hide forever! I want to be brave, just like you told me before!"

"Shh, my darling; it's okay; please don't shout," Izzy said as her shoulders slumped in defeat.

"Why does it matter? You said they were just memories, and they can't hurt us. Is that not true? Did you lie?"

"I'm not exactly sure how it works, baby. I just know you are safe with me."

"I love you." Ellie rose quickly to her feet. "But if you keep me trapped here, you're no better than him, trying to keep me in that box!"

"I love you too, baby, but please stay quiet; we can discuss it." Izzy reached for Ellie, only grasping her pajama top.

Ellie looked at the door that led to the house, then back at the box that had brought her here and screamed. "Here! I'm in here! Come out here and get me!"

"No, Ellie, please," Izzy said, louder this time.

Ellie rushed to the workbench and grabbed the first thing

she could find—a wrench—and threw it at the door, where it clanged off to the floor.

"No, baby!" Now Izzy, too, was shouting. She tried to grab Ellie, but the girl was too quick. Ellie reached for a screwdriver on the bench, and this time, she threw it at the door with even more force, yelling for him to come and get her the whole time. She was halfway to the hammer when the door cracked open. Tear-streaked, Izzy ran to her spot behind the car, beckoning Ellie to come to her.

"I'm sorry. I love you," Ellie said, and as quickly as she had ever done before, ran to the box, opened the lid, jumped inside, and closed it above her. She cried silently to herself, "I'm sorry. I'm sorry. I'm sorry. Please let her be okay." But deep down, she knew she would be, because her other mom had always only been a ghost. *And you can't kill a ghost, can you?*

Ellie could still hear noises from outside the box—someone picking up the tools she had thrown, she guessed. If she stayed focused on what was happening in the garage, she would stay there. So instead, she tried focusing hard on the last thing she remembered when she was in her own body: her head resting on her mother's lap as she ran her fingers through her hair.

Ellie's breathing slowed, and she could swear she felt her mom's fingers getting caught in her knots and gently untangling them. She could even feel her mother's breath on her face. She could hear the rumbling sounds of her stomach that always made her giggle, and she could even feel the warmth of her mother's jean-clad leg on her ear.

Ellie opened her eyes and could no longer hear the clanking of metal. She was afraid to open the box. What if the man was being quiet to trick her into coming out? But couldn't he just open the lid himself if he wanted her? Or maybe it didn't work that way. How was she supposed to know anything about anything? She was just a kid, and none of this was fair.

Ellie wasn't patient enough to let even fear keep her in the box any longer. She slowly opened the lid. Light shone through as she did, and her weight shifted. Suddenly, what was once the side of the box was now the floor, and instead of stepping out of the box through the top, when the lid opened, it spilled her out onto something soft.

It was the bed in Mark's cabin. Only moments ago, she'd felt nothing; now, she felt the wound in her hand and noticed some blood had seeped through the bandage. Her entire hand felt sore and stiff. She was also exhausted. All of this, she thought, could only mean one thing. She was back in her own body.

"Mom!" She suddenly remembered why she had wanted to get back here so badly. She scanned the room and found her mom sitting upright in an uncomfortable position on the couch. She couldn't help but wonder why her mother hadn't come to her when she awoke and called to her.

"Momma?" she said, climbing off the bed and going to her mother's side. She sat next to her on the couch and hugged her. She squeezed her so tight that she would've had no choice but to register her presence.

"Momma, what's wrong?" Ellie grabbed her mother's shoulder and shook her as hard as she could, but Julia just stared ahead with a blank expression. She stood up before her mother and waved her arms frantically, trying to get her attention, so engrossed with her task that she hadn't even noticed Mark in the center of the room, bound and gagged.

It wasn't until she heard a series of muffled mumbles that she finally turned to see him. She rushed over to him, eyes bulging with disbelief. "Mark? Oh my gosh, are you okay?"

He shook his head and mumbled something else. Just then, her mother made a sound, a tiny squeak followed by a choked gargling sound. Yet her facial expression never changed.

"Momma?" Ellie said, but Mark became louder still, trying to tell her something. Ellie grabbed the necktie wrapped around Mark's face, trying to pull it off his mouth, but it was so tight that, as she dug her fingers behind the cloth, her nails dug further into the skin of his cheek. He winced in pain, and anger flashed in his eyes. She backed away, startled by the emotion.

"I'm sorry," she said, and instead of trying again, she found the knot at the back of his head and started working to untie it.

"I can't get it. The knot is too tight. Maybe I can find something to cut it." Ellie was about to start her search, but Mark moaned at her, trying to move his head toward his side. She couldn't figure out exactly what he was trying to say, but she could tell he was getting frustrated, which made her nervous for some reason. Mark wiggled his fingers at her, and she finally understood that he wanted her to work on getting his hands untied, so she did.

She freed his hands, and he worked on the tie around his mouth as she moved to his feet. She'd just released the last knot when the front door shot open, and a large man rushed inside.

The man stopped when he saw her and held his hands up to her, one empty and one with a roll of duct tape around its wrist.

"Ellie, listen to me," said the man. "This is not how it looks." She instinctively moved closer to Mark, who was still working on untying his mouth gag.

"That man is your father."

"I know," Ellie squeaked out. "But how did you know? Who are you?"

"No, that's not what I mean—"

Ted/Mark reached out and grabbed Ellie around her chest and shoulder, pulling her into him tightly.

"No!" the large man said, jumping forward, but Ted/Mark's hand moved up as he did. One hand encircled her throat, and the other finally loosened the tie as he rose from his chair. The washcloth fell to the floor, and Julia gurgled pitifully behind them. Ellie didn't know what was going on; this didn't feel like protection. Was Mark putting on a show for this man? Was she supposed to go along with it?

"Please don't hurt her," said the large man. "I'll do anything. You can just walk out of here a free man."

Has Mark done something wrong? Ellie wondered as his grip tightened around her throat.

"Ellie, it's me, Mark. I know this doesn't make any sense, but—"

Without saying a word, all the man had to do was squeeze, and Ellie saw stars. That was when Ellie remembered Mark's eyes and the anger in them. At first, she mistook the familiarity, but now she understood. The eyes were familiar because she'd feared them her entire life. They were the eyes of her real father. Ted's eyes.

But now it seemed too late; his grip tightened, and Ellie could only think of one thing. She reached her arms out and wrapped them around his waist. She closed her eyes and brought up the only memories of love she had ever felt. Her mother's face was the one that popped up, and Ellie drove her emotions with the thought of her. Ted's grip weakened with the surge of love he felt. He didn't hug her back, but his rage lessened just enough to offer a window of opportunity.

Ellie pulled back slowly to look him in the eye. She let her gaze convey all the love she could find in herself. A violent shudder passed through him, and a single tear dripped down his cheek. She let the moment linger for only a second longer, then reared back and thrust her knee forward, making direct contact with his groin. He let out a painful moan as his body curled inward while he slowly dropped to the floor.

Ellie ran to her mother, who seemed to be coming out of her trance. She shook her head as Ellie pulled her to her feet. "We have to go!" Ellie yelled at her mother. Still confused and groggy, she grabbed her daughter's hand and followed, trying not to stumble over her newfound feet.

"That won't hold him long," she said to the large man standing in the doorway with his mouth hanging open.

"Are you coming?" she asked.

"Hide your mother," Mark said as he followed them out of the cabin's front door, pulling it closed behind them. "He can control her."

"Not in the office!" Mark shouted to her as they ran in that direction. Ellie turned and gave the man a confused look.

"Trust me, find another place."

Ellie's eyes searched her surroundings and when her gaze landed on the woods beyond the cabins she gave a nod of affirmation, then directed that gaze back at Mark/Phillips.

"What are we going to do?" she asked.

"I'll take care of him—just hide, please."

Ellie nodded, then continued dragging her mother toward the tree line.

"Oh, Ellie?" the big man shouted after her. She turned to look back at him. "That was awesome."

She gave him a big smile, and they continued on their way.

CHAPTER 39

ANITA

"Is this good?"

The sound of the Uber driver's voice startled Anita awake. She sat up and looked around at the street, her eyes settling on a mailbox outside of her window—1207, at least a few houses away from Ted and Julia's.

"Yeah, this is good, thank you," Anita said as she exited the car. She expected to see a crowd in front of the Barnet house, news vans, paparazzi, and police cars, but there was nothing. Not even lookie-loo neighbors. It was very early in the morning. *Maybe the press sleeps after all?*

Even though the street looked deserted, Anita still wished Laura had given her a back door key instead of the one to the front, but it was all she had, so Anita would have to take the risk. She walked with a purpose to the front door of the Barnet's house. Hiding in plain sight was her only option, so she would try not to look too suspicious.

She slid the key into the door lock with ease, like she had done it a thousand times before, and stepped inside, then closed it behind her.

Despite her earlier expectations, the door had no police

tape on it to block her entry. This being an affluent neigh-borhood probably had something to do with it. They didn't want the eyesore, or any negative reminders that the real world could get in. She supposed the police had come in, taken pictures, made reports, and left. Had they even searched the house for cameras? Anita looked around at the ceiling for small red lights indicating a recording device, but from what she'd learned about Ted on this dreadfully long night, she could safely assume he wouldn't be that obvious.

If she hadn't been so exhausted, she would've googled types of hidden cameras, or where to hide cameras on her drive over. She didn't want to waste time now, so she thought she'd look around first. She took a step toward the stairs and almost stepped into a pool of blood.

"Ewe, disgusting," she said, side-stepping around it to climb the stairs. The staircase was steep. She could imagine what it might feel like to fall down it—or, even worse, to be pushed. When she reached the landing, she noticed the family pictures on the wall; they were disturbing, at the very least, because the smiles of the woman and the little girl in them never reached their eyes.

The woman, who Anita surmised was Julia, looked almost trapped in her own body, like those ventriloquist dummies, and Ellie, who looked nothing as she'd pictured her, was smil-ing a forced a smile, but her eyes looked off in the distance in every picture, as though she were noticing something or someone out of frame.

Anita lifted the photos off the wall, checking behind them for cameras. Finding nothing, she scanned the landing and tried to think of where she would hide a camera if she were psychotic enough to spy on her family.

She looked up to find a light fixture on the hallway ceil-ing and wondered if there could be a camera hidden inside.

It was frosted glass, so it wasn't unreasonable to think so, but she would have to get a chair and tools to look inside. She surveyed the scene, trying to decipher which tools she would need, when her glance landed on the hallway light switch.

There was something strange about it, so she moved closer to inspect it. A standard light switch would have one screw above and one below the actual switch. This one had both holes—only the screw on the bottom was missing. She needed a flathead screwdriver, she decided, and went to the kitchen, assuming everyone keeps at least one in a kitchen drawer. She prayed she was right and that it wouldn't be a Phillips head.

The Barnet's junk drawer was much tidier than her own— one could even say it wasn't a junk drawer at all but an expertly curated drawer of only useful items. Anita found a screwdriver, and alas, it was a Phillips head, but upon further inspection, Anita discovered that with a simple push and twist, the head of the screwdriver flipped around to become a flathead.

"Cool," she said, speeding back up the stairs and once again narrowly avoiding the bloodstain. After quickly removing the top screw of the light switch, the entire panel fell off into her hand; it looked as she expected a normal light switch would, connected to electric wires that held it in place instead of allowing it to fall to the floor.

She searched its components, looking for who knows what because she'd never even seen the inside of a light switch before. Was she really expecting to turn into MacGyver right now, in order to save these people she'd never met before? Why was she doing any of this? She was just so tired, and even if this thing she held *was* a camera, what were the odds that it would stream directly to Ted's phone? A phone that was likely to be sitting in an evidence locker somewhere, never to be seen again, if this house was any indication of the current state of this investigation.

Her frustration grew as she stared at the switch, not knowing what she was looking at. She finally slammed it back against the wall, ready to leave it hanging there as she continued her search. The force of her slam, however, seemed to have knocked a component loose. A small black piece of gold-edged plastic lay on the wooden floor. She bent down, first assuming she'd broken something, then realizing happily that it was not an old piece of plastic but a microSD card—one that would likely contain countless hours of videos.

Anita looked behind her to check where the camera's line of sight might be. It may well have caught a good deal of any struggle that had taken place on this landing.

Hell, Anita thought, *if this doctor thing doesn't last, I could make a damn good private eye. Maybe both? Wasn't Dick Van Dyke in a TV show where he played a doctor and a detective?* She would have to google it.

But for now, before she went back to the hospital to check this card, she would make sure there were no more SD cards left to find.

CHAPTER 40

MARK

MARK/PHILLIPS STOOD OUTSIDE the cabin in the predawn light and watched Ellie and Julia until they were out of sight. He quickly searched the space, trying to think of what to do next, how to distract Ted, or better yet, erase him completely, but coming up blank. It was all too much; there were so many choices, but very few good options.

Ted/Mark burst through the cabin door. To Mark, the sight of his own body in front of him still felt surreal, but he was beginning to hate the sight of it. "Julia," Ted roared, "get back here right now!"

Mark could only pray that Ellie had covered her mother's ears, but he guessed he would know soon enough. "It's over, Ted!" Mark shouted.

Ted/Mark hadn't seemed to notice the detective standing outside the cabin. Either that, or he didn't care.

"Just leave. Walk out of here and never contact them again. You're a free man." Ted didn't acknowledge Mark, only scanned his sightline for movement.

"What's your end goal here?" Mark asked, following Ted/Mark as he lumbered toward the wooded area lining the resort's edge. He grabbed his collar and yanked him around. "What do you fucking want? Tell me! What will it take?"

"They took my life. I want them dead."

A shudder went through Mark's spine—or, more accurately, Detective Phillips's—on hearing the certainty in Ted's words. The sun was breaking through the trees now. It would only be a matter of time before he found them out here, or at least got close enough to make Julia show herself.

"They went that way," Mark said, pointing in the direction he last saw Ellie and Julia.

"Right," Ted said and made off in the opposite direction.

He'd bought them some time, but he still didn't know what to do next. He could attempt to call someone, maybe from the office. If he knew the Langsteds like he thought he did, they would have a landline. He didn't want to go back in there with the dead police officer, but if he had to, he would. *Police*, he thought, *why didn't I think of that before? The police car will have a radio.*

Mark/Phillips sprinted to the car, tore open the door, and found it there shining like a diamond. He didn't know how to use it, but after fumbling with knobs and buttons, he heard a static sound from the other end. Following what he'd seen cops do in movies, he held the button on the handpiece down and spoke into it: "Hello? Is someone there? Hello?"

He released the button, but nothing came in response. He turned the dial to another channel and tried again. After a few repeated attempts, there was a garbled voice.

"Hello, hello? Can you hear me?"

"Who... this?" The static broke up the words midsentence, but he could tell it was a woman's voice.

"Send help to the Lakeview Resort!" he yelled into the handpiece.

"Sir... you'll... to... I can't."

"Lakeview! Help!" Mark repeated over and over until a loud beep sounded in his ear.

A now-clear voice took over: "Can I take your order?"

Unsure what to say, Mark just repeated himself. "Send help to the Lakeview Resort."

"Would you like hot peppers on that?" asked the cheery voice. Mark looked up through the front windshield of the detective's car to see Ted standing there in his body about fifty yards away in the dusky morning.

Mark didn't take any time to think. He placed the handpiece back in its place on the radio and reached for the car keys in his pocket. He never took his eyes off Ted as he inserted the key into the ignition, assuming the man would run at the sound of the engine, though he didn't, which was even more concerning. Mark put his foot on the gas pedal and pressed it to the floor. The tires spun out in the dirt and caught traction. The car lurched forward. Ted still didn't move. Mark zoomed forward, was about five yards away now, focused on one thing—destroying that motherfucker—but the wheel jerked in his grasp.

Mark tried to slam on the brakes, but the pedal was frozen in place, and the gas remained pushed to the metal. He was so busy focusing on the pedals that he never saw the tree growing closer in the windshield. Then, without warning, there came the sound of crunching metal, broken glass, and the intrusive "*poof*" of the airbag deploying before it slammed into him.

CHAPTER 41

THE HOSPITAL

KUNAL WOKE TO the sound of a rain shower of plastic hitting his desk. Anita stood above him, having dropped at least twenty microSD cards in front of his face.

"What?" was all he could think to say.

Laura came over from where she'd been resting—not exactly sleeping—on the loveseat in the corner.

"Geez, that's a lot of memory cards," she said, having expected a few SD cards after her text messages with Anita, letting her know of her discovery.

"I don't even think this is all of them," Anita said.

"Why did you bring them here? Shouldn't you take them"—Kunal yawned midsentence—"to the police?"

"And have the police destroy them under Ted's mind control? No way! It doesn't even look like they're investigating. There is absolutely no police presence at their house. It's strange. I want to have the evidence in hand."

"And copies made," Laura added.

"Exactly."

"Okay, so how do we do that?" asked Kunal.

"I thought you would know," Anita said.

"Why would you think that? This seems like outdated technology to me. Everything is digital now."

"Okay, but they still exist, so there must be a way to see what's on them, right?"

"Wait," Kunal said. "I have an idea, Radio Shack."

"Okay, you don't have to be a smart-ass."

"No, Gerry, our night janitor. They call him Radio Shack because he knows all about tech gadgets. He may still be here. Hold on." Kunal jumped up from the desk and fled his office.

Anita and Laura waited for him to return while googling microSD card reading devices.

"It looks like Walmart has one!" Laura said before frowning. "Oh, shit, two-day delivery."

The two searched for a while before Kunal finally burst back into his office. "I had to track him down," he said. "He's carrying not only a few different devices but also what looks like an old laptop computer. He had the card reader, but I can't read it on my Mac, so we had to track down a PC." Kunal set the computer down, opened it, and turned it on. He grabbed one of the SD cards, then placed it into what looked like a larger memory card and slid it in a slot on the side of the computer then sat back and waited.

"What now?" Anita asked anxiously.

"It has to boot up."

"Jesus Christ," she said.

"Why do you think I have a Mac?"

Laura's phone rang in her hand, and she answered Evan's call on the first ring. "What's going on?"

"Nothing," Evan said. "Nothing has happened since Mark. What's the plan here?"

"We're looking for evidence to clear Julia and Ellie."

Evan sighed. "You know I'll do anything to help Ellie, but I'm not sure what good I'm doing here, and I think it's going to get much harder to stay hidden when the morning shift takes over."

"Well, we still have about an hour and a half before the shift change." Laura glanced at her phone to make sure she was right about the time. She couldn't believe how much time had passed since the first phone call from her sister yesterday morning. "I just don't want her waking up there scared and alone, you know?"

"I know, I know. I'll stay as long as I can."

"I love you, you know that?" Laura said.

"I mean, how could you not?" Evan said, his tone brightening as he smiled.

"Shut up." A genuine laugh escaped her mouth, and it felt odd but a little cleansing. "I'll keep you updated."

"Me too," he said before hanging up the phone.

"Holy shit, look at this," Kunal said, turning the computer around to show his sister and Laura. The screen showed Ted standing at a kitchen counter as Julia washed the dishes at the sink. They couldn't hear what was being said, but they could see his mouth moving.

Ted picked up items from the kitchen—a napkin holder, a saltshaker, a set of keys—and one by one, threw them at Julia's back as she worked. She flinched as the items struck her; one even struck her in the back of the head. Her back hitched in what appeared to be sobs as he pummeled her with seemingly endless objects.

Laura's mouth hung open, and she could barely get out the words, "I had no idea."

Kunal turned the computer back around and switched out the SD card for another. Some cards held footage of only hallways. Others showed more of Ted's abusive behavior toward Julia. After the fourth card, Kunal realized the volume was turned down on the computer.

Once he turned it up, however, they all wished he hadn't. Hearing Ellie's voice begging for Ted to stop was heartbreaking. They watched her try to help her mother, only for her father to retaliate with more humiliation. He never laid hands on his daughter, and not one of the three people in the room believed it was because he loved her.

They could clearly see that he just wasn't capable of it, for whatever reason. They all hoped that whatever transcendent ability she held would keep her safe in whatever hell she was experiencing right now. For their part, they would sort through every miserable second of these files just to be sure to clear their names, even if that meant destroying evidence.

CHAPTER 42

ELLIE

ELLIE HEARD THE crash and hoped it was her father who'd been hit, though she feared it was Mark.

Sitting in the woods, just waiting to be found, didn't feel right to her. She was tired of waiting for someone to save her and her mother. She was tired of it all, and she was just *tired*. Her body had gotten some sleep, but her mind was exhausted. As much as she didn't want to leave her mother in the woods alone, sitting behind a tree, she would not wait anymore. She was going to save them.

She kissed her mother on the cheek and whispered in her ear: "I'm going to get help. Stay here, and if he comes for you, fight him, Mom. I know you can." She hugged her mom tight, trying harder than ever before to pass her love on to her, and if she was lucky, just a little bit of her own power. "I love you. I'll be back soon."

Her mother stared ahead with no reaction, but Ellie knew she could hear her, so she fled back to Lakeview.

When she came into the clearing, she saw that the detective's car had smashed into a tree. Inside sat the detective, whose body Mark occupied. She felt a strange disconnect—there was this stranger, unconscious from the accident, and she knew it was Mark, but she wasn't sure if she should, or could, take the time to help him.

She reached into the car and shook the big man, trying to wake him. To her surprise, he groaned and raised his head before dropping it again.

"I'm going to get help," she said, and ran for the Langsteds' home. Ellie pounded her fists on the closed door as hard as she could. "Hello! Help us, please! Help us!"

There was no sound from inside. She looked around for something she could use to break a window; she found a concrete goose, but it was too heavy to lift high enough to break a window, so she kept searching. She found a smaller lawn gnome, picked it up, and threw it as hard as she could toward the Langsteds' large picture window. It bounced off without so much as a crack.

"I know I raised you better than that," said a voice behind her. "It won't help anyway. They won't wake until I tell them to." She knew the sound of the voice was Mark's, but something integral was missing. A softness. Even a soul? Shivers ran through her, and she turned to see him there. There was a chance she could run past him without getting caught, but he saw her eyes shift to the side.

"Uh-uh, don't try it," he said. "You won't make it."

"What do you want? Why don't you just leave us alone!" She grabbed the gnome from the ground and tried throwing it at him. It landed about a foot in front of him, and he laughed, which enraged her even more. She attacked him with her fists, but he easily held her back. He turned her around and grabbed her from behind, bear-hugging her and trapping her arms.

"I want to offer you a deal," he said into her ear, "and if you accept, you and your mother can walk out of here free and clear. Are you going to listen?"

"No!" she screamed, kicking her feet as hard as she could until she finally caught his shin and he dropped her.

"Damn it! You little shit!" She wasn't sure why she'd done it. He still had her cornered. Maybe she wanted to hurt him as much as she could, as much as he had hurt her mother.

"Are you done?"

"No!" she cried.

"Then I guess this night will just go on forever."

"I guess it will!"

"Or maybe I will just go into the woods over there, get your mother, and have her kill your friend, Mark, then you, before killing herself."

Ellie wanted to scream and fight him and never stop until one or both of them were dead, but she knew he could do precisely what he claimed he would, and that scared her enough to keep her quiet.

"Now," he said, "are you ready to make a deal?"

Ellie's father scanned text messages on her mother's phone as she watched the front door of Mark's cabin, praying someone would burst through it. Ellie sat in a kitchen chair, makeshift ties wrapped around the spindles, but Ted hadn't bothered tying her up. He must've assumed that the threat alone was enough to make her stay put, and he was right. She would not let anyone get hurt to protect her.

Once he found what he was looking for, he searched through the pill bottles still scattered on the kitchen table. He found the bottle he was looking for and shook it, looking disappointed. He tried to open the bottle but couldn't. He looked at his new hand and turned it over and back, flexing and extending the fingers. To Ellie, it looked like he couldn't figure out how to use his hands.

Good, she thought. *Maybe Mr. Mark's body is rejecting my father; and it will spit him out, and he can float away like a balloon and explode somewhere in the atmosphere.*

He tried the bottle again, and this time, it opened. He looked inside, then whipped the bottle across the room. A single pill fell out. He picked up one bottle after another, clearly not finding what he was looking for.

"Well, these aren't going to help me," Ted said. "I could just knock you out, but I don't want to wake up with a headache." Ellie's head tilted to one side, and her father smiled.

"You haven't figured it out yet, have you?" he continued. "We're going to switch bodies. You see, since you are my daughter, I am going to let you live, but since you took my body away from me, I'm going to take back those years and then some."

Ellie shook her head frantically. "I didn't!"

"There is no use denying it. To be honest, I admire you for taking some action instead of just taking it like your mother always has. Maybe you've got some of me in you after all."

Ellie began to cry. *What if he's right? What if I am like him? What if he was just like me as a kid, and then at some point, he changed, and so will I? But Izzy said it was trauma that caused him to change.* If she could end this trauma before it was too late, could she be saved?

"Oh, don't start that blubbering," he said. "I don't have time for that. We need to figure out how to get you to sleep."

There was a problem, Ellie realized, something putting a hold on the process. *We can't switch unless we're both sleeping. So all I need to do*, she thought, *is stay awake.*

"So now what?" Ted said, picking up a random pill bottle. "I don't want to give you these, because there is a good chance they will kill you." He looked at her for a long while, then shrugged. "I guess it's worth the risk."

He opened the bottle and poured the pills into his hand.

"No, no, wait!" Ellie begged, racking her brain for anything that could help her. *Sleep—how does a kid sleep?* "Benadryl!" she yelled. "Mom brought Benadryl!"

Ted raised an eyebrow. "That would work. Where is it?"

Ellie had no idea if her mother had brought Benadryl. In fact, she could almost guarantee that she didn't, since they had packed in such a hurry after the accident. Her father, though, had no way of knowing that.

"In our cabin, in Mom's bag."

"Okay, let's go. And if I find out you are lying to me, I'm going to slit your throat."

Ellie instinctively reached for her throat and swallowed. Ted gave a nod, then grabbed Ellie by the arm, pulled her to her feet, and dragged her out of the cabin.

Before the door could close behind them, something knocked Ted/Mark down, pulling Ellie along with him. There was another presence—the big guy (Mark/Phillips!)—working to untangle them, and then a fist slammed into Ted's cheek.

"Run!" Mark said to Ellie as he worked to keep Ted down. He was wobbly on his feet, but his size was his advantage, and he used it against Ted as Ellie rose to her feet and did what she was directed to do. She ran away, with no specific direction in mind. Her father's voice broke out in a scream of anger and frustration, which only made her run faster. She remembered earlier, when she'd run from who she thought was Mark, how the water had stopped him in his tracks, so she ran and ran toward the lake.

CHAPTER 43

JULIA

JULIA STOOD IN a black room no larger than a bathroom stall. The full-length pane of glass before her showed an image of what her physical body's eyes were seeing, yet she had no control over what was happening to her. She saw the detective try to help her; she heard some of what he was saying, but it was distorted and confusing, like the adults in a *Peanuts* cartoon.

Then she saw her baby.

Ellie was back, and she seemed okay. The girl pleaded with her to stand, to move, but Julia couldn't. She was stuck, trapped in this box. She pounded on the glass, screamed, and railed out in anger, but nothing changed; she couldn't do or say anything unless *he* told her to.

But then she did: Ellie grabbed her by the hand, and she somehow stood, as if the spell had been broken, or at least temporarily disabled. She followed her daughter outside. Inside, she dared to feel some relief.

Now, the forest stretched before her. She begged Ellie not to go, to stay here, so they could be safe and together, but she could do nothing to make her stay. She sobbed as her daughter walked away, not knowing if she would ever have the chance to hold her again or to tell her she was sorry for all of it.

Julia threw her body against the walls on either side of her, not caring how much it hurt. She kicked, scraped, and punched, eventually falling backward into nothing. She skittered to her feet and turned around. In front of her was a long expanse of darkness, illuminated only by the light shining in from outside. If she couldn't go through the glass, she thought, maybe she could find another way.

She felt her hands against the wall as she made her way down the dark hallway before she stopped. The light from behind her was invisible now—she'd gone too far. So she felt the wall in front of her, and her hands eventually grazed what felt like a doorknob. She twisted it and, without a second thought, opened the door and walked through.

The red car sat in front of her, and she knew where she was. She felt instantly sick to her stomach, knowing her daughter had been trapped here, alone and afraid, only she wasn't alone now; just past the car now stood a woman about her age. She was beautiful, with long, golden blonde curls falling past her shoulders. Her eyes darted around the room.

"Hello?" Julia said to the woman.

"Where is she?" the woman asked, her eyes pleading.

"Ellie? She's back there." Julia gestured to wherever she had just come from, though the door behind her looked as if it led into a house. "I mean, back at the resort."

"How did you get here?" the woman asked.

"I'm Julia, I'm—"

"I know who you are," the woman said harshly. "Why are you here? And why is she not with you?"

"Excuse me? Who are you?"

She looked annoyed, but Julia didn't know why. It appeared she had no desire to explain her presence.

"How do you know my daughter?" Julia asked.

"*My* daughter," the woman said through gritted teeth.

"Okay," Julia said, dragging out the word. "I'm just going to go back." She walked to the door and reached for the knob.

"No, wait! You can't get back that way."

"Why not?" Just as Julia asked, the door swung in toward her. The woman rushed to her side, grabbing her arm and dragging her back behind the rear of the car. She squatted down and pulled her close, closer than Julia cared to be with this stranger, who now gestured firmly for her to shush and to stop moving.

"Dad?" Ted called into the garage through the open door. He wasn't a teenager, but he was young, probably early twenties. When there was no response, he entered the garage, followed by two uniformed police officers, a man and a woman.

"He's always out here when I get home," young Ted remarked. "He works on cars, so he pretty much lives out here."

The female officer spoke. "The neighbors said the screams sounded like they were coming from the garage, so we just need to check and make sure he isn't injured."

"I understand. You're welcome to look around, but like I said, I haven't seen him today."

The two officers separated and perused the garage, passing right by Julia and the woman but not seeming to register their presence. Julia looked down and to the left of her and noticed what appeared to be a large spatter of blood just under the rear bumper of the car. The male police officer spotted it. He crouched down right next to Julia, touched the blood, and rubbed it between his fingers.

"How do you explain this?" the officer asked, standing and holding out his two slick fingers to Ted.

"Oh, that? That's. Just. Motor oil."

"Right," the officer stated. "It's just motor oil."

The female officer stood at the workbench. She picked up a hammer, the claw end of which was wrapped in what looked like blood-matted hair. Her eyes widened as she stared at the gory tool. Ted calmy sidestepped over to her.

"That. Is. The cleanest. Hammer. You. Have. Ever. Seen."

"This is the cleanest hammer I have ever seen," she repeated.

"Everything. Seems. Fine. Here. You won't. Be bothering. Me again."

"Well," said the male officer, wiping his bloody fingers on his uniform pants. "Everything seems to be fine here. We won't be bothering you again." The officers walked out of the garage door. Ted calmly followed.

When the door closed, Julia peeked over the top of the car to make sure they were alone. "What the fuck was that? Was that Ted?"

The woman nodded in response.

"And they can't see us?"

"The others can't, but he sometimes can."

"Jesus, this is nuts." Julia stood, readying herself to flee. "We have to get out of here."

"I can't leave," the woman said.

"Why not?"

"Because I don't know what will happen to me if I do, and this is the only place I can talk to her and hold her and that she can talk to me."

"Who? Ellie? Why the fuck do you need to talk to my daughter? Did you put your hands on her? I swear to God I will—"

"She was my daughter *first*," the woman said.

"Okay, lady, you're crazy, and I am going back to my daughter."

"You don't understand. I lost her, but then found her

again. She was reborn, but this time, in you. I've protected her from that monster ever since."

The last thing Julia needed right now was more crazy shit to wrap her mind around, though she couldn't help but remember some peculiarities since Ellie was a baby. When she would look in the distance, and smile and laugh, or as a toddler, being able to entertain herself for hours. She knew her daughter had always been special, but it really was more than a parent could ask for.

Julia was sure she could recall more memories of times when things should've been much worse than they were. Was this woman to thank for that?

"Okay, but I still have to get back to her," Julia said, "and I think you of all people can understand that, right?"

The woman nodded.

"There is only one way for you to get back," the woman said, indicating the direction of the large chest in the corner.

"Seriously?" Julia asked, but before the woman could respond, Ted burst back through the door with cleaning supplies in hand. They hid in their designated hiding spot, and Julia whispered to the woman, "What's your name?"

The woman whispered back, "Izzy."

CHAPTER 44

LAKEVIEW

MARK WOKE UP yet again with the metallic taste of blood in his mouth. He tongued his top row of teeth and felt them shift, but he had no way of knowing if this man's teeth were loose because of damage caused by Ted's fist or if they had been loose to begin with.

He supposed the car wreck had something to do with how easily he'd lost consciousness. It also could've been a sign that Phillips's already-broken body was failing. Ted was nowhere in sight—never a good thing. He had to be careful as he searched for Ellie, but he felt he knew where to find her.

Staggering, he made off for the lake.

"Hello, Julia, I've got a gift for you," Ted said. Julia was frozen in place, still sitting where her daughter had hidden her behind the largest tree she could find.

"Take. This. Don't. Lose it," he said, handing her one of the large kitchen knives that once lived in Mark's cabin's kitchen drawer. "Stand up. Follow me. I have a job for you."

The Julia puppet did as she was told, and together, they walked through the woods. If anyone had seen them—and couldn't hear them—they would've thought they were just taking a leisurely morning stroll.

Ted was giving Julia her instructions, and she was committing them to memory.

⁂

Mark/Phillips waved to Ellie from the beach. She was about chest-high in the water, and even from far away, he could see that she was shivering. He wondered if it was from the cold or fear. Both, he guessed. He wanted to wrap his arms around her and warm her, to comfort her. He didn't think she'd seen him, because she didn't wave back, and he hoped she wasn't falling asleep in there. She was so smart to take to the water, knowing her father was frightened of it. A swell of pride welled up in Mark's chest.

He raised his arms again to wave to her, and as he did, Ellie finally waved back. She also tried to yell something to him.

"What?" he yelled back. As he struggled to decipher Ellie's words, he felt a jolt of pain emanating from the center of his back. That was when he realized what she had been trying to tell him. Ted was back. Mark slowly turned, preparing to see his own face staring back at him, bloodied knife in hand. Instead, what he saw was Julia's blank gaze. And again, a sharp, piercing pain struck him, this time in his abdomen.

Julia shoved the kitchen knife into the detective's body once, twice, three times, exactly as she was told to, hard, fast, and deep. He hardly had time to register what was happening, let alone fend off his attacker. His eyes pleaded with her for help, but hers held no sympathy. They held nothing at all.

He tried to speak, but even the simple act of taking a

breath was too painful. Ellie screamed in the distance, and as he fell to the ground, the last thing he saw was Julia slowly entering the water.

∽

When Mark opened his eyes again, there was only darkness. He hadn't pictured death this way—he'd imagined light not darkness, but maybe this is what he deserved for not saving Ellie. Maybe he deserved to be alone in the dark forever.

Then suddenly, light shone down on him from up above, dissipating the darkness. There was Julia's shocked face too. *Has she somehow died as well?* But then she reached down and grabbed his hand and pulled him upright. He stepped out of the trunk and into the garage. Julia hugged him, and he could see Izzy wince as he hugged her back. He then reached for Izzy and kissed her, as if her mouth were the breath of life.

"So, this really is *your* Izzy?" Julia asked.

"Yes, *my* Izzy," Mark said, not taking his eyes off her.

"Where's Ellie?" both women asked, almost in unison, before glaring at one another.

"Oh, my God, Julia," Mark said, suddenly remembering the scene he had just left behind. "Ted is controlling your body! You're in the water going after Ellie as we speak!"

"You have to go back," said Izzy. "You have to be strong enough to fight back. You can't let him hurt her."

"How? How do I do that? I've never been able to resist his control. I don't know *how*."

Izzy grabbed Julia by the arm and dragged her to the open chest. She forced her to step inside, and before closing the lid, she said, "Be a mother and figure it out."

Julia stiffened. Anger flooded her. She lay curled on the hard floor for only a moment before everything below her turned to liquid, and she descended into water with seemingly no bottom in sight. She looked up toward the surface and saw her body standing above her, holding her daughter under the water, watching as Ellie struggled and scratched at her arms. One scratch drew blood, causing "Julia" to release her long enough to grasp at the wound. Ellie's head popped out of the water, and she gasped for air.

"Finish. it. Julia," Ted called from the beach, knee-deep in water.

Julia's body grabbed Ellie again and held her under. Ellie opened her eyes to see her real mother trapped below an invisible barrier. She mouthed the words, "Mom, help me," as the last of her air bubbles escaped her mouth.

The real Julia kicked her legs upward as hard as she could before grabbing puppet Julia's leg and pulling her down. She lost her hold on Ellie, who popped up and took another deep breath of air. Julia continued pulling her body down, using it to push herself up before stepping on her own head to break the surface. She gasped for air, then found Ellie panting hard in the water next to her. She reached for her daughter, but Ellie fought her off.

"It's okay; it's okay," Julia stammered. "It's me. I'm back. I'm so sorry."

On hearing her mother's voice, Ellie wrapped her arms around her waist and squeezed tighter than she ever had before.

"I'm so sorry. I'm so sorry. I'm so sorry," Julia said over and over, kissing her daughter all over her head and face. "Are you okay?" she asked, and Ellie nodded through her tears.

"I think you killed Mark," Ellie said.

"He's okay. I just saw him. He's with Izzy."

Ellie hugged her mother in response. They continued to embrace, all while knowing they were not yet out of danger. Ted was moving toward them cautiously.

"Julia!" he bellowed. "Kill. Her. Right. Now!"

Julia glared at Ted as she held her daughter close. "Should we try to swim away?"

"I'm so tired, Mama." Ellie always called her *mama* when she was tired or sick. Her heart sank. Her daughter was losing the energy to fight. Julia was going to have to fight for both of them.

"Me too, baby. And I'm done with this bullshit." Julia pulled herself out of Ellie's hug and moved until she was directly in front of Ellie, between her and Ted/Mark.

Ted must've forgotten about his fear of water, because he made it to waist level—only a few feet away from them.

"Julia! Do. As. You're. Told!"

"No!" Julia bellowed. "*You* do what you're told and fuck off and die!"

"I have to do fucking everything for you, don't I!" Ted growled as he lunged toward Julia. It was so strange to have what looked like Mark in front of her acting so aggressive. She didn't want to hurt Mark's body, but she was going to anyway. Julia kneed Ted in the groin, and he doubled over in pain, but as soon as his face touched water, he began flailing his limbs in a desperate bid to be upright again.

"Oh, are you scared of this?" Julia said, splashing water on Mark's face. "Ellie, get to the beach, baby." But as Ellie swam by, Ted/Mark grabbed her by the leg and pulled her down into the water. "No!" Julia screeched, suddenly jumping onto Ted/Mark's back, wrapping her arms around his throat and squeezing. He still held Ellie down, but when her foot kicked out, she felt something on the bottom of the lake. Instead of fighting toward the surface, though, Ellie kicked him and pushed herself down to the bottom and out of Ted's grasp.

Ted used Mark's neglected fingernails to rip into Julia's skin, pulling her off him and throwing her back into the water.

She came up to the surface, breathing heavily and yelling for her daughter. They both grew silent as they waited for her to pop up.

Ellie's face broke the water first, followed by her shoulders, then finally her chest, arms, and hands, holding Detective Phillips's gun.

She pointed it at her father's head. Julia let out a gasp. Ted looked at her as though she were crazy.

"First of all, you don't know how to use that thing," he said. "Second, it has to be waterlogged. Do you even know if it's loaded? Because if you take even a moment to check, I guarantee I'll have it out of your hands so fast you won't even know what hit you; or should I say, what hit your mother—because she will be the first to go."

"Mama?" Ellie asked, terrified of making the wrong choice.

"You do what you gotta do, baby."

"Kill. Yourself. Julia," Ted said, and Ellie pulled back the mechanism on the gun just like she had seen in the movies.

"Put. Your. Head. Under the. Water. And. don't. come. up."

Ellie's whole body was shaking, but she felt the little button near the handle of the gun and slid it over to the other side. She hoped it was the safety.

"Die. Julia."

Ellie pulled the trigger. It made a wet clunking sound, but nothing else. Ted smiled and moved toward Julia. The gun almost slipped out of her wet fingers, but she recovered it. She cocked the gun again and fired. This time, it worked—a bullet shot out next to Ted's ear, so close he reached up to check for damage.

Ted laughed.

"You fucking stupid piece of—"

She cocked the gun again, and this time, she didn't miss.

His shoulder was jerked backward; he remained upright but unsteady. It wasn't enough. She fired again, burying the next one in his gut. That one knocked him off his feet. Once his shoulders became submerged, he began to panic.

He attempted to get to his feet, but when the water entered his mouth, he lost any control he may have once had over Mark's body. His arms flailed around on the water's surface as he appeared to fight an invisible force. To Julia, it looked as if he were being attacked by a shark. Ellie began to cock the gun again, but Julia went to her side and gently touched her hand.

"Wait. Look," Julia said as they both watched Ted/Mark's head slip further under the water the more he struggled.

Julia took the gun from Ellie's hands and held her close as they watched the monster fight for his life. They waited for what must've been three full minutes after his head went under for the last time.

They both shook uncontrollably as they looked at each other for confirmation. Julia looked at the gun in her hand and wanted to toss in anywhere else, but she knew better than to let go of it because, as she'd recently learned, this man didn't die easily.

She took the gun and stuck it in the back of her sopping wet blue jeans, then picked her daughter up in her arms. She walked them back toward the shore, and with Julia's lips next to her daughter's ear, she whispered, "Great shots, baby."

CHAPTER 45

THE HOSPITAL

A SICKENING GURGLING sound came from Ted's mouth. Evan wondered who he was about to meet this time until the man's body began convulsing. Machines beeped. Alarms sounded. Evan got to his feet just before the nurses rushed into the room, grabbing at chords and devices, confused about how this could be happening. No one registered Evan was in the room, so he stayed, peeking around the curtain, out of the way of the medical professionals.

Someone pulled a crash cart inside as a flurry of doctors and nurses stood dumbfounded around Ted's bedside. Ted continued to seize and gurgle until a spurt of dirty water erupted from his slack mouth. Evan looked on in horror at what looked like seaweed sliding down the man's arm. Once the projectile finally came to an end, the monitor screamed one long earsplitting beep. The stunned hospital staff then began CPR.

After only a few minutes, however, they called it.

"Time of death, 5:36 a.m."

Theodore James Barnet was finally dead.

Evan's spirit lifted. Soon, he was escorted into Kunal's

office by one of the morning shift nurses, where Anita, Kunal, and Laura all looked up from their computer screens.

"He's... dead," Evan remarked. "It's over."

Laura rushed to his side and hugged him, reserving her giddiness for more of a confirmation.

"Are you sure?" she asked.

"Yep, just watched him die." She hugged him again, then pulled back for a moment.

"How? How did it happen?"

"Jesus, Laura, I was just sitting there, and he started choking and coughing, and then the nurses came in and started working on him. It was the strangest thing I've ever seen. I swear to God I saw water come out of his mouth. They finally gave up and called it. He looked like someone they had just pulled out of a lake or something. It made no sense!"

Laura hugged him again, so excited they were practically jumping in place together. Then a thought came to her, and she pulled back from Evan's embrace. "What about Ellie? And Julia?" she said to no one in particular.

Just then, her phone rang.

"Julia?" Laura answered, putting her on speaker so everyone could hear.

"I'm not really sure, but I think it's finally over," Julia said from the other end.

"It is!" Ellie said in the background. "This time, I know it!"

"How do you know it, baby?" Laura heard Julia ask her daughter.

"I felt it. All the pain and anger left him; all the sadness drifted away. When he died. When I killed him." The last sentence sounded slightly regretful to Laura, but that would have to be worked through at a later date. She glanced over at Kunal, who stood enthralled in what was being said—still shocked, but enthralled nonetheless. Laura believed he would be the one to help her through it. She felt a wave of love wash over her as she watched her new friends—hell, they felt like family at this point—celebrate and congratulate each other.

"Ellie is okay?" Laura asked her sister.

"She's safe; she's here with me." No one would've guessed four exhausted adults could make so much noise as they all hooted and hollered with joy. Anita hugged her brother, who spun her around in circles as Evan and Laura grabbed papers from the desk, whipping them in the air in celebration.

"Hey, that's my stuff!" Kunal said, then broke into a grin and joined them. He peeled off sticky notes and flung them into the air.

"I have to go," Julia said. "The police just pulled up."

"What happened?"

"I'll tell you all about it later. I cannot possibly thank you all enough for what you did."

"Call me after. I love you," Laura said.

"Love you too."

"I love you, Auntie Laura and Uncle Evan!" Ellie called out to them.

"We love you too, baby!" Laura said, tears now streaming freely down her rosy cheeks.

"Thank you, Dr. Anita and Dr. Kunal," Ellie added.

Anita and Kunal looked at each other, the shock slowly draining from their faces.

"Yeah, yeah, of course; you're welcome," said Anita.

"Dr. Kunal?" Ellie said.

Kunal found it so strange to hear his name from this girl he'd never properly met.

"Uh, yes, Ellie?"

"You owe me an ice cream."

Kunal smiled and shook his head. "You are absolutely right."

After they hung up, Evan, looking more toward Kunal than anyone else, said, "So, what now?"

"Now I'm going home and getting some sleep," said Kunal. "I suggest you all do the same."

"Sounds good to me," Laura said, popping up from the edge of the seat she had been sitting on. She grabbed Evan by the elbow. "You heard the doctor."

"Not so fast," said Kunal. "For the time being, your home is right down the hall."

Laura's face fell. "Really?" The nurse side of her knew full well that they would not let her out of the psych ward just because the worst was over.

"Yes," Kunal went on, "I'm not going to risk my job when we're so close to being done with this. Plus, if you give me time, I can probably figure out a way to 'lose' your hand injury footage. With the help of Radio Shack, of course."

Evan looked at Laura and raised his eyebrows, his expression leaving no doubt that he agreed with Kunal.

She gave a huff, but relented. "What about you?" she asked Anita, noticing she hadn't taken her eyes off the computer screen for quite some time.

"I have to make a trip to the police station," Anita said, turning the computer around for the group to see.

The screen showed a paused picture of the Barnet's staircase landing with three figures frozen in time—Ellie, Ted, and Julia. Ted's large hands were wrapped around Julia's throat at the top of the staircase.

"Watch," Anita said grimly.

Laura moved closer to the screen and took a deep breath, preparing herself for what was to come.

She hit the play button. It was disturbing to listen to Julia gasping for air as she struggled to free herself from Ted's grasp. Ellie stood in her bedroom doorway, sobbing and begging for him to stop. Finally, Ellie garnered enough courage to reach out for her mother's legs to try and pull her away from the edge of the stairs, tripping Ted's balance long enough to let Julia go. All three fell to the ground. But he wasn't done with her yet.

As Ellie and her mother cowered on the floor, Ted entered the bedroom, emerging moments later with an electrical cord.

"No, no, no," Laura whispered as she watched.

He pulled the door closed behind him, then moved so fast that Ellie didn't have the time to register what he was doing. He wrapped the cord around Julia's throat and dragged her to the bedroom door. Now he looked less enraged and more calculated as he wrapped the other end of the cord around the doorknob multiple times, locking Julia in place by her neck. Ellie tried to shove Ted away from her mother, but he dodged her flailing hands.

Soon, Julia passed out from lack of oxygen, her head hanging heavier on the cord.

Laura whispered, "Oh, my God," and raised her trembling hand to her mouth. Suddenly, by some invisible force, Ted was shoved back hard toward the top of the staircase.

Laura reached out and paused the video. "There! Did you see that?"

"It looked like he got shoved," Kunal said.

"By whom?" Anita asked, then pressed the play button to restart the video.

Ted growled. "What did you do, you little—"

But Ellie's hands were clearly at work, trying to release her mother from the strangling cord.

Before he could finish his sentence, Ted's body folded forward as if something or someone had shoved him, and he fell hard and fast down the staircase. Ellie released the last bit of cord from the doorknob and gently lowered her mother's upper body to the floor. She laid her head on her mother's chest, checking for breath, Laura assumed. "Good girl," she said, already knowing the outcome but rooting for her niece just the same.

Ellie's father made gasping and spurting sounds from his stopping point at the bottom of the stairs, but it was only after the house went quiet that she dared to look at what lay beneath them. Ellie had to take at least five steps to get to the edge of the staircase to look down. Five steps too far to have in any way pushed him, even if the police didn't believe the evidence on the tape.

Anita paused the screen just as Julia rose to a sitting position and grasped at her throat.

"So, it was an accident," Anita said.

"I'm not sure about that," Laura added. "But this proves that neither Julia nor Ellie could've been responsible."

"And I'm going to make sure everyone knows." Anita then went to grab the SD card from the slot in the computer.

Before she could, though, Evan, Laura, and Kunal all shouted in unison, "Make a copy!"

CHAPTER 46

LAKEVIEW

"Mr. and Mrs. Langsted! This is the police!"

On hearing their names, Dave and Mary Beth shot up from bed. They looked at each other in a state of confusion and clutched the blankets as men with large guns and riot gear burst through their door.

꙳

The office at the Lakeview Resort was now a taped-off crime scene, along with the beach where Detective Phillips's body lay in the sand.

"Looks like this one has been gone for a few hours at least; rigor mortis has set in," the medical examiner said to some important-looking man in uniform.

Julia cocked her head to the side, baffled by the examiner's comment. She'd stabbed that man to death only forty minutes ago, not that she knew anything about what happened to the body after death, especially when that body was possessed. She wasn't about to tell them, "No, no, I killed that man myself; let me give you the exact time," but she decided to leave it all be. Worst-case scenario, a lawyer would have to figure out how to defend her. Good luck to that poor soul.

From the water, a man in diving gear called to her: "This area, ma'am?"

"A couple of feet back!" she called back from her spot next to Ellie on the beach. Despite being wrapped in warming blankets supplied by the police, they still shivered.

She watched as the owners of the resort were escorted from their home. They wore the strangest clothes. Julia remembered Mark saying he had interrupted something strange earlier in the night.

A police officer sidled up to Julia and her daughter, note pad in hand. "I'm sorry to bother you, ma'am, but I just have a few quick questions."

Julia nodded. "Okay."

"You say that this Mark person was renting the cabin right there with the view of the lake, correct?"

"That's right, that one right there," she said, pointing at the cabin in which they'd spent so much time last night.

"Well, ma'am, the thing is, we can't seem to find any of his belongings inside the cabin. Did he have a car, by any chance?"

"Yeah, I think so? Wait, I don't know." Julia scanned the area. "I thought I remembered seeing a car, but then it was gone."

"Do you happen to have any more information about him? Next of kin, perhaps?"

"No, we just met last night. I don't think he had anybody. Wait a minute. The Langsteds had to have known him, or at least they took down his information when he checked in. Let me ask them." The officer attempted to stop her, but she didn't seem to notice.

Julia and Ellie walked over to the ambulance, where the

Langsteds were waiting temporarily while the police searched their house.

"Are you both okay?" Mary Beth asked on seeing Julia and Ellie walk up.

"We've been better," Ellie said.

"We're okay," Julia added.

"But I can't say the same for Mark, unfortunately."

"Mark?" Mary Beth asked.

"Yes, Mark, the guest who was staying at the Lakeview Cabin last night," Julia said.

Mary Beth and Dave gave each other quizzical looks.

"I'm sorry, dear, but no one was staying in the Lakeview Cabin last night," Mary Beth said with a pitying look.

"Don't you remember? You had to switch our cabin last minute because Mark was staying there."

When they didn't respond, Julia's frustration grew. She issued a small, incredulous laugh.

"You said that the Lakeview Cabin was already reserved, and you had forgotten... so you gave us the other cabin."

Dave gave a little shrug and a laugh. "Oh, no, we didn't switch you because there was another guest staying there; it's just..."

"It's just what?" Julia asked, not able to help the tone of frustration in her voice.

"I don't want you to go around telling people about this, but you see, an incident occurred in that cabin, and on the anniversary of that incident, some guests have reported strange things happening—items being moved, things disappearing. Most of all, though, they would report feeling sick or angry when they walked into the cabin. So we just make sure not to put anyone in the Lakeview Cabin on that anniversary." Dave's eyes were evasive. "Do you understand?"

"No, I can't say that I do..." Julia said.

"What kind of incident?" Ellie asked.

"Well, now," Mary Beth said, "that's not really something for young ears, if you catch my drift?"

"Her ears are anything but young at this point," Julia said. "You have my permission to say it."

Mary Beth and Dave looked at each other for a long time, a practiced and weighty gaze, probably, whenever this topic arose.

Julia could tell that they were judging her parenting, but she didn't care. She was done being told what she could and couldn't do, especially when it came to parenting, so she crossed her arms and waited.

Mary Beth gave Dave a nudge, and he relented. "A nice young man about your age decided to..." Dave made a slicing gesture across his throat. "He took a bunch of his wife's pills with a bottle of whiskey. His wife had passed earlier. Cancer, I think. Real friendly folks too. They used to come up on their anniversary every year. I think they had been expecting a baby before she died, so I'm sure that pushed him over the edge. He just couldn't get over the loss.

"Mary Beth found him two days later when she went in to clean the cabin. He looked real peaceful, like he'd been watching a movie. We left his tapes in the cabin, to I don't know, commemorate the two. It was really sad. Definitely a shock, especially to Mary Beth."

"I just can't understand how a person could be so hopeless," Mary Bath said. "But I've never suffered what he went through, so how can I know?"

"In fact, his name was Mark too, now that I think of it. Mark Peters. That was"—Mary Beth thought for a moment—"nine years ago yesterday."

Julia tried to swallow, but the saliva had dried up in her throat. She looked at her daughter, whose mouth hung open in horror. When she could finally produce enough saliva to help speak, she said, "Mark and Izzy Peters?"

Mary Beth blinked. "That's right, did you know them?"

But Julia just grabbed Ellie by the shoulders and walked away.

"Ma'am? Young lady?" Dave and Mary Beth called to them, but they just kept walking.

They walked to the beach and tapped the slightly disheveled yet important-looking man on the shoulder. His name tag said: Chief Stevens. "They don't have to look anymore," Julia said, gesturing at the divers. "They won't find him."

She took Ellie by the hand and walked toward their car.

"What about the police?" Ellie asked, trying to keep in step with her mother.

"They can track us down if they need us. Let's get the keys and find a La Quinta."

They were relieved. Of course, they were. How could they not be? The monster that had plagued them for years was finally dead.

But so was Mark. And it just wasn't possible, Julia thought, driving down Highway F, away from the Lakeview Resort and all the horrors they'd experienced there. She had gotten to know him. He'd *helped* her. Neither of them would be alive now if it weren't for him. How could that not be real?

They should've been celebrating right now, but they were too tired and too sad, a little too everything, really. They didn't know if Ted was still out there somehow, and they didn't know if either of them, or both, would be found guilty of his death. For now, they were just thankful to leave the resort.

Julia took a deep breath and exhaled slowly, trying to release stress incrementally, to stave off a panic attack.

"They're probably still there," Ellie said, unintentionally pulling her mother out of her own thoughts.

"What? Who? Still where?" Julia asked.

"Mark and Izzy, in the garage; that's where you left them, right?"

"I didn't leave them there. I had to come back for you."

Ellie looked at her mother with a slight head tilt. "I know, Mom, I just meant that's where you last saw them."

She hadn't realized it until that moment, but she finally knew what was eating at her: the guilt she felt for leaving them alone in that garage, knowing she may never get back, after all Mark had done for her and all that Izzy had supposedly done for Ellie, even before last night.

"Yeah, the last time I saw them, they were in the garage."

"I can just talk to them," Ellie said. "Make sure they're okay."

"No! Absolutely not! You are never going there again. Ever. Ever."

Julia paced the floor of the La Quinta Inn and Suites as her daughter sat on the bed and brushed through her freshly washed hair. They had on new Walmart pajamas, as just the thought of entering their cabin to retrieve their things made them both want to vomit in terror. Julia was sure the important things would be returned to them, either by the Langsteds or the police, and, if not, they would get over it. They would move on.

"At least I didn't kill him," Ellie said, and Julia stopped dead in her tracks.

How had she not thought of that? Of course, Ellie would be worried about the fact that she'd just killed another human being. Even if it was Ted.

Friend? First father? Spirit guide? Ghost? Was that what Mark Peters was? After everything they had experienced over the last twelve hours, why was this the thing she couldn't get past? Julia went to Ellie's side and sat next to her on the bed.

"I don't know how it was possible," she said, "how he did all those things to help us, but you're right, you didn't kill him. He was already gone. For nine years now." Julia shook her head. "I don't want you, even for a second, to think that you did anything wrong. I would not be alive right now if it weren't for you. Do you understand?"

Ellie nodded. "I keep seeing him, with the holes in him, right before he fell in the water." Her eyes glistened, and Julia could see that she was trying to hold back her tears. Julia bit her cheek, working even harder to hold back her own.

"What would you say to them?" Julia asked. PTSD was real. She'd suffered from it herself after years of abuse. The last thing she wanted was for her daughter to see the man she killed every time she closed her eyes. If she could see him alive, or at least whatever version of him that remained in that garage one more time, she just might replace that memory with a better one. What kind of mother would she be if she didn't at least try to give her daughter that gift? Even if it meant that she herself would suffer for it.

"What would you say to them?" Julia asked.

Ellie shrugged. "I haven't really thought about what I would say. I just want to make sure they're okay, y'know?"

"And you are positive you know how to get back now?"

"Yes."

"But how do you get there?"

"I'm not really sure how to explain it. But I can do it."

"And will you tell them—"

"I'll tell them, Mom, I promise. I am really tired, though. Can I please go to sleep now?"

"Okay, I'm sorry. Just please be careful. Otherwise, I'm going to learn how to astral travel and come and find you."

"You already did it once, so it shouldn't be too hard."

"Hah, hilarious. I love you, sweetie."

Julia tucked her daughter in, terrified at the prospect of her little empty vessel lying in the bed next to her, her spirit traveling to wherever that garage existed in space and time.

"I love you too, Mama," Ellie said.

At that name, Julia's teeth bit down hard on the inside of her cheek, metallic blood coating her taste buds. She then crawled into bed beside her daughter and pulled her close, listening to her breath, deepening and slowing as she drifted off to sleep.

CHAPTER 47

ELLIE

MARK AND IZZY sat huddled together on the floor of the garage, still not willing to take their hands off each other when the lid of the chest opened.

Their eyes widened as they watched Ellie step out in what looked like fresh new PJs, her hair now damp. She jumped out and ran to them before they could get to their feet. They felt her arms and legs in disbelief. They sniffed her fresh coconut-scented hair as they kissed the top of her head.

"Baby, baby, baby," Izzy repeated. "You're so warm. Mark, I can feel her warmth. I haven't felt that in so long."

"Wait, does this mean…?" Mark asked, pulling her out to arm's length so he could look at her.

"I'm okay," said Ellie. "I mean, I'm alive, and so is Mom. We got away. I killed him."

Mark's eyes widened. "Your father?"

Ellie nodded.

"Oh, baby," Izzy said. "I'm so sorry."

"I'm not," Ellie said to Izzy. "I'm glad he's dead. And I'm glad you pushed him down those stairs."

"I… how did you know?" Izzy asked.

"I realized it when I first saw you in the garage. The feeling I got when I hugged you, it was the same one I've felt every time you've been near me, for as long as I can remember. You've always protected me."

Izzy pulled her close. "Always, my dear."

They sat together for a moment, their little family together at last, but they couldn't stay that way forever, and everyone but Izzy knew it. Mark could see the look in her eyes—the relief that she had finally gotten her family back for good. But that wasn't how the story would end.

"Did you come here to tell us you were okay?" Mark asked.

"Yes, and to tell you something that I don't think you remember."

"What's that, sweetheart?"

"Do you remember the night you went to the resort with other mommy's bottles?" she asked.

"Of course, I remember; it was just yesterday," Mark said, looking ashamed.

"But it wasn't. It was nine years ago," Ellie said. Mark laughed, but when he studied her face, he could see that she wasn't joking. He looked at Izzy, who looked down but nodded her head.

"What?"

"Think about it," Ellie said. "I think you have to remember. I think that's the only way."

Mark's mind flashed back to the letter he'd written not even a day ago. He remembered stopping at the convenience store for Jack Daniel's and meeting the girl who reminded him of Izzy, driving to the resort, unpacking the pill bottles… but then, things clouded over. Images so clear only hours ago— watching Ellie and her mother drive up, going to the vending machine, touching her hand—were replaced with other scenes: Mark, without a chaser, downing gulps of whiskey, followed by handfuls of pills and throwing up on himself before attempting to swallow more.

Mark jumped to his feet. "What the hell is this? What is happening to me?"

"It's okay," Izzy said, gently taking his hand in hers. "You couldn't remember, so you just kept repeating it—every single year, the same day, over and over again. I knew it would take something big to break the cycle, something important. I couldn't watch you suffer anymore, not over me—so I started something that had to end with you."

Mark let her confession sink in. "I remember it now, the numb feeling of the drugs entering my bloodstream. I remember falling and then waking up over and over again. Does this mean... does this mean it's finally over now?"

Ellie and her other mommy looked at each other and smiled.

"I think it does," Izzy said.

Mark's heart swelled with a feeling of intense calm. A warmth spread throughout his body. He glowed from the inside, and the glow was so bright that Ellie had to shield her eyes to look at him. Izzy glanced at Mark, worried that whatever was occurring was happening without her.

"Wait," she said, "you can't go without me. I can't leave her."

"Mom," Ellie said, taking Izzy's hand. "It's okay. I'm safe now. You made it so I'm safe now, you saved me from him. Now you can go. You can be with Dad. I promise I'll see you both again one day. I love you."

A light flickered inside Izzy, dim at first but growing brighter every second.

"We love you," Izzy said.

But the two of them didn't disappear like Ellie had expected them to. They stayed there, still lit up like torches. A kind of sunlight shone around them; each of them felt the warmth of it on their skin. They were outside now, at the resort, but at a different, happier time.

Boaters cheered on the lake as they pulled water skiers behind them, and kids played happily in the sand. The smell of barbeque wafted over to them from the grill at the cabin next door. A man waved a bottle of beer in his wife's direction, indicating the need for a refill, she laughed at him and pointed at the cooler.

"Is this?" Mark asked. "Are you doing this?"

Ellie smiled and nodded. "The garage doesn't exist anymore. This is our happy place now. And I think we may be able to see each other here."

"You wrote us a story," he said.

Ellie shook her head. "I got it from you when I hugged you the first time. I saw this place how you remembered it, or at least wished it could be."

"I feel it," Izzy said. "Whenever we need each other, whenever you need us, we can meet here. We will always be with you. I know that now."

"But where is the chest?" Mark asked. "How will you get back?"

"I'm never going in that thing again," Ellie said, guiding her first parents to the lake's edge.

They hugged her one last time as they walked her ankle-deep into the sun-warmed water. The warmth of their touch reminded her of what she'd passed to others—an all-encompassing love.

"Take care of your mother," Mark said, and Izzy jabbed him in the ribs. Mark laughed. "I love you, kid; thanks for saving me."

"I love you too." Ellie lay down on her back in the water, and the blinding light emanating from Mark and Izzy was the last thing she saw as she let herself slide beneath it.

EPILOGUE
FIVE MONTHS LATER

"THERE HE IS!" Ellie said, running to the black BMW parked out front of the Original Rainbow Cone ice cream shop.

"Be careful, please!" Julia shouted.

Julia walked slower than usual, realizing she was nervous. She had heard from Ellie how handsome Dr. Sengupta was, and she was still working on building up her own confidence. She wasn't quite sure how to act around good-looking men, especially one for whom she was so grateful.

At least she was able to convince Dr. Taylor to join them to help break the ice. She just hoped their budding friendship wasn't one-sided.

Ellie wasn't shy at all with Dr. Sengupta. She had visited him multiple times with her Aunt Laura since that day, and they had also become fast friends. Now she pulled him by the hand, back toward her mother.

"Mom, this is Kunal," Ellie said, practically forcing their hands together.

"Hi," Julia said, shaking Kunal's hand, then brushing her hair behind her ear. She still wasn't used to having short hair or the bob style. Ted had never let her. And even though her sister and Ellie raved about how great the style looked on her, she was still learning to accept their compliments.

Kunal smiled wide. "It's great to finally meet you."

"You too."

The four of them sat around a table before getting into a casual competition about which ice cream flavor was the best. By sheer force of her opinion, Ellie seemed to win with her classic rainbow cone. Once they finished their cones and small talk, they got up, picked up their trash from the table, and walked back outside to their cars.

Julia was nervous, but she couldn't let this moment pass without one last thing. She turned to face them. "I know I've said it over the phone, but I have to say it in person. You both saved our lives that night, and there couldn't possibly be enough words to express how grateful I am to you for that."

Anita looked at her brother, and they both looked at Ellie.

"Come on, bring it in," Anita said, spreading her arms out for a group hug. They all squeezed around Ellie, squishing her in the middle.

"Okay guys, I can't breathe," Ellie said, and they finally released her. They walked Julia and Ellie to the car, Kunal holding Ellie's hand the whole way.

"So, everything is well with you, I mean with the police and the detective?" Anita asked. "I didn't want to ask in front of Ellie." She glanced toward her brother, who pulled his hand away as Ellie tried to slap him a low five.

"They confirmed that his cause of death was suffocation. None of it adds up, and they will probably be trying to figure it out for some time, but I've been cleared of any wrongdoing."

"That's wonderful! Really. Congratulations," Anita said.

"Thank you; it's such a relief to finally have it all behind us."

"What is it?" Anita asked after seeing Julia's face change, becoming contemplative.

"I just…" Julia said, glancing at her daughter, who was still enthralled with her friend's game, and lowering her voice to a whisper. "I still don't understand what happened to Ted. He was inhabiting a body that didn't exist. Ellie couldn't have shot him if he didn't even have a physical body."

"Kunal has some interesting theories about that," Anita said. "The one I am leaning toward is that Ted's *belief* that he was being shot was enough to incapacitate him, causing him to fall in the water and drown. At least in his own mind."

"Hmm, that *is* interesting. It makes as much sense as everything else that happened. I'd like to hear some more of these theories sometime."

"It's funny that you mention that. We're having a family dinner on Sunday night," said Anita. "Our parents are very Indian, and very annoying. You should come."

"Well, with an invitation like that, how could we refuse?" Julia said, giving Anita another hug before getting into her car.

"I am not kidding. You need to be there. I cannot handle them without strangers in the room, as they have to be on their best behavior with others around."

"She's not lying!" Kunal shouted from the other side of the car, having overheard the tail end of their conversation.

Anita gave her a nod that seemed to say, *See, I told you.*

"Got it, we'll be there," Julia said.

Anita closed her car door for her. "You owe me!" she mouthed, and Julia gave her a thumbs up.

Kunal walked Ellie to the back passenger seat of Julia's car and helped her inside. He gave her a big hug. "I'll see you on Sunday," he said, bopping her on the nose with his finger.

"Wait," Ellie said, before Kunal could close the car door. "One more thing."

Kunal leaned in close, so Ellie could whisper whatever it was into his ear: "You. Should. Date. My. Mom."

ACKNOWLEDGEMENTS

This book would not be what it is today without my editorial team at Ebook Launch. They are the most talented and supportive editors I have ever worked with. I take full credit for any additional mistakes or inconsistencies.

My beautiful book cover, graphics and formatting are all thanks to the wonderful design team at Damonza. Please, judge this book by its cover, because it is spectacular.

I would also like to thank my family. I already thanked my husband in this book's dedication, but I feel it necessary to include him here as well because, without his support, I never would've taken my writing career seriously. I would've just kept on having crazy dreams, then waking up to tell him every detail and how it would be a great book, only to let them die in the notes on my phone. Thank you for believing in me, babe. Here's to celebrating many more books together.

To my kids, for being the brightest source of light in the dark world that exists in my head, and for loving me, even in the times I had to write instead of playing Roblox. I promise we will get to 99 nights!

Thank you to my mom for always reading my stories, even if they make you say, "I don't know how this stuff came out of your brain"—which I take as the highest of compliments. Don't worry, your book is also in the works.

Thank you to my brother for supporting me since my first

acting showcase all the way to this book (which I'm not sure you've read yet? Maybe if I tell you I mentioned you here, you'll give it a shot).

And yes, as a matter of fact, I am *The Lizard Queen.*

I love you all,
Colleen

ABOUT THE AUTHOR

Originally from the suburbs of Chicago, Colleen Bite now resides on the East Coast with her family, where writing fills her time between parenting, exploring theme parks, movie-watching and indulging all things dark and eerie. She is completely normal. Really.

Lost in Lakeview is her debut novel, to be followed by the highly anticipated *Loomis Falls* series.